MW01102445

THE HEART OF THE MATTER

OUR RECENT RELEASES

Short Fiction

That's It But
By SuRaa

Short Shorts Long Shots
By Uday Prakash
Trans by Robert A Hueckstedt &
Amit Tripuraneni

Asomiya: Handpicked Fictions
Selected by NEWF

Inspector Matadeen on the Moon
By Harishankar Parsai
Trans by C M Naim

Hindi: Handpicked Fictions
Trans & Ed by Sara Rai

Ambai: Two Novellas and a Story
Trans by C T Indra,
Prema Seetharam & Uma Narayanan

Paul Zacharia: Two Novellas
Trans by Gita Krishnankutty

Waterness
By Na Muthuswamy
Trans by Lakshmi Holmström

Downfall by Degrees
By Abdullah Hussein
Trans by Mohammad Umar Memon

The Resthouse
By Ahmad Nadeem Qasimi
Trans by Faruq Hassan

Katha Prize Stories 12
Ed Geeta Dharmarajan

Best of the Nineties:Katha Prize Stories 11
Ed Geeta Dharmarajan

Novels

JJ: Some Jottings
By SuRaa
Trans by A R Venkatachalapathy

Seven Sixes are Forty Three
By Kiran Nagarkar
Trans by Shubha Slee

Ashokamitran: Water
Trans by Lakshmi Holmström

Singarevva and the Palace
By Chandrasekhar Kambar
Trans by Laxmi Chandrashekar

Pages Stained with Blood
By Indira Goswami
Trans by Pradeep Acharya

A Madhaviah: Padmavati
Trans by Meenakshi Tyagarajan

Listen Girl!
By Krishna Sobti
Trans by Shivanath

Non-Fiction

Upendranath Ashk: A Critical Biography
By Daisy Rockwell

Rajaji
By Monica Felton

A Child Widow's Story
By Monica Felton

Links in the Chain
By Mahadevi Varma
Trans by Neera Kuckreja Sohoni

Travel Writing and the Empire
Ed Sachidananda Mohanty

Translating Desire
Ed Brinda Bose

Translating Caste
Ed Tapan Basu

Translating Partition
Eds Ravikant & Tarun K Saint

Vijay Tendulkar

Ismat: Her Life, Her Times
Eds Sukrita Paul Kumar &
Sadique

Katha Classics

Pudumaippittan
Ed Lakshmi Holmström

Basheer Ed Vanajam Ravindran

Mauni Ed Lakshmi Holmström

Raja Rao Ed Makarand Paranjape

Masti Ed Ramachandra Sharma

THE HEART OF THE MATTER

Selected by
The North East Writers' Forum

KATHA

First published by Katha in 2004

KATHA
A3 Sarvodaya Enclave
Sri Aurobindo Marg,
New Delhi 110 017
Phone: 2652 4350, 2652 4511
Fax: 2651 4373

E-mail: kathavilasam@katha.org
Internet address: www.katha.org

KATHA is a registered nonprofit society
devoted to enhancing the pleasures of reading.
KATHA VILASAM is its story research and resource centre.

Cover Design: Geeta Dharmarajan
Cover Painting: Shalini Patel
Courtesy: www.saffronart.com

Edited by Geeta Dharmarajan
In-house Editor: Gita Rajan
Assistant Editor: Anjulika Thingnam
Production Coordinator: Sanjeev Palliwal

Typeset in 11 on 14.5pt ElegaGaramond BT at Katha
Printed at Usha Offset, New Delhi

Distributed by KathaMela, a distributor of quality books.
A-3 Sarvodaya Enclave, Sri Aurobindo Marg, New Delhi 110 017

Katha has planted two trees to replace the tree that was used to make
the paper on which this book is printed.

ISBN 81-87649-43-7

1 3 5 7 9 10 8 6 4 2

CONTENTS

INTRODUCTION

The twenty one short stories in this volume takes you on a tour of five of the eight "North East" states of India – Assam, Manipur, Meghalaya, Mizoram and Nagaland – tracing not only their rich culture and colourful history, but also the bleak, darker present. It is perhaps for the first time that Asomiya, Khasi, Meiteilon, Mizo and Naga stories have been compiled together in an anthology – either in the original form or as translations into English. Not just that, most of them have been translated into English for the first time.

The Heart of the Matter is the second of six books that have resulted from a unique collaboration between Katha and the North East Writers' Forum (NEWF), a collaboration that aims to bring to the forefront, through translations, the rich treasure trove of literature that the northeastern states of India house. The series includes collections of short stories, novellas, folktales, plays and children's stories. Both Katha and the NEWF have taken great care to make each volume distinctive, given the diversity of the region, and ensuring that there is a fair and faithful representation of most of the main language and geographical groups. The combined efforts have resulted in a volume that is homogenous in that the stories are all about the human predicament, but diverse in that the cultural codes which govern human behaviour and responses are unique to this region.

While *Asomiya: Handpicked Fictions*, the first in the series, is an anthology of short stories written originally in Asomiya, and depicting the sights and sounds of Assam and its people, *The Heart of the Matter* is a window to Assam as well as Manipur, Meghalaya, Mizoram and Nagaland, a window revealing an India that to date has not been so beautifully represented or translated.

The term "North East" is a geographical, linguistic and ethnic stereotyping that clubs together these often misconstrued, misjudged and misunderstood eight states – Arunachal Pradesh, Assam, Manipur, Meghalaya, Mizoram, Nagaland, Sikkim and Tripura – in the northeastern geographical periphery of the Indian union. Our series, we hope, will create greater awareness of the variety, the diversity and the plurality of the region and through its literature, dispel the misconceptions.

The northeastern region, which accounts for 7.8 per cent of the total land space of the country, is different from the rest of India in almost every way – be it in terms of culture, tradition, language and ethnicity or of history, physicality, cuisine, dress and indeed, the very cosmology and ethos of life of the people here. This diversity is further reflected within the region itself –

each state, and, indeed, even each small region within the states, has its own distinct tradition, lore, music, myths, language and even cuisine, though separated by only a few kilometres in physical terms.

From the matrilineal society of Meghalaya to the patriarchal traditions of Assam, from the Bihu dance of Assam to Cheraw of Mizoram and the Lai Haraoba and Ras Leela of Manipur, from the Moatsü and Hornbill festivals of Nagaland to the Gompas of Arunachal – each state is a storehouse of an immense wealth of traditions, customs and artistic forms that are as lush and abundant as they are unique. And all these coexist with modernity's influences. While Hinduism has ingrained itself in the lifestyle, ethos and literature of Assam, Manipur, Tripura and Sikkim, Mahayana Buddhism is found in Arunachal Pradesh and Sikkim, and Christianity in the hills of Manipur, Meghalaya, Mizoram and Nagaland, the people in this region have their own unique religious practices which have been kept alive till date even after the entry and acceptance of more "foreign" religions like Hinduism, Buddhism and Christianity. Thus the Adis, Akas, Apatanis, Bangnis, Mishmis, Mijis, Nishis and Thongsas of Arunachal worship the sun and the moon as Donyi Polo and Abo Tani, the original ancestors for most of these tribes, while the Meiteis of Manipur worship household deities like Lainingdhou and Umang Lai, sylvan deities, among others.

This uniqueness and these diversities are what *The Heart of the Matter* attempts to present – through varied narratives and through a variety of themes. And each of the twenty one stories in this volume depicts the close link that the writers have with their cultural moorings, and it is primarily this deep-rooted bond with one's culture, tradition and history that gives substance to the stories in this volume. Thus, Kaphleia's short story "Chhingpuii" depicts a Mizoram in the late nineteenth century. Set against the backdrop of an inter-tribal war, the story interweaves a tragic tale of love, war and headhunting with a portrait of the Mizo culture and society. Easterine Iralu's strange narrative "Death by Apotia" introduces the reader to the cultural belief and superstitions surrounding apotia deaths or unnatural deaths in an Angami village of Nagaland, and the denial of burial rites of passage to such victims in a society whose very existence is governed by rigid customs.

The advent and acceptance of Christianity and its values of universal brotherhood by the people of the North East, especially in the hills, find itself reflected in many of the stories. The main Christian themes of sin, remorse, repentance and ultimately, forgiveness are dealt with in C Thuamluaia's love story with a twist, "Sialton Official." The narrator is the Sialton official whose past love overshadows his present resulting in the loss of his wife and children, and how his remorse and repentance finally finds expression in a new code of life for him. "Lali" by Biakliana has the distinction of being the first Mizo short story and dates back to 1937. It not only depicts the life and status of women in traditional Mizo society, but also delineates the initial refusal to accept Christianity by some people in a hill village and the ultimate acceptance. S J Duncan's "A Christmas Story" depicts the trials and tribulations of a Khasi widow, and of the true gift of Christmas that saves her little family from ruin.

But the serenity and mysticism that these stories conjure up about the North East are as deceptive as they are real. Exotic, colourful and beautiful the North East might seem to most outsiders, but in truth, the region is also a hotbed of conflict and violence. Almost all the eight states face the problem of insurgency, with more than fifty insurgent groups operating in these states, which together has a population of 3.85 crore, according to the 2001 census – about 3.75 per cent of the total population of the country. Thus, today for the common people in the region, life is an everyday existential crisis, caught as they are in the crossfire between the insurgents, the government's counter-insurgency operations and the resultant vicious circle of insecurity, vulnerability, hopelessness, death and violence in addition to the ever-present problems of corruption, poverty and unemployment.

The deceptively leisurely pace of Arupa Patangia Kalita's "Someday, Sometime Numoli" juxtaposes the peaceful life of an innocent, trusting village girl with the shattering brutality of guns to which she falls a silent victim. This strain of senseless violence has sadly enough become a part of life in the North East, and consequently, a common theme to many creative works that emerge from the region. Sebastian Zümvü's "Son of the Soil" traces the life of a village youth in the backdrop of the insurgency movement in Nagaland, while also exploring another aspect of the movement. The protagonist tries to make it "big" by extorting money in the false garb of an insurgent with severe repercussions. Caught by the army, no one now believes that he is not part of any insurgent group but was merely out to get easy money, and he is tortured and crippled in custody.

Mohon in Keisham Priyokumar's "The Bomb," is a young man already in a no-win situation because of poverty, unemployment and corruption. He gets caught in another dilemma when an unknown youth gives him a bomb for safekeeping. Lamabam Viramani's "Thabellei," dwells on another terrifying aspect of insurgency and counter-insurgency – rape of women by army personnel, a sad reality in every conflict zone. Bimabati Thiyam Ongbi's "He's Still Alive," is the haunting story of Thamcha, whose only son goes "missing" without a trace and of her hopeful yet endless wait for his safe return. The story reflects the social reality of Manipur and of the North East where cases of people being picked up by security personnel and then vanishing without a trace and also incidents of people going underground are everyday occurrences.

The universal conditions of suppression and rebellion are dealt with in a sympathetic, yet hard hitting practical way by Nongthombam Kunjamohon Singh in "Ine Leipaklei" – an interesting tale of the transformation of a simple, meek lady who runs a little teashop and whose only concern is to educate her son, into a rebel conditioned by the oppressive forces in an unequal society. This theme of the common man caught in a world he/she fails to fathom is again dwelt upon in Yumlembam Ibomcha's "Oja Dinachandra's Dream," which highlights the plight of the common man in a corrupt, bureaucratic society, while also touching upon the lottery mania in Manipur – a simple and often disastrous means of escape from mundane reality. "The Adventures of Bah Ta En" by Wan Kharkrang narrated with sardonic humour brings home the cruel world of corrupt officialdom.

But life in the North East is not always bleak, tragic or violent. From Meghalaya, the abode of clouds, we have S J Duncan's "Civility Is All That Counts," a hilarious tongue-in-cheek comedy exploring the transformation of the honest, simple Father of Bor into a nasty, suspicious character and how he subsequently regains his lost faith in his fellow beings. M K Binodini's Ramduiali in "Itamacha" is a little non-Manipuri girl who isn't troubled by questions of identity, homeland and belongingness. To her young mind, and to her father, Ramprasad, who was born and brought up in Manipur, home is where the heart is.

Where life is, love reigns despite all hardships. Harekrishna Deka's "The River Within" is the poignant tale of a woman whose secret love for the son of the family she once worked for only comes to light on her deathbed. "Bats" by Bhabendranath Saikia is a heartwarming story of Loknath, a widower, and of how love and human bonding take precedence over material considerations like the guarding of his litchi trees from marauding bats.

The portrayal of the indomitable human spirit in Vanneihtluanga's "Thunderbird," Homen Borgohain's narrative "Fear" which is weighted with symbolism, Saurabh Kumar Chaliha's science fiction "The Final Request" exploring the question of death wish and euthanasia, and K C Lalvunga's compact, well-structured story of the supernatural, "Hostel Sentinel" add to the variety of technique, style and treatment in this anthology. These stories, while remaining true to the locale in which they are set, are also as sophisticated in their narration and form as any other story set anywhere else in the world in a similar genre.

All the writers who have contributed to this volume are well-known literary personalities in their own states and languages. Many of them have won recognition for their work not only at the national level but also at the international level. This volume brings to you some of their most interesting reads, beautifully and sensitively translated by some of the best translators available in each language. Happy reading!

December 2003   Margaret Chalthantluangi Zama

CIVILITY IS ALL THAT COUNTS

I tendered my jeep for sale. A man came to negotiate. Where are you from, who are you, I asked, for in selling and buying you should ask such questions.

I Haripod, he replied. You sell car, he asked. Yes, I said. I look at car, he said. Okay, I said. When he had had a good look, he said, I go try ... no try, no can tell good or bad. Okay, I said, for in selling and buying you should indicate you have absolute trust in your customer. I come back very soon, he added. All right, I agreed.

Roar-r-r, the jeep rumbled and in a moment he was gone. All I could see was a dense cloud of black smoke. But his "very soon" took a very long time.

S J Duncan
translated by Kynpham Sing Nongkynrih

Father of Bor, I told myself, you must not be too gullible. But at that very moment the jeep returned. Purr-r-r, it stopped. No good, he said, I not buy. All right, I said. That was that.

The next morning when I went to clean the jeep (for I used to wash, scrub and groom it every day, so it could fetch an extra value,) I discovered that the rear wheels were not of my jeep. Mine were bought only a short while ago, but these were worn out and completely treadless. Hei, I started, that rascal has cheated me. Now I see, it is decidedly unsafe to let a stranger go for a trial all by himself. But where and how will I find that son of a thief again! Father of Bor, I counselled myself, from now on you must clutch your ear tightly, you must beware. I reached for my left ear. From now on never will I be swindled again, I vowed.

Three days after that another man came. He too wanted to buy the jeep. I felt for my left ear and held it firmly. Who are you, where are you from, I asked. You must quiz them like this every time, otherwise you'll end up in a soup.

I'm Holira, he answered, I live at Nongthymmai.

Oh, a neighbour, I told myself. After inspecting the jeep for some time he said he wanted to go for a test run. Father of Bor, I cautioned myself, remember. I twisted my left ear till it hurt. I remembered Haripod. So you wish to try it out, I said, come, we'll go together. In selling and buying you should sweat it out a little, otherwise you won't make much of a profit.

Soon we were in the jeep. He was in such a tearing hurry, as if he was going to miss his bus. My god, how he zoomed. Even I, who had been driving for years, was so thoroughly disorientated that I simply couldn't make out if I were sitting in a jeep or flying in a jet. I felt as if all my entrails were trying to leap out of my stomach. With one hand I clutched my belly, for fear that my guts would spill out, and with the other I hung on for dear life. Fortunately, we soon arrived at the bus station or else I was sure my entrails would have been hopelessly entangled. But this hurricane, I mean this Holira, seemed unperturbed. He got down quickly and said, Please wait a moment, I'll go in for a little while.

It was right then that the buses were preparing to leave for Gauhati. Fifteen minutes, he did not return. A neighbour from Nongthymmai is harmless, I comforted myself, for at that moment, quite by chance, I happened to twist my left ear. Half an hour, and still he did not come. The man speaks Khasi like a khasi, he must be harmless, I'm sure he is absolutely straight – I comforted myself some more because I was beginning to worry. The Gauhati-bound buses were departing one by one, and it had been a whole hour since he left. What is taking him so long? Where has he vanished?

I went to look for him in the station's compound. There was no one there except a coolie or two. This will not do. In selling and buying you must do a little hard work, otherwise you simply won't be able to keep your business going. I went to the station's office. Scanned the entire place. Looked high and low. For whom are you searching, enquired one of the clerks. I'm looking for Holira, babu. He told me he would come in here for a little while, but he hasn't returned, though it has been more than an hour since he left.

Oh, you are looking for Holira, he said. But he left for Gauhati in one of the buses. It's been quite some time now. I nearly fell flat on my back in shock, but I braced my legs as best as I could and told myself sternly, Father of Bor, don't be a fool, preserve your dignity. In selling and buying you should not expose yourself as an idiot, otherwise you'll be swindled right and left. But why was a man like me conned by those two impostors? Father of Bor, I said, from now on you must clutch both your ears. The left hand, because it was used to the practice, went straightway for the left ear. But the right hand, being inexperienced, tried to pull at my nose. It was only when I grimaced with pain that it let go and grasped the right ear.

One day, a roly-poly man, with a belly bulging like a large cooking pot, came to my house. Where to ... I nearly addressed him as "Potbelly," but remembered in time that in buying and selling one should never be rude to anyone. So I coughed instead and asked him, Who are you, where are you from, why are you here? You not know me, I know you, he said, I Dadakhwandew, you not know me. O yes, I answered for the heck of it, otherwise how am I supposed to know my Khakhwan, the fish of Khwan river, from my Khabyrini, those from Byrini river.

You sell car, he asked.

Both my hands immediately clutched their respective ears. Why, you deaf, he asked, as he saw me holding fast to my ears. He thought I was deaf, but he was quite unaware of the profound motive behind my ear twisting. Yes, I would like to sell my jeep, I said. And I'm not deaf. Then in a louder voice, Do you want to try it out, I asked (the image of Haripod, with his small beady eyes, was staring at me) or do you want to go for a test run (the memory of that gut jerking hurricane Holira was still fresh.) You must always be on guard with drifters like these. My hands were still clasping their respective ears. No, he said, I look at jeep, I know everything. The right hand relaxed and let go of its ear.

He examined the jeep. How much price you say, he enquired. Three thousand, I replied, twirling my moustache as if to imply that I too was perfectly used to talking in terms of thousands. When it noticed the right hand twirling my moustache, the left one too came down from the left ear and delved into my shirt pocket for a Navy Cut. But as I was in the act of putting it in my mouth, Dadakhwandew suddenly gave a snort of utter disgust. Phooey, what's this?

I was so shocked that I dropped my cigarette. Three thousand for this car, he bawled, staring at me as if he would eat me up. I know this car very old. I give eight hundred, he said, reaching for his pocket with his right hand as if to take out the money. With his left, he picked up my cigarette from the ground. No, I yelped, I will not settle for less than three thousand. His right hand came out from his pocket and felt for a matchbox. Why you speak so, he said, lighting the cigarette.

No, no, mahajon, I won't give, I repeated, addressing him as a merchant, shaking my head once. Take nine hundred, he urged. His right hand was already feeling for his wallet. No, I said quickly, shaking my head vigorously. You have no idea about jeeps, he stated. Look this ispring broken in a week. I know about car, he went on. Inside engine gone bad, piston must change, carbetar also must change, kalatch also gone bad, birake also not working. I give one thousand one hundred, he concluded. No, I said. And this time I did not shake my head. I stared, instead, at his face. Maybe this potbelly is a nutcase, maybe he is just pretending to know everything about my jeep. I never knew, no, I never dreamt that my jeep would be so derelict, so worthless. Listen I tell you, he said again, taking out a bunch of bank notes, diphrenshal gear also no good, costing lot of money, new bearing also not getting now, you take one thousand five hundred.

I was now really furious. But, on the other hand, maybe some crooks had raided the garage at night and swapped the parts. I thought, let me see for myself. I opened the bonnet and looked around. Everything was fine. I stepped on the brake and checked every other part. There was nothing wrong anywhere, everything was as it should be. My anger flared up, he had denounced and discredited my car out of hand. I thought of giving him a befitting dressing down and heaping him with curses he wouldn't forget for the rest of his life. When I approached him, however, there he was, huge and fleshy like a calf elephant, and it seemed to me that even dynamite would have trouble moving him. Father of Bor, I counselled myself once again, be careful. And as I told myself that, both my hands grabbed their ears straightway. Even the right hand did not make the same nose yanking error again.

This business with this potbelly is no Holira-Haripod encounter. This must be tackled in an entirely different manner. But how do I confront this potbelly?

While deep in these profound reflections (for in selling and buying you should mull over things carefully, otherwise you'll end up in the woods,) I heard him say again, Okay, okay, take this two thousand, and so saying produce another wad of bank notes. That blazing anger was racing to my head again, but before I could counsel myself, I blurted out, Mahajon, when my jeep becomes lame, deaf and blind, when all the bones in its body are broken, and when it has been reduced to a pile of scrap iron, then is the time you should come for it. And bring that two thousand, and I will sell the jeep to no one else but you. I hurled at him, sweating all the while, for fear that he would reach out and wring my neck. But to my great relief, he left without making too much of a fuss.

I entered the house. Mother of Bor, I confided, since I have been holding both my ears I've become much wiser, but when hagglers like that potbelly turn up what will I do to keep my anger from going to my head. Bite the tip of your tongue, she replied. Mother of Bor never said more than was necessary. Oh yes, of course, why did I forget to bite the tip of my tongue? A little later Mother of Bor said, Father of Bor, left to you that jeep will stay there till it gives birth to a child. I laughed aloud, Ha, ha, ha. Mother of Bor is given to jesting like this.

Don't laugh like a nitwit, she chided and added, Father of Bor, if any other customer shows up, call me. Mother of Bor is pragmatic, she thinks of everything. She never wants to put anyone to trouble. She had seen how hard I had tried to sell the jeep. She must be feeling sorry for me.

For a while there was not a single jeep buyer to be seen. But one morning, as I was washing, scrubbing and polishing the jeep in the garage, I heard someone cough behind me. I turned. Who are you, where are you from, have you come to buy the jeep, I fired my questions at him. My hands were about to twist their ears, the tip of my tongue too was already out, ready to be bitten.

I'm here because I heard you've offered your jeep for sale. My name's Horshon, you don't remember me, he asked. Both my hands clutched their respective ears tightly. I bit the tip of my tongue but had to let go of it very quickly – partly because of the pain and also because I had to answer Horshon. Oh yes, I agreed, I have offered the jeep for sale (the left hand gave the left ear a hard pinch.) You want to go for a test run, I asked (the right hand too gave the right ear a hard pinch.) Let us go together. I want five thousand for the jeep, I declared, but you, how much will you offer, five hundred? I asked, giving the tip of my tongue another bite for I suddenly remembered that potbelly.

Horshon stared at me, stupefied. It seemed that my outbursts had really offended his feelings. In selling and buying, if you are doubtful of your man, you should hit him where it hurts. They thought I was an idiot whom they could trick into selling the jeep for peanuts. What do you think, I queried, as I removed the right hand from its ear and twirled my moustache to show that I was not someone he could fool around with.

I came to take a look at your car and to buy it if the price is right, he said. But since you've treated me so uncivilly, and stuck out your tongue at me, I have no other choice but to leave. I didn't come here to steal, he retorted, upset. I haven't seen a man anywhere, he said, who'd stick out his tongue at his own customers so frequently and abuse them as you do, even before they started bargaining. I too have my own business. I too have my own investment. Between businessmen, he said, we first look the commodity over and then talk about the price. I don't know what you think I am.

He went on and on and on. I started biting the tip of my tongue more frequently, hoping it would help me out of this vexed situation, but it bled instead. His words stabbed my heart like red-hot iron rods. But just when I was about to dive underneath the car and pretend to examine the differential gear, Mother of Bor arrived on the scene.

Oh, it's Bah Horshon, I didn't know you were here, she said. And right away they struck up an intimate conversation as if they were long lost friends. I left them together and crept backwards out of sight, for sweat was flowing from my body as water from a bamboo tube. Phooey, I said to myself, what made me so crazy as to speak like that to Bah Horshon? I went inside the house, not to hide myself in shame as you might suppose, but to have a sip of water. Father of Bor, I said, cool down. But I kept seeing visions of Haripod, Holira and Dadakhwandew. Those churlish, hoggish swindlers had made me so suspicious and ill humoured that I could not even be civil to Bah Horshon.

A little later I heard the jeep rumble to life in the garage. I peeped from a window. There he was, Bah Horshon, bent over the engine. He looked up, looked down, and walked around the jeep, no doubt giving the tyres a once-over. Then he sat close to the jeep with Mother of Bor by his side. Hei, what was he doing? I stared at them. I saw him fish out some money, count the notes and hand out some to Mother of Bor, who accepted them without a murmur. Earlier, as he was counting, I too had counted along from the window. I counted as far as two bundles of ten rupee notes, but after that I could no longer count, for Mother of Bor was looking towards me and I had to duck out of sight.

I waited inside the house. I heard them discussing something and then Mother of Bor called out to me. Father of Bor, she shouted. Yes, I replied. Why don't you come out? Bah Horshon is just leaving. I almost ran out of the house. I kept my eyes fixed on the ground lest I should trip (but you know what, later people scoffed at me, saying I did that because I couldn't look Bah Horshon in the eye.)

Goodbye Um, he said, I'm going. But I did not reply for I was still biting the tip of my tongue. Mind your manners, Mother of Bor demanded, staring at me. I let go of my tongue. Oh, sorry Um, I said. I'm leaving for Mawsynram today, he told me. I don't think these rear wheels would give me any problem, would they, Um, he asked. All of a sudden I remembered Haripod. Son of a thief, I said, shouting at the top of my voice, because I was still smouldering with pent up fury.

Father of Bor, take it easy, why did you address Bah Hor in such a manner, Mother of Bor chided me. Uh, sorry Um, I apologized. These tyres are actually quite new (I started explaining) but, son of a thief ...

Father of Bor, what are you saying, interrupted Mother of Bor, why are you making these wild accusations at Bah Hor.

I'm very sorry Um, a thousand apologies, I said, trying to appease him and explaining that I did not refer to him – all the while fuming inwardly at the thought of those scoundrels. I opened my mouth to say something more but Mother of Bor came quickly to my side and waving the bundles of money at me, said, Here, take this three thousand, Bah Hor has already paid for the jeep. The pupils of my eyes dilated as I ogled at the money. Three thousand, I repeated, excited and incredulous. But son of a thief, I exclaimed, no, no, I didn't mean you Um, I clarified hastily, I was only referring to that rogue ...

Vroom-m-m, the jeep roared to life at the moment. Okay Kong, I'm leaving, he thanked Mother of Bor, driving away before I could clarify the cause of my seething rage. When the jeep was out of the courtyard, he stole a look at me. Goodbye Um, he said, and then he was gone.

As soon as he was out of range I asked Mother of Bor what she had done to strike such a quick bargain and that too at three thousand rupees. What did I do, she replied, Bah Hor inspected the car. More

Um: Brother-in-law, also used to indicate cordiality. **Kong**: Madam.

than three thousand I cannot manage, he said. And I too did not haggle. I said, Bah Hor, when you've inspected the car and when you're prepared to pay that much, it's all right with me. That was all. We didn't really talk about it.

Father of Bor, she said, when she saw me still holding on to the three thousand as if I were in a daze, in selling and buying, civility is all that counts, it pays its own price. She stretched out her hand and gently eased the three thousand out of my hand. When you take anything out of a person's hand, you must do it graciously, she said.

Civility is all that counts, I told myself and let out a sigh when I saw that three thousand resting snugly in Mother of Bor's hand.

S J DUNCAN wrote short stories, plays and poems. A bureaucrat with the Assam Civil Services, he started writing quite early. All his major works were however written after he retired from service as the Chairman of the Assam Public Services Commission. His most popular collection is *Phuit! Ka Sabuit!* (1968). He died in 1984.

KYNPHAM SING NONGKYNRIH translates from Khasi to English and vice versa. He also writes short stories and poems in both Khasi and English, which have been anthologized in two volumes, *Moments* (1992) and *The Sieve* (1992). His other works include a collection of folk-based short stories, *Death in a Hut and Other Stories from the Khasi Hills*, a book on understanding poetry *Ban Sngewthuh ia ka Poitri*, anthologies of Khasi poems *Ka Samoi Jong ka Lyer, Ki Mawsiang ka Sohra* and *Ki Jingkynmaw*. He also edits various literary journals in Meghalaya.

CIVILITY IS ALL THAT COUNTS was originally published in Khasi as "Ka Jingiathuh Khana Khrismas" in *Phuit! Ka Sabuit!*, 1968.

Put out the light, will you? You can daydream with it off. What people say is also important."

The sun had set. My mother's nagging had started. As usual. Closing the doors and windows as soon as darkness fell, putting out the lights she starts her daily ritual. One thing or the other. "Since dawn, the roads and lanes had been dark with siphais, it's only now that they have left."

"What have they done, Ima? They're there to protect us."

"Is that why they're said to have done this and that, day in, day out? Pretending to be courageous, uhng? I'm warning you, you'll meet your end unexpectedly."

————

Lamabam Viramani
translated by *Tayenjam Bijoykumar*

She'd potter around till I put the lights out. Checking already closed doors and windows, jabbering, jabbering, "Don't say I didn't warn you. Just because you want to disobey me, disregard my words, don't go when someone calls you out late. You're to wake me up immediately."

Knowing it was useless to argue, I went to bed. After double checking the entire house, she too went to bed. And then all was finally quiet.

Ah, the pleasure of life in such moments. I had no job, no workplace. So no earnings. No food nor clothes to my heart's content. I didn't mind this much – it's my fate! A time will surely come, I told myself. But then unbidden the thought arises – this inability to laugh freely, to cry when the feeling arises, to say what you want to ... about this life in which you have no knowledge of what will happen later in the day, what the morrow will bring ...

It's too damned early. What else but to dream. That freedom's all I have. I have to call Thaballei now ...

I remember her, Thaballei arrives. Smiling, she comes to sit by me.

"What's it, Tai'bi? Want me to massage you?"

The only one who still loves me, who worries for me. Eager to please, actions match words. Her tender hands press my back, waist and legs. What pleasure! The honest, sincere caress from the heart's chosen! Her bangles danced, providing the rhythm to her sweet words. The song.

"How I'd have enjoyed had someone also massaged me like this!"

Thaballei's words startled me. Could she say such things!

"What did you say, Thaballei?"

"Tai'bi, what happened about your job? I'm just saying that there's one who'd become old before that."

Tai'bi: A shortened form of address, made up of the generic "Ta" a marker of respect for elder brother/older man, and "I'bi" possibly from the name Ibotombi or Tombi.

"Don't change the topic, Thaballei. Say again what you just said."

"It's just this: Men pretend not to know a woman's heart."

"You mean, I'm a coward?" I made to get up. But Thaballei was up and quite far away.

"Thaballei, Thaballei! I say, wait, Thaballei."

"Ahng! What happened? To whom?"

Ima got up in panic. My dreams have woken her. Such embarrassing moments are beyond count.

"It's nothing, Ima."

She took a deep breath. "It's strange. Even in my dreams my mind is disturbed." She drifted back to sleep. It was quite late, past eleven. I decided not to think of anything. Breathing deeply, I tried to sleep.

Suddenly I heard the sound of a vehicle stopping at the gate. I pricked up my ears. Some people walking. Ima's words came to my mind. "No going out when someone calls you."

The sound of heavy footsteps. Then they moved, towards Thaballei's house. Voices. That abruptly stop. Now pindrop silence. But no one leaves. The Takyelpat incident which rocked the state came to mind – the rape of a married woman. In front of her young son and crippled husband late one night. By siphais.

Surely Thaballei's feeling let down. She must be saying, What use are you as a neighbour?

And we were not neighbours alone, she was also my love, my heart's companion. Just mother and daughter alone in the house. How meek they must be now!

About two years ago they moved in next door. To my delight. At last a neighbour who was a bit better off than us, someone good hearted. Unfortunately, within a year Thaballei's father died. She was secure in the knowledge that a younger brother was there. Where had he gone?

I had also asked around and searched. Now I was the only male member in the two families.

That is why Thaballei often says, "Tai'bi, let's do something so we live together."

But I haven't had the courage to say yes. She'd ask every single day, "Tai'bi! When will your job be settled? If there's no money, we'll think up something."

Whenever this talk came up, anger simmered within me. But whom to blame? After graduating, many were the tests I took, but I always got left behind in the interview. I know the reason too. But my heart could never agree to kowtowing and bribing. I didn't have the money either.

In the end I too was caught in Shija Yaima's trap. How she knew that I had sat for the written test for that particular job is a mystery. On the very day the result was out, she landed up at our doorstep.

"Let's not miss this chance. The interview starts tomorrow."

Ima and I paid no attention. Ima merely said, "What's the use, Ibemma, of becoming one of the singers in the pala?"

The woman was not deterred. "Don't join the chorus, and you don't get the khudei. No matter how sweet the voice, or how well-versed, if you don't fawn over a teacher, there won't be any invitations. That's how the times are. If you want to snap up the khudei, do what others do."

"A hundred or two hundred is not much. But from where can I, a widow, get that much money?"

"Would we starve ourselves saying we have nothing, Iche? There's something called compulsion. And even if someone can afford to pay,

---

Pala: Nat sankirtan singers. Invitation to a Manipuri Hindu religious ceremony is usually in the name of a lead singer, who then invites others, his pala (usually his favourite students) to form a chorus. All the singers get cash and other benefits like the khudei, the striped cloth worn by men. Iche: Elder sister, also used as a marker of respect.

his money won't be accepted if he hasn't cleared the written test. There are also many who don't know where and to whom the money is to be given. And tomorrow when the age limit to join the service is crossed, what earthly use is money? I'm just saying that you'll repent afterwards."

Undeniable truths. My mother was caught. I did not interfere. A portion of my father's plot of land was mortgaged off to Thaballei's family.

But the money paid, the result of the interview, that had seemed as though it would be out any day, was stalled. Tomorrow, the day after tomorrow, a week, a month. After some time Shija Yaima arrived again, saying, "It's hard, but wait another week. This time, it's for sure. The paper's with the minister. If you don't believe me, send someone known to the minister to find out. I've even arranged to have you posted at Imphal."

And the talk came round to money. "But then, Ibungo, a little more money has to be necessarily added."

It was as if she was asking us to return money she had lent us, so vehement was her insistence. So finally a portion of our plot was sold to Thaballei's family. But seriously, I might not have met Thaballei if the land had not been sold off to her family.

What angered Thaballei most was my silence. What was I to reply? I am not fond of lying or bluffing. Neither was she. No way except to turn it into a joke.

"If you're tired of waiting, why don't you obey your mother?"

These words infuriated her further and enraged, she would walk away. It would take a week at least to bring her around.

It's been a while. I still haven't heard the heavy footsteps leaving their house, nor the sound of the vehicle driving away. What *are* they doing inside that house? I worry. Thaballei, how are you! And your mother?

Someone knocks at the door. Ima wakes up. She murmurs to me, "Don't come out." Then lantern in hand, she goes, opens the door. "Thaballei, you?" she asks.

I don't hear Thaballei's reply. Ima says, "Hei listen, don't you even know the meaning of shame?"

No reply to that either. They entered my room. In the light of the lantern, I see a frightening figure coming slowly towards me. Thaballei! Not a shred of cloth on her body, her breasts smeared red. Nail marks had left no part of her breasts untouched.

She approaches me steadily. Ima brings her a cloth. Thaballei throws it violently away. She's neither laughing nor crying. Her eyes bloodshot, she stares as if she wants to devour me. And she moves, relentlessly moving forward. She scares me. The Thaballei whom I never wanted away from me for even a moment – I fear her now.

Standing there like the fierce goddess Bhairabi, not a bit of shame in exposing those parts of her body that she had always kept hidden behind her clothes, she says, "Look Tai'bi, this body which I guarded with great care, for you, isn't it beautiful?"

It was revolting. I could not watch. Nor speak.

"Why turn away? This is the body you treasured ... Thaballei's body. These imprints left by various hands – you hate it as you do leftover food, don't you?"

My lips seem glued together. My body is numb, I can neither move nor turn, except turn my face away.

"That won't do, Tai'bi. See! See the beauty of a violated woman's body."

Ima tries hard to stop her, but Thaballei comes and climbs on top of me.

"You coward! Eat the leftovers." She holds one blood smeared breast with her hands, shoves it into my mouth, filling it completely. I cannot breathe. I try to shout.

"Is anybody there? I'm dying!"

"Ibobi, can you hear me, Ibobi."
Ima shook me awake, her hands on my shoulders.
"Move. Sit up." I was drenched in sweat.
Ima's shouts bring Thaballei and her mother running.
Thaballei asked in a voice of concern. "What happened, Tai'bi?"
Taking a deep breath, I answered. "Nothing."

LAMABAM VIRAMANI writes short stories and plays, besides children's books, travelogues, science books and articles. His published works include the short story collections – *Picnic Picnic, Chekla Paikhrabada, Kwak-ki Macha Kwak, Urok-ki Macha Urok* and *Ukhrul-dei*, besides a travelogue, *Machin Moupwa*, a radio play, *Nongphadok Lakpada*, a children's book, *Ishing Nungshit Amasung Ingocha* and a handbook for Science teachers, *Environmental Studies Tambiba*. He has received various awards including the Katha Award for Creative Fiction, the Sahitya Akademi Award, the Manipur State Kala Akademi Award, the State Children Literature Award, the Akash Vani Playwright Award, the Jamini Sundar Guha Gold Medal. He has been an active member in various councils and fora relating to literature and teaching and has also worked as an editor with some leading journals.

TAYENJAM BIJOYKUMAR has translated several short stories and poems from Meiteilon into English, besides the script of a Manipuri film. He also writes short stories and poems in English and Meiteilon. He has to his credit a collection of Meiteilon short stories, *Turoi Ngamloiba Wagi Lanban*, besides various short stories and poems in both Meiteilon and English published in leading newspapers and literary journals in Manipur and outside. An electrical engineer, he is an active member of many literary fora.

THABALLEI was first published in Meiteilon as "Thaballeigi Wakat" in *Sahitya*, 2000.

Someday, Sometime Numoli

> What is Freedom
> For him or her, for you or me?
> What does it mean
> To each one of us?
> Freedom means to love
> And to share,
> To help and to care,
> To be unafraid
> And to love everyone.
>
> — Safdar Hashmi

Numoli's fingers were aching. She had been working at the loom since daybreak. Leaving the shuttle on the unfinished pattern, she cracked her knuckles and looked deeply at the gradually emerging motif. Her brothers would be really impressed. They always teased her, calling her a bengi and an idiot – this time they

Arupa Patangia Kalita
translated by Meenaxi Barkotoki

would realize her true worth. This was no common pattern she had copied from somewhere. It came straight out of a book that Makon's citybred sister-in-law had brought.

Coming out of her reverie, she worked the loom faster and soon finished the pattern. She thought of wrapping the woven towel around the beam, but stopped and ran her fingers lovingly over it once again. How lovely the red sarais looked, their tiny tips complete against the heron white background. Resting her hand on the narrow movable reed frame separating the threads of the warp, she called out to her mother excitedly, "Bouti, o, Bouti, I've finished another one."

A little sparrow fluttered down to sit on a pole of the loom, then flew off again suddenly, frightened by the sound of the treadle, to sit on the fruiting mango tree nearby. Laughing, she called out, "You're scared, aren't you? But I know you're the one who sat on the flower on Majuda's gamosa yesterday and tangled the yarn, I know."

The song of a kuli cuckoo. She looked around, searching for the bird, and noticed a beautiful orchid on a fork of the mango tree. It seemed as if suddenly that row of red sarais in the gamosa had spread out over the mango tree, the kuli's song, the orchid petals and the whole sky. Touching the woven sarais yet again, she called out, "Bouti, o, Bouti, please come. Help me wrap the cloth around the beam."

Numoli's mother was cleaning fish for her sons' lunch. The eldest, a teacher, would go to school, the second to his office. The youngest had already taken out his bicycle to go to college. Her daughter-in-law was at her parents' place for the delivery of her first child. Numoli's mother had to manage everything herself and at such times, she wished her second son too would get married. But he was adamant: he would not bring home a wife before he had built a decent house.

She walked out of the kitchen, hands unwashed, leaving the fish in the bamboo sieve. "Why are you bringing down the sky with your shouts?" she scolded. She wanted to say something more but stopped at the sight of her daughter's innocent face looking fondly at the red pattern on the just completed gamosa. How quickly she had grown! Soon it would be time to marry her off.

Last week a proposal had come from her sakhi. She really liked that healthy, hardworking son of her best friend who had crossed the river to set up his own fields on the riverbank. But the brothers did not want to give away their only sister to an uneducated farmer, though they teased her constantly, "You couldn't even complete your matriculation. Who, but a village bumpkin, will marry you now?"

She, the mother, was touched to the quick. How did it matter if her daughter could not finish her schooling and go to college? Not many girls could work such intricate patterns on the loom. The sight of her daughter at work, humming a bihu song or a marriage song, was so soothing. The brass plates she cleaned gleamed like gold, the tangy fish tenga she cooked was like nectar, the sweet coconut laroo she prepared were as white as tagar blossoms, the pithas she made with rice powder, coconut and jaggery were very special.

Numoli was not like other fashionable college girls. She had been embarrassed seeing the silk churidar kameez that her youngest brother had bought for her from the city, last puja. "O Bouti, look what Saruda has brought for me. Where and when will I wear such fancy stuff?" And sure enough, that pretty dress, mauve like the ejar flowers, was left unworn in the case where she kept her clothes. She only wore the traditional cotton mekhela sadors that she wove herself. How she had cried when they had bought for her a silk mekhela sador set for a thousand rupees from a Sualkuchi trader! "After Pitai died, my brothers work so hard to keep our house going. And now they go and waste their hard earned money to buy silk clothes for me. That old travelling salesman counted and took not one, not two but ten hundred rupee notes in front of our very eyes. We could have bought a cow or a bundle of corrugated iron sheets for our roof with that money." The girl cared about nothing else except the house. She did not go anywhere, nor did she spend a paisa on herself. It was hard to find a young girl as homely as she was.

Numoli's mother could not help sighing.

Saruda was getting ready for college, wrapping a book with a newspaper. Numoli tried to take it away from him. "What do you do with these old newspapers? Do you ever read a word from any of them? Is there anything in your head that you will be able to read? Whenever someone takes an old newspaper to wrap something, you come swooping down," he shouted. Numoli began to weep, holding on to the batten.

Numoli's mother stroked her daughter's head, glared at her son and said, "With the money she gets from selling the papers in Ramu's shop, she buys things for the three of you. These soap dishes, the shaving bowls are from that trader who sells everything at three rupees a piece."

Hearing raised voices, Numoli's Majuda, her second brother, who was polishing his shoes getting ready for work, said, "If she didn't waste her time on all these useless things, we could have got her admitted into a college in town by now."

Numoli's mother took her daughter's hand. "Come with me, Maajoni, and help me in the kitchen. "

Wiping her tears with the end of her sador, Numoli started cleaning the fish. But when her eldest son came in to check whether the food was ready, the mother burst out. "Why scold and taunt her? God did not give her the brains to go to college. A goddess for a god, a mare for a horse. Like everyone else, she too must have someone destined for her."

The eldest son sat down on a low wooden pira. "Bouti, you're the one who has pampered and spoilt her."

The spoilt daughter of the over indulgent mother was at that moment gazing at a bheseli fish, leaving half-done the fish she was cleaning. She'd put the bheseli in a bowl of water, and was down on her knees in front of it. "Look, Bouti, how beautiful it is. As if someone has streaked its body with red and silver. Bouti, it's still alive. Isn't it so pretty when it swims?"

Her mother took some of the fish that Numoli had cleaned. She then washed and deep fried them, all the while chiding Numoli. "Your brothers don't scold you for nothing. All you need is a little fish or a bird to forget everything. You're old enough to look after a household all by yourself, but you still haven't lost your childishness."

"Whose, Khurideo?" The deep voice and the sound of boots approaching made everyone turn around. Prasanta!

Prasanta was Numoli's cousin, her paternal uncle's son. Even on this warm April afternoon, he wore a loose jacket. As he pulled up a murha to sit down, there was a clinking sound from inside his jacket. He pulled down the chain of the jacket, and Numoli got a glimpse of the three revolvers nestling inside. She wanted to scream but stopped, biting her lips. Once before, seeing a revolver in his pocket, she had asked, "Kokaideo, why do you carry it around?" and had been scolded by her mother and brothers.

How Prasanta had changed in the last few years. Two years ago he had gone away, returning home only now and then. They were seeing him now after nearly six months. Whenever Prasanta came, there was silence.

Her eldest brother was already locking the main door. "But, Sarubapu, tomorrow we have a meeting of the organization in our house." Prasanta said, leaving as abruptly as he had entered.

The whole kitchen reeked of stale sweat, wiping out even the smell of fried fish.

"Sarubapu, what did he ask you to do?" Numoli's eldest brother, asked worriedly.

"I have to keep my eyes and ears open. The whole village is swarming with the military. It's only because of Prasanta that they're after all of us. Prasanta killed two of their men in our village, didn't he?"

"Who knows what will happen next?" Numoli's mother cradled her head in her hands and sat down near the hearth.

Numoli did not like all this moaning and sighing. Moments like these – when one could not laugh, or say anything – weighed on her like a curse. How could people live like this? She felt like teasing that little kuli singing away on the mango tree or sucking a piece of the sour ou-tenga vegetable drying in the sun. But how could she do that when everyone else was so grave, sitting around like numb doves? Let Prasanta do what he wanted, what difference did it make? Saruda had given up Prasanta's company after Bordada had scolded him, and the military filled every cranny of the village. They had swooped down in truckloads after two army personnel had been killed in the fields. Before she could even understand what was happening, Bordada had taken her and his wife to his in-laws' place. But where was the military now?

She had finished cleaning the fish ages ago. The little bheseli fish was still swimming in the half bowl of water – like a little red and silver petal. She would have to keep it alive in a bottle. She wanted to get up to look for a bottle, but how could she do anything at a time like this?

"Bouti, are there any military here these days?" she asked, unable to bear the silence.

All of them turned to look at her. Her doe-like eyes gave her face the innocence of a little girl.

"Maajoni! These things are beyond you. You've been working on the loom since dawn. It's almost ten o'clock. Go eat something."

Picking up the fish in her hands, she glanced at her mother who was on the verge of tears, her face pale with fear. She was saying, "The other day, I heard in the naamghar that the soldiers do not come openly like before. It seems ten military men roamed around for a long time in Bongaon disguised as fishermen before they were found."

"Very bad times," muttered Numoli's Bordada, as he poured water over his half-eaten meal and got up. Even Sarubapu who was always on the lookout for something to eat, went out without eating. The food served to her Majuda remained on the plate, untouched.

Numoli's eyes moistened – her brothers would remain hungry all day. She sat down on the kitchen doorstep, her head between her knees, dejected, large teardrops wetting her mekhela.

Saruda returned soon after. Pushing back the bamboo pole across the gate, he entered the compound and rested his bicycle against the wall. Noticing Numoli at the doorstep, he stopped. All three brothers loved to hear Numoli calling out to her mother, announcing their arrival the moment they touched the bamboo wicket gate. They would first look at Numoli's face, say something to her and only then get on with other things. Something was really amiss if she did not go about her work humming a cheerful tune.

Last night six of Prasanta's accomplices had entered the village. Of course no military or police had been spotted yet. Still, if what their mother had heard in the naamghar was ... Sarubapu shuddered involuntarily. His chest felt like a field of dried hay that could catch fire at the smallest spark. He had got ready to go to college but, his elder brothers were not home. If something happened, what would his mother and sister do on their own? The sounds of little Numoli's sobs distressed him. "Numoli, what's the matter?" he asked.

She looked up, a little surprised that he called her by her given name – he usually found other names to tease her with. "Dada, didn't you go to college?"

"No, don't know what might happen ..." he started to say but stopped short. He did not want to frighten her unnecessarily.

"You did well. What would you have learnt cycling ten miles to college on an empty stomach?"

"Did you eat something? Bouti was saying you've been at the loom all morning." He placed his hand gently on her back.

The affectionate pat made her happy again. She wiped away her tears. "Let's go and eat. The food must be cold by now. Wait! I'll go pick a few pudina leaves. They'll taste good ground with a little tamarind."

She knelt near the lush mint patch in the garden – thin blades of sorrel were pushing up their heads through the earth in between the aromatic herb. She plucked a couple of stems with little violet flowers. The flowers wilted instantly. How easily these tiny plants wilt! She thought of weeding out the sorrel but felt, Let them be. They are not doing the mint any harm.

Spotting some little yellow flowers growing in the grass nearby, she stopped plucking the mint again. How pretty they looked! Like gold! If only I could wear one as an earring! She plucked two tiny flowers and placed them on her palm. Makon's sister-in-law wore a pair of earrings that looked like these flowers, only slightly bigger. She was, in any case, a very smart city lady. On top of that, her stylish woven clothes and sparkling earrings set off her beauty. When she became a bride, would she too ...

Her mother's best friend had taken the size of her bangles when she had come last time. Would she really become her daughter-in-law? Her mother had told her about her sakhi's home – she had fish swimming in her pond, there was no kind of tree that was not to be found in her backyard. They said that the boy was very hardworking. Tall, tanned and handsome, he had come to their home one day, bringing with him three kinds of bananas from his kitchen garden – malbhog, jahaji and senisampa. What ripe and firm bananas! Her brothers had teased her while eating them, "Did the ploughman bring these for our little bengi?" He tilled his own land, how could he be called a mere ploughman? If everyone went to work in offices and schools, who would work on the land? She would also go to the fields, to sow and reap. Not once had she been to the fields, even to take food for her brothers. They wouldn't allow her.

She opened her palm. Although wilted, the two little flowers were not completely crushed. In front of her floated the spectacle of the tall, tanned son, her mother's sakhi standing beside a bride dressed in beautiful handwoven clothes, those golden earrings in her ears like the flowers in her hand. No, how silly they would look, like ivory and ebony. The sharp tongued women who sang wedding songs might even start singing, Oh, my little heart, how pretty is the bride, but the groom? Oh, my little heart!

She had actually started singing the refrain aloud, "Oh, my little heart..."

"Come on, bengi! You went to pick pudina and now you sit here singing wedding songs. Let's go."

Hearing her brother's voice she covered her flushed face with both hands. As if he had caught her in the middle of a golden mustard field, hiding in the arms of a tall, tanned, well-built lad. Three kuli birds started singing from three directions all at once, as if to tease her. A flush crept up on her childlike face.

"My stomach is growling. Half the day is over while I wait for a meal with pudina chutney."

The youth in the mustard field vanished. She took the mint leaves and ran to the kitchen, "Bouti, o, Bouti, where did you keep the tamarind?"

She had found everything a little strange since the morning. Saruda usually studied through the night and slept late. On other days, as soon as he woke up, he would start shouting for his tea and would not leave his bed before she had served him a cup with lots of milk and sugar. But today he was up early, just a little after her. He had left untouched the tea she had lovingly poured out for him. Instead, he set off towards the village crossroad, even before washing his face and returned to say, "Nobody should go anywhere near Borpitai's house today."

Numoli and her mother would go to her borpitai's house, which was just beyond the mound, several times a day. What was special about today? Was it because Prasanta was there? What had he done that people lost their voices the moment he arrived? How would the police or the military know that he had come? Why was Saruda so upset? Numoli sat at the loom, the shuttle in her hands, motionless.

In came Ratul and Prabin – Saruda's friends. Normally they sat in the soraghar or the bat soraghar, but today they walked straight to the backyard. She got up from the loom to go make tea for them when she overheard them talking about various people being put up at various places. They left without the tea.

Bordada was not at home. Although he did not speak much, the sight of her grave and dignified brother sitting in the veranda would make Numoli very happy. She glanced at the chair on which he usually sat in the mornings. If only he were home she would not feel so uneasy. Her sister-in-law's baby was due any day. She was at her parents and Bordada had gone to see her directly after school yesterday. He would return home only this evening, after school. Her other two brothers were sitting with their mother in the kitchen. Again that numb, uncomfortable, frightening period. She was scared of sitting alone at the loom. God knows what was going on. She was scared in her own house. Everything was just the same – the mango tree drooping under the weight of its blossoms, the lau gourd creeping over the kitchen roof, the rows of tamul trees with betel leaf creeper growing on them lining the path, the backyard garden, the pebbled road in front of their house, the people going back and forth, the lemon trees growing on the little mound near their borpitai's house ... nothing had changed. She took out some seera on a sieve and started cleaning it for her brothers' snack later in the day.

Her ever smiling Saruda seemed so different today – he seemed frightened about something. "Majuda," he asked, "can you not stay at home today? What if something happens?"

"How long will they be here?"

"Prasanta had said that they'd disperse tonight immediately after the meeting."

"Has he kept anything in our house?"

"He wanted to, but I didn't let him," Numoli's mother answered.

Numoli wanted to ask her what it was that they had wanted to keep but didn't. But Ma would get irritated if she asked her anything. Numoli poured water in a big bowl and soaked the flattened rice she had been cleaning in it. Then, she went to get four bowls to serve it in, but on second thoughts, left one behind. She did not feel like eating. With what would she serve the seera? She had not milked the cow yet. What was wrong with her today? Ordinarily, she'd not only have milked the cows and cleaned the courtyard, she would have also worked on her loom for a while by now. She waited for some time, the bowls in front of her, and then asked her mother softly, "Bouti, I'm going to milk the cow ..."

Saruda interrupted, "No, you musn't go to the cowshed. In the room next to it ..." he swallowed hard.

"I'll go," Majuda said, and headed for the cowshed.

The cowshed was located in the backyard, right next to the house, as cows often got stolen. Of course there weren't as many cows now as there were in her father's time. Numoli's Bordada had sold them. All three brothers went out early in the morning. How could the two women alone manage so many cows? Now there was only a year old calf and its mother.

The cowshed was very close to the front room of Borpitai's house next door. Their father had built the house close to his brother's so that they could call out to each other in case of an emergency. Numoli had often asked her brothers to move it away and have a garden there instead. The flowers would make her borpitai's new soraghar with its full brick walls, built at the time of her cousin's wedding, look so much nicer. Although they kept promising, nobody had done anything about it. Next to the cowshed, Saruda had planted a little sapling that he had bought in the city. She could never remember the name of the plant. That little plant grew tall and luxuriant in no time. Last year it was so laden with orange coloured blossoms that passersby stopped in their tracks to look at it. The soil around there was very fertile – the betel leaves that grew there had a very special flavour and each leaf as soft as the tender segun leaf.

She felt a little sorry to see her Majuda in his white pyjama kurta going to the cowshed with the dung pail. She ran and snatched the pail. "Majuda, I'll do that. You go and get the cow instead. I need to milk her, the calf is crying for milk."

"No need to throw out the dung today. Just milk the cow," said her brother, putting the pail down.

Prabin and Ratul came in. Her mother gave them murhas to sit on in the courtyard. The very fair Ratul was flushed and agitated about something, beads of sweat glistening on his forehead. "We shall tell Prasanta this time, he can do whatever he wants to outside the village. We cannot tolerate this anymore. Last time they killed two military men and vanished, and we had to pay the price for that." Ratul seemed really scared, uttering the words one by one, "How many days has it been since we've started sleeping in our houses again? We had to hide in jungles and forests."

Numoli's hands, milking the cow, started trembling. The cow got annoyed and lifted one of her hind legs. What was Ratul saying? Will it all happen again? Last time, after staying at her sister-in-law's house for a fortnight, she had come home to find everything in a mess. The ripe and heavy paddy lay trampled in the mud. The young men would go to the Reserve every night. Truckloads of military men everywhere. For days on end nobody in the village could rest for even a moment. Those days again! She could not milk the cow today with her trembling hands. After getting only about three quarters of a litre, she tied the cow near the haystack and returned.

Majuda went in and said to his mother, "It doesn't look as if anything untoward will happen. Let me go to work. I'll work half day and return early. Sarubapu will be here. I'll eat when I return." He left after having some seera. He went out a little early today since he wanted to have a quick look around the village.

Her youngest brother was digging worms near the rubbish heap. She wrapped them in a kosu leaf. "Saruda, are you going fishing?"

"Yes."

"Can I come too? I don't need worms, I'll use atta instead."

She wanted to run to the kitchen to fetch some wheat flour, but her brother's voice stopped her. "No," he said sternly. "I'm not going fishing. I just want to keep an eye on the road."

It was possible to sit on the bridge over the pond and keep an eye on the main road. But who was her brother going to keep an eye on? She couldn't stop herself from asking.

"Why do you need to know? Go and do your work. And listen, if anybody asks you anything about Prasanta, say you don't know. And if you see the police or the military, tell me, but don't come out."

She wanted to squat near her brother and ask him what Prasanta and his friends had done to be hounded thus by the police and the military. Where do the military and the police come from? What meeting was Prasanta and his group having today? Why did her brother have to use fishing as an excuse to keep an eye on the road? Who could come? Their village was a full ten miles away from the town, and then her borpitai's home and theirs were in the Baruasuk locality of this remote village. How would anyone get wind of when and with whom Prasanta was having a meeting there?

Her mind was in a flutter. The consequence of working on the loom with a restless mind reflected clearly in her weaving – the red sarai pattern appearing in two disjointed bits separated by a white line, as if someone had driven a sharp knife through it. It was as if someone had run a knife through her mind too, leaving one half muddled while the other remained focused on the pattern. She sat staring at the two bits of the sarai, holding her face in her hands. Even this dull afternoon held something frightening. On other days, her mother would have by then joined her after finishing her work, and helped her fill a shuttle or untangle the yarn. Today her mother was still groping around in the kitchen. She had not even finished cooking. First she had burnt the vegetables, then she spilt some water, and then the milk boiled over even as she was watching. Should she go to help her mother? She decided she should but kept sitting. Somehow she didn't feel like going into the kitchen.

Suddenly the godhuligopal tree near the fence came to life. She stood up. Had the cat got in, chasing a mouse? When she clapped her hands saying, "Shoo ..." a big, fat snake came out and disappeared. That snake did the rounds of the backyards in the neighbourhood. She had seen it many times. At least four or five yards long and pitch black, it usually kept away from people. Today it had come as close as the threshold, probably to catch some frogs thinking nobody was around. There were many frogs under the godhuligopal tree. She would have to tell her brothers to get that place cleaned – nobody could tell if there were even five snakes lying in wait there.

Saruda emptied the fish he had caught onto the sieve. All sorts of fish ... garai, magur, rohu and puthi. Seeing the fish jumping about on the sieve she jumped up too, "Dada, that's a lot of fish you caught today." She touched the fish, turned them over and then cried out again with childish pleasure, "Saruda, look at these two tiny xenduri puthi."

Scraping the husky covering of a large ripe tamul with his sharp curved knife, he answered, "Fry those two for me today."

"No." She sounded so sad and upset that her brother stopped scraping the nut.

"Okay, you eat them."

"How can anyone eat such lovely fish? They're still alive, I'll keep them."

"Fish caught with a bait don't survive too long."

"They will, I'll take care of them."

"The tamul tree near the pond has given very good fruit this year," he said, splitting the nut into two, revealing its thick white kernel.

Numoli did not hear anything. The two tiny fish, jumping around like two streaks of vermilion, occupied her mind completely. Those unnecessary worries, the sarai, the big, fat snake under the godhuligopal tree – all these thoughts were left behind, like the outer covering of the areca nut that Saruda was peeling. Her long braid trailing in the dust she sat on her haunches staring at the fish.

"Oi, bengi, go and get me a paan leaf. Don't forget to put some lime on it," her brother said, lifting her braid gently from the ground.

Everyone in the house called her names and asked her to run small errands. And her overwhelming love for her brothers found expression and fulfilment in these little chores. That day nobody had asked her to do anything. Now Saruda had asked her to fetch paan, and her suspended breath seemed to flow again.

"In just a minute, Saruda!" she ran to the kitchen, her braid flying. Not a single paan leaf in the broken handled bowl – just a black, rotting remnant. She ran towards the cowshed to get a fresh leaf from every one's favourite creeper. The leaves from the others were either sold or given away to neighbours on festive occasions. The long handled hook stood against the fence. Reaching out for it, her eyes fell on the flowering tree her brother had brought from the city. What a strange plant it was. New leaves were sprouting on all the other trees nearby, but not on this one. Was it dying? She scratched the stem – it was still juicy and soft green like young leaves.

While she was stooping to check it, a man came up. Tall, stiff, dark, strange – she could not remember having seen him before. Dressed in a dhuti and punjabi, a gamosa with a large flowery pattern on his shoulders, and a golden coloured, ornamental seleng sador with a jari border over his body. Who was this man with closely cropped hair and a big impressive moustache? He was not from this village. Who was he looking for? Was he a relation of Makon's sister-in-law? The man came very close to the fence.

"Which is Prasanta Hazarika's house?" His voice was as rough as he was stiff. The tone was somewhat unpleasant. Why did he want to know Borpitai's house? There was a marriage proposal for Lata who was doing her MA in the city. This man looked like someone from that family. One did not dress up so much unless one was visiting for an auspicious occasion. She hesitated a moment before pointing out the house to him. If somehow this man went back to the city without finding her borpitai's house, everyone would blame her. They would accuse her of sending him away out of jealousy, for not having made it to college herself.

In her mind's eye, she could see the picture of her citybred cousin with her cropped hair and red lipstick, wearing a bright coloured, flower patterned sari. How distasteful that sight was! But why would she be jealous? She was happy if everyone was happy.

Instantly the man straightened. Suddenly, the whole area reverberated with the sound of bullet shots coming from the direction of her borpitai's house. The air was filled with the smell of explosives. Before she knew what was happening, the man caught hold of her, his strong hands pressing her against his chest like a shield, aiming his revolver at her uncle's house. In reply to every shot of his, bullets were raining on them from all sides. The man kept jumping up and down like a cat, forward, then backward. Suddenly something pierced the left side of her bosom. She wanted to cry out, O, Bouti, but could not roll her tongue. She heard her mother's voice once, "What happened to my dear Maajoni?" After that a deafening sound behind the cowshed. And with that sound, her little world of red dotted fish, singing cuckoos, blossoming mango flowers, her mother's love, her brothers' affection and the red patterns on the gamosa that sparkled on her loom – all fell silent. Her head wilted and drooped like the plucked blades of sorrel. On her white sador appeared the red colour of blood, the stains rough and ugly ... as if some careless unskilled weaver had tried to weave a confused border on sparkling white cotton. The man lowered her to the ground, her body writhing and shaking, like the two red dotted fish flipping on the sieve. Kneeling, he fired a round of bullets in the air and then took out a walkie talkie from the pocket of his punjabi.

The spring wind seemed to carry the smell of the blood through the entire village. Like her limp and drooping head, the whole village seemed to wither away at the smell of explosives, the sound of firing and the deafening roar of grenades. The notes coming from pipes and horns fell silent. People on the streets and in the fields hurried home and locked their doors. The strangely dressed military man kept guard over Numoli's body. The news spread from house to house in no time. Those who heard it could not restrain their tears. How could that innocent girl who never went out of the house without her mother die such an unnatural death? In everyone's cooking pots food remained uneaten. Those whose food was already served fed it to cats and dogs. The terror stricken people got to hear another piece of news – Prasanta and his gang had fled by the side of the naamghar through the fields. And in their mind's eyes floated the spectacle of the paddy fields laid waste last year, laden paddy sheaves trampled flat by military boots. Those wounds had not healed yet, and now, once again ...

When the first round of shots were fired, Numoli's mother was in the kitchen, washing and straining rice. She had called out, "Sarubapu, what is that sound?" And when she heard round after round of the same sound, she stiffened, the steaming pot of rice still in her hands. She put the pot down and started looking for her daughter. She heard her youngest son's anguished voice from the living room, "Bouti! We're finished, our fates are sealed." When she reached the living room she found him sobbing. Looking out of the window she saw the man with the gun, holding her daughter to his chest to shield himself from the bullets raining from Prasanta's house. The mother could not see her daughter clearly. She could not hear her voice either. In the midst of the smell of gunpowder and smoke, her daughter's thick serpent-like braid would suddenly swing in the air, only to vanish from sight again.

Seeing his mother trying to open the front door, Sarubapu went and locked it. "Bouti! Pitai is already gone, now if you too ..." They saw blood red flowers sparkle on Numoli's white dress. A frightening, ear shattering roar. This time Sarubapu, red with fury, tried to open the door to go to Numoli's side. But his mother held him back, "I've already lost one child, how can I bear the loss of another ...?" Her voice faded as she lost consciousness. Sarubapu laid her on the floor, brought some water from the kitchen and sprinkled it on her. She opened her eyes and started mumbling, "My dear, sweet Maajoni ..." Prasanta's house had fallen silent. On seeing the injured man firing in the air and trying to contact his associates, Sarubapu wanted to go out again but stopped. The man was like an injured tiger guarding its prey. If he went and something happened to him, what would his mother do?

In his mother's distraught mind, drifting between consciousness and unconsciousness, floated the picture of her Numoli, walking back from the pond, crying in pain. Once, during their holidays, all three brothers had together drained the pond. Numoli had hovered around like a little girl, running small errands for them, helping them, when a tiny sting fish had pierced her finger. She had run crying to her mother, "O, Bouti!" She had cried so much on being pricked by a little fish ... Her mother tried to get up again and open the door to go out – Numoli was lying face down on the stones of the road, a pool of blood around her. Sitting beside her was the big man, revolver in hand. He too was bloodstained. Every now and then he let out a roar like an injured tiger, in Hindi, "Keep away!"

The line between consciousness and unconsciousness blurred in the mother's mind.

Not too long into the afternoon, four truckloads of military men descended on the village. People returning from work, students returning from school or college, small traders returning home with empty baskets after selling their wares in the city – all were stopped on the road to the village and asked to turn back.

That day, Raghu had got a good price for the ahu-jika gourd from his garden. He had bought half a kilo of fish with the money, and was already thinking how tasty the fish would be when cooked with fresh gourd, when he was stopped by the military. Their guns terrified him. Girls returning from college had to seek shelter in the hospital, while most of the men decided to pass the night in Ramu's little teashop at the end of the road. They sat up the whole night.

Numoli's Bordada was returning home from school after spending the previous night at his in-laws' house. The bag on his bicycle was bursting with things his wife had sent for Numoli – patterns for the loom, some bamboo shoot pickle, some kharoli made from pressed mustard seeds ... The whole night at Ramu's shop, he hadn't been able to sleep. All night he kept hearing of the girl, sometimes they said bride, killed in the firing. Worry for his mother and little sister made his heart throb like a paddy thresher.

Numoli's Majuda had also returned home early as promised. On the way he too heard about a girl who had been killed in the firing. His heart had missed a beat – they were assembling near their house, and there weren't any girls in his borpitai's house. For a while he had been overwhelmed. God knows what had happened.

Cycling furiously he had tried to enter the village, but the military had obstructed his way. Orders from above. Nobody to enter the village or leave it. He almost forced his way in. Partly in Asomiya and partly in broken Hindi, he tried to tell them that his mother and sister were alone at home. But they did not relent. There was the whole village inside. Why was he so worried? How could he tell them what was going on in the house next to theirs? Seeing him standing on the road with his bicycle, one of them pushed him aside. With a heavy mind, he proceeded to the quarters of a friend who worked in the hospital, to spend the night there. Throughout the night, he kept hearing about the girl lying on the road. And every time it was mentioned, a shiver went down his spine. His friend had often invited him to stay overnight. Today, he had even put together a nice dinner for him, but Majuda could not eat a single morsel.

Towards evening they loaded Numoli's body onto a truck. Sarubapu, fanning his unconscious mother, caught a glimpse of it – his sister's body, lying amidst upright guns and khaki uniforms, he could not contain himself – he went to the edge of the pond and wept, biting his lips hard until they bled, so that his mother might not hear him. Nothing stirred anywhere – his unconscious mother, his sister's lifeless body being carried away in the truck. In his life of one score years he had never encountered a crisis like this. His father had died in that very house two years ago. The whole village had come and seen them through that crisis.

Some had taken charge of their distraught mother, others had showered all four of them with affection and understanding. Yet others had cooked and made sure they got the vegetarian baratia meals prescribed for relations after a death in the family in time. The whole village had surrounded them, protecting them like a big bird guarding her eggs. In the warmth of their affection their wounds had healed quickly. Remembering the hustle and bustle of people going in and out of their house, bringing them food, provisions, fruits and vegetables, he suddenly felt very lonely. He was not a city lad. He had been nurtured on the affection of an entire village. He succumbed to the terror of the present situation, and his stifled sobs rolled down the banks of the pond.

The sun had set into the reserved forests. In the gradually increasing darkness, the military went from house to house. They collected all the men in the big yard in front of the naamghar. They gave Rajat Barua, who had come to the village from the city to meet his sick mother, an extra kick or two when they came to know he taught in a college – for being an educated man, yet allowing terrorists to enter the village. For that same crime, they also kicked around the old arthritic village headman. Old and sick, young and immature – all sat quietly, shivering. In the houses where there were no men, they left a trail of devastation behind, trying to find the birds that had flown, in the pots of rice and the jars of salt.

When Sarubapu walked by the edge of the pond and reached the naamghar they all looked at him. The dried coagulated blood on his lips and his bloodshot eyes swollen with incessant crying were of the same colour. Seeing all those familiar faces, he started weeping again, tucking his head between his knees.

The jawans who went into Sarubapu's house looking for terrorists knew only one thing – the gang of terrorists had fled from somewhere very close by. They entered Sarubapu's house in the middle of the night. The doors were still open.

After searching the whole house they reached the front room where Sarubapu's mother was still lying, almost unconscious. "Dead or alive?" they asked in Hindi and left, after prodding her from side to side with the muzzle of their guns. The flash of guns, the sound of boots and the unfamiliar smell brought Sarubapu's mother back to consciousness. She sat up on the floor with a start. And her mind saw again and again the image of a long braid swaying in the wind like a big, fat snake. She felt like getting up and screaming, "O, my dear Maajoni," but stopped, seeing the armed men swarming her courtyard. She wanted to call out to Sarubapu but her voice choked. When she thought one or two of them were approaching, their boots crunching, she crawled under the bed, like an animal. A sharp sliver of light licked the house. The woman tried to shrink further into herself. After that the sound of boots died down. Numoli's mother shivered and sobbed silently with a terror she had never experienced in her entire life.

Numoli's body was returned to the village just before dawn. Her virgin body had been cut open by a doctor's scalpel and sewn together again. After Numoli entered the village, the blocked road was opened. When they set foot on the road, the frightened villagers saw the body of the much loved girl that they all knew lying on a little wheeled carriage that looked like a cow cart attached behind the jeep. Her body jumped with the jeep as it drove over the bumpy, potholed road. It seemed as if she would sit up that moment, flash a smile and say, "Raghukai, have you come back from the market?" Raghu would stop for a moment. And from his basket he would take out a paper packet and show it to Numoli. "I've bought a sador for your mami. It cost me twenty five rupees." She would inspect it closely, "It's quite nice. But the woven ones are much better, this is flimsy." Raghu would let out a sigh, "What can one do? The woman who used to weave for everyone in the house is now crippled with pain." Once, during that Bihu, Raghu's sick wife had cried inconsolably after putting on a green bordered white sador

Numoli had woven for her. That same Numoli was today reduced to this. Raghu sat down on the roadside and started to howl.

A military man standing nearby started hurling abuses at him, "Your own boys have become terrorists, you've hidden them in your houses ... those terrorists kill your own people, and now you sit and cry ..." He abused in Hindi, of which Raghu did not understand a word. In his bosom then was a heart full of love for a white sador with a green border. He kept crying.

The jeep carrying Numoli began to circle the village, a loud voice announcing – "Your own people are being killed by them, this is what will happen if you shelter terrorists. Cooperate with the police and the military. Otherwise such incidents will keep happening." Most of the villagers understood not a word. No one was allowed to come close to Numoli. When the jeep passed by Makon's house, she, mad with grief, tried to touch Numoli, but was sternly stopped.

Almost all of those who had spent the night waiting outside the village had also returned by then. But nobody entered their homes. The wicket of Numoli's house was wide open. The villagers entered the courtyard, one by one, silently. In their houses, their cows and calves were still in the sheds. Nobody had swept their courtyards. Those who had eaten nothing since the afternoon of the previous day had still not thought about lighting their kitchen fires. The housewives had fed the very young, the very old and the very sick with whatever was available and rushed to be beside Numoli's mother. No one bothered about the neighbour's cows ruining their gardens, no one checked whether the ducks and hens had all returned to their coops or had been devoured by cats and jackals. In their minds was an overpowering, overwhelming fear – an all consuming terror.

Meanwhile, Numoli's two other brothers had returned home. Their mother was still semi-conscious. And Sarubapu? Four or five men together could not hold him down. He was screaming, "What did she know of terrorists, or the army? Why was she killed?" He was banging his head on the floor. Those trying to restrain him almost toppled over. Seeing his brothers, he started rolling on the floor, like an old tree that had just been felled, "I couldn't save her. In front of my eyes, they ..."

At that moment, the jeep halted in front of the house. Numoli came home borne by two jawans. She was laid down in the courtyard. Over her body, covered by her bloodstained clothes, a military officer laid a garland of roses and took off his hat. The other jawans, jostled in with their boots and guns. They too placed garlands of roses on her. The handsome and polite officer stood for a while with his head bowed. The truckload of jawans who had accompanied Numoli's jeep, and now filled her house and compound, also followed suit. The waiting villagers realized they were looking once more for Prasanta and his gang. One of them even pulled up Sarubapu, whose tear stricken face was hidden between his knees, to look at his face. After about five minutes they all trooped out, the sound of their marching boots echoing, and climbed into the truck. The officer saluted Numoli's body once more and got ready to leave. Before getting into the jeep he said in English, "If you shelter terrorists, things like this will happen."

Sarubapu shouted back, "Everyone tries to victimize the innocent. I'll have my revenge on all of you. Just wait ..." This time his brothers held him back.

His old borpita, Prasanta's father, approached him slowly, weeping uncontrollably. "O Bapu, don't try to stir up a hornet's nest." He had heard again and again, throughout the night, that the bullet riddled body of his six foot tall, well-built son, who had been away from home these last two years, was lying in the reserved forests, in some fields, on the riverbank.

Numoli was lying asleep in the courtyard – the garland of roses on her bosom, her long plait trailing on the grass – encircled by a ring of dumbstruck people whose stomachs ached with hunger and whose eyes were stinging because they had not slept all night. No elder was trying to remind the others about the rules and rituals of performing the last rites, nobody was trying to organize the wood for the pyre, no one had even thought of taking the body to the tulosi plant, no lamp had been lit near the head, no incense had been burnt near the body, no joss stick had been lit ... Only the occasional sobs, quickly stifled, and Sarubapu's screams, "I'll teach them all a lesson, I'll spare no one ..." broke the silence.

Who would put Numoli's body on a bamboo bier and take her to the riverside cremation ground? How would they do that? Numoli seemed to spread over the entire village. There sat Numoli on the tree of large, oval kaji limes in Raghu's garden, bursting into a song if anyone came near, like Tejimola,

> *O cowherd of the village,*
> *My dear friend and my brother,*
> *O, listen to my plea,*
> *Pluck not this lime or the other.*

She'd become a gourd creeper and spread over the mounds of the village, breaking into sobs if anyone came near. She bloomed and swayed as lotuses in the pond, crying out if anyone tried to pluck her. One day someone would come to her and say, " If you're the little Numoli, then eat this little bit of chewed tamul." She will eat that and turn into a little sparrow. Then he would say again, "If you're the little Numoli, if you have love in your heart, then wear this gamosa and you will become a human again." Numoli will come back to life. Her heart is full of love. She will wait till she can come back to life.

Tejimola: Main protagonist of a popular Asomiya folktale. She was killed by her stepmother, but turned into a tree, bird and finally a lotus, before coming back to life when her father gave her tamul to chew, and threw a gamosa over her.

ARUPA PATANGIA KALITA writes short stories, novellas and novels both for adults as well as for children. Her published works include *Mriganabhi, Ayananta* and *Kaitat Ketaki* (for children,) *Moruyatra Aru Anyanya, Morubhumit Menaka Aru Anyanya* and *Deopaharar Bhagnastupat* (short story collections) and *Arunimar Swadesh,* a collection of three novellas. She has won a number of awards including the Katha Award for Creative Fiction, the Sarlesh Chandra Dasgupta Sahitya Setu Award and the Bharatiya Bhasha Parishad Award. Besides writing features for Asomiya journals, she also edits (with her husband) a little magazine called *Damal* (The Bridge.) She has translated a collection of Chinese folktales, entitled *Maple Habir Rang.* She teaches English Literature at Tangla College, Assam.

MEENAXI BARKOTOKI (Bhattacharjee) translates poetry and short fiction from Asomiya to English. She also writes short stories and travelogues. She teaches Mathematics at at the Indian Institute of Technology (IIT) Guwahati. The founder treasurer of the North East Writers' Forum, she is presently working on a research project in Germany.

SOMEDAY, SOMETIME NUMOLI was first published in Asomiya as "Ketiyara Numoli Aydin" in *Saadin, 1998.*

THE BOMB

Mohon was in a fix. He had to find a place to explode the bomb.

This thought had tormented him for the last few days, keeping him awake at night. Tired out, he confined himself to his room even during the day, spending most of his time on the chair near the window and watching the passersby wearily. All this was new to Mohon. It was also his agony.

The day was already dawning when he managed to drift into sleep. But all too soon, it seemed, his father's persistent coughing woke him up. The morning had advanced quite a bit. In the room next door, his father was probably still in bed. He had been coughing like this for some days now.

Keisham Priyokumar
translated by Tayenjam Bijoykumar

Mohon thought of getting up to attend to him. But what could he do even if he did? What was the use of superficial compassion? He closed his eyes and tried to go back to sleep. But thoughts of the bomb came rushing back. Is it right to explode the bomb – In a train full of innocent people? At a crowded corner of the city? There is a reason behind every action. But is every reason right? How do you measure another's inner thoughts? Trivial issues maybe. Still, the bomb, exploding all of a sudden, people blown into pieces, others crippled and dying. Seeing it all with one's own eyes or hearing it over the radio! It might be seen as fun, but that wasn't what Mohon wanted. Every action ought to have a right and just cause.

Where was the youth planning to explode the bomb? And why had he handed over the unexploded bomb to him?

"It's going to be a little difficult enroute. Please let me leave this with you. I'll come and collect it in a day or two." It was the middle of an afternoon when no one was around. Coming in hurriedly into his room, the youth had shoved the bag at him and left quickly before Mohon could get over the surprise or ask any questions.

Mohon had opened the bag and found the bomb inside. He had been stunned. Alarm followed. For a while he could not decide what to do. Calming himself, he wrapped the bomb in a plastic bag and stealthily buried it near the lavatory in the backyard.

The youth did not come back the next day or the day after. Many days have passed. Mohon has been uneasy. Tense. Full of fear. Cannot eat or sleep. The youth had courageously carried the bomb around in a bag. But now, it was lying buried in Mohon's backyard. Why should he be afraid? But he seemed to be bathed in cold sweat whenever he saw army personnel or the police on the road. Now, after so many days, he was able to calm himself down a little. Sometimes now he felt he was the new owner of the bomb.

"Baji, why are you getting dressed so early in the morning? Where are you going? And here I am, to ask you to go with me to the doctor's." His sister's voice brought him back to the present.

"Forget the doctor. The under secretary – I have to go to his house. I hear that the file has been sent to him again," his father answered.

"Won't it be better to meet him later in the office after taking your meals? You don't look too well."

"Nothing's wrong with me. At the office I will have to stand at the gate, the guards won't allow anyone to enter. And while I wait in the shade of the tree in front of the secretariat the file will be shunted up and down."

"But then, even if you meet him at his house, without money, it will be futile."

"The under secretary's father and I were teachers together. We were very close friends. I'll ask his father to plead on my behalf."

"In case you need this, here, use it."

"Where did you get this money?"

"I sold off my earrings."

They were silent for a while. Then his sister said, "It's not really compulsory to wear gold ornaments ... they're anyway meant to be sold off when the need arises."

His father didn't reply.

Mohon heard them go down the wooden staircase with heavy steps. He kept lying on the bed, trying in vain to go back to sleep.

It has been about a year since his father had retired as a junior high school teacher. But he hadn't received his pension till date. How long has it been since this old man's been running around? Had it not been for the rent they received from Ram Prasad, how would they have survived? His father had received some money at the time of his retirement. That had been given to the minister to secure a job for him, Mohon. It was gone like a pebble dropped into water. He had tried innumerable times to retrieve the money. A petty teacher can't save much, and he had two children to educate. Mohon's father had lived his life as a simple and honest teacher. And now? Would he be able to accept all this? At the treasury, at the bank, in the scorching sun, among the old men and women – how long would he have to stand?

Mohon, who had been lying on his back, turned on his side. He didn't want to think of his father anymore. Instead he started thinking of the bomb again.

"You haven't got up yet?"

He opened his eyes. "Your tea and breakfast," his sister said, placing the same on the table.

What a surprise. It was a long time since morning tea had been made in the house. He went down once in a while to Ram Prasad's hotel for a cup.

He looked out of the window. The sky was clear and greenish. He saw the sunlit crowns of the multi storeyed buildings of Thangal Bazar in the distance. He glanced again at the tea on the table ... and remembered the earrings.

"Nowadays you hardly ever leave your room. What's wrong?"

"Nothing."

He didn't say more. After a while, his sister said hesitantly, "I was thinking of making a partition in the ground floor kitchen to start a small shop. But Baji isn't willing."

She became silent, her eyes on the table, her face ashen even in the daylight. Suddenly she smiled, saying, "I wanted to tell you something, but forgot ... Listen, considering the subjects you've studied, you shouldn't think too deeply. I'm worried about you."

Mohon did not smile. She had joked about his studying philosophy and psychology. But there was something else she wanted to say.

There were only two rooms on the ground floor. The bigger room was Ram Prasad's hotel. It was also home for Ram Prasad, his wife and their three children. During the day it was the eating place for the customers. At night they kept their folded clothes in a corner, spread themselves out on the benches and slept.

The smaller room was their kitchen. Once Mohon's sister had suggested starting a small shop in the kitchen itself. Their father had refused. Mohon too had not liked the idea, but had kept silent. Why then was she trying to reopen the topic? Was she trying to remind him of the problems in the family? Or, did she want to entrust something to him?

Once born, one has to stay alive ... live in the society. While a student, he had known Shankaracharya, discussed the Gita and the Vedanta, atma, paramatma, cosmos, maya. But can anyone run away from society saying that the world itself is maya? Act, Arjun. One has to live. But what does one need to live? Wasn't this what his sister was saying? But he didn't ask her.

"Why are you sad again? What are you thinking of?"

"Nothing."

"Don't think. It's not right to think so deeply about life. You might not have brushed your teeth yet. Still, there's no harm in having tea."

She left the room and went downstairs, probably to the kitchen. He asked himself again – how far has he understood his sister? Was it possible to say that even siblings know each other?

His sister had returned home unexpectedly one day less than a year into her marriage. Hers was a love marriage, an elopement. Mohon was surprised, but had thought it was a petty quarrel that would not last long. After two or three days his brother-in-law had come to take her back. But his sister did not go back. His brother-in-law too was a man of few words. He had his pride, probably wanting to maintain his status as an officer, no matter how low ranking it was. But Mohon was not interested in thinking about other people. He had remained detached then too. Their father had tried to reason with her, as a father should. He had even suggested that he would accompany her if she was embarrassed to go by herself. She had refused, and their father did not pursue the matter further. His brother-in-law did not come again.

"Iche, why did you quarrel with Ebai?" Mohon had asked her one day.

"I didn't."

"If you didn't quarrel, why did you come back?"

His sister had looked hard at him and asked, "Are you unhappy with my staying here?"

For a moment, Mohon hadn't been able to answer. He could only look at her. Then he had said, "It's not that, Iche."

"You had studied psychology, hadn't you? Though I haven't, I can grasp the inner meaning of another person's words. Instinctively. Neither earnings nor dowry – when someone makes even the slightest remark to a girl not belonging to a rich family, I find it hard to tolerate."

Fear cropped up in his mind. His sister didn't continue either ... She went out. Alone, Mohon was lost in himself, thinking, The distance between one person and another only become wider. Love is a great joke. Something that can be broken into pieces.

Mohon's thought turned to the bomb again. His tea remained untouched.

Sitting on the chair near the window Mohon watched the road below. As Ram Prasad's hotel was near the bus parking, there were many people entering and leaving the hotel. Many more were getting into the buses. Another bus arrived, from somewhere. Many people got down. Where had they come from, where did they go? There ought to be a reason for every journey. A bird fluttered past in the distance. Destination and journey ...

Mohon was brought back to reality when he heard his father coughing. When had he returned?

"Did you meet the person, Baji?"

His sister was with their father.

"Yes." He seemed to take a long, deep breath. After a while he said, "We'll need about ten thousand rupees. Should we borrow it from Ram Prasad?"

"The twenty thousand rupees that we borrowed for Ibungo's job have not been returned yet. He also pays the room rent every month. We are surviving on that," his sister said softly.

"Once I receive the general provident fund, gratuity and the rest, it will all be returned."

He heard them go downstairs. This time Mohon did not look out of the window, but kept gazing at the ceiling, closely. He did not look at his father entering Ram Prasad's hotel.

Mohon is flattening out dough for rotis in Ram Prasad's hotel. His father sits on a low cane stool, near an oven with leaping flames, dropping the rotis into a frying pan. Both father and son are drenched in sweat. But they do not stop working, not even to wipe the sweat. Wearing a sparkling white dhoti and shirt, Ram Prasad sits near the door with his legs crossed, sipping tea. Mohon looks at Ram Prasad now and then with fear. His hands do not cease their work, but the hullabaloo of young men in his sister's paan shop in the next room also reach his ears.

The soul is immortal. Nainang chindanti shastrani, nainang dahati pavakaha ...! What is the harm even if the soul dies? Why did I study books that weaken the mind? Whether the soul dies or not, whether the body dies or not, the bomb has to be exploded. His bomb has to be used today. It could be anywhere. Mohon stops abruptly.

"Tamo, Tamo!"

Mohon woke up suddenly, startled, his eyes bright and unfocused. Then realization dawned. He must have fallen asleep, his whole body drenched in sweat. He looked at the window. Outside, the sun was blazing.

"Tamo, it's me. Let me take away that thing. I had gone to a far off place for some time. Please don't mind."

Mohon turned to stare at the youth, not a single word escaping his mouth.

Tamo: Elder brother, also used to address a man senior in age.

KEISHAM PRIYOKUMAR has three anthologies of short stories to his credit – *Awaoba Punshi* (1971,) *Eikhoigi Yumlonnaba* (1990,) *Nongdi Tarakkhidare* (1995) and *Lan Amasung Mang* (2000.) A recipient of the Katha Award for Creative Fiction, his book *Nongdi Tarakkhidare* won him several awards, including the Sahitya Akademi Award, the Manipuri State Kala Akademi Award, the Dr Khoirom Tomchou Memorial Gold Medal, the Telem Abir Memorial Award and the Dineswori Sahitya Award. A civil engineer by profession, he has edited the literary journals – *Wakhal*, *Sahitya* and *Meirik*, and a literary bulletin, *Sahityagi Pao*.

TAYENJAM BIJOYKUMAR has translated several short stories and poems from Meiteilon into English, besides the script of a Manipuri film. He also writes short stories and poems in English and Meiteilon. He has to his credit a collection of Meiteilon short stories, *Turoi Ngamloiba Wagi Lanban*, besides various short stories and poems in both Meiteilon and English published in leading newspapers and literary journals in Manipur and outside. An electrical engineer, he is an active member of many literary fora.

THE BOMB was first published in Meiteilon as "Bomb" in *Lan Amasung Mang*, 2000.

A CHRISTMAS STORY

U Kyuin, an amusing name, but Khasi sounding to the very bone, is, come to think of it, pleasant sounding too, although it means nothing.

U Kyuin's father, U Myllon, was a good natured youth of twenty five, well-built and muscular. Used to labouring in the fields since his childhood, he was as swift as the wind. And U Kyuin's mother, twenty two year old Ka Irbon, was so in love with her work, she was never given to wasting her time in gossip.

Ka Irbon had two farms besides a paddy field at Umjarain. And both she and U Myllon worked steadily to improve and extend the field. This particular year they

---

S J Duncan
translated by *Ivan M Simon*

were able to gather three bushels of paddy, each bushel twice the length of a grown man's arm. So they had enough rice, potatoes, millet and various seasonal vegetables to last them through the year.

A year into their happy marriage, their first child was born, who, as the months went by, grew up into a handsome child.

Yet, the life of man hangs from the hands of the one above, from god the dispenser. There came a winter, after the harvest, when U Kyuin was three years old, U Myllon went hunting in the Bhoi country with his friends. Three weeks after his return, he was suddenly afflicted with fever, and within six days, to the great grief of Ka Irbon and all the people in her village, he died.

Ka Irbon, then pregnant with her second child, was distraught with grief. It was the support of her relatives that somehow managed to get her back to work again, and the immediate future. Two months after U Myllon's death, she gave birth to a daughter, joy of her life. Only to lose her a year later. Misfortune and sorrow seldom come singly. Ka Irbon, heartbroken once again, thought of herself as a monster of sorts. But when she heard U Kyuin calling "Mei," she collected herself. "Forgive me, a fool and a mad woman, o god!" she prayed. The sight of U Kyuin made her heart glow afresh with love for her son.

When U Kyuin turned six his mother sent him to the village school. U Kyuin proved to be an earnest pupil. Rain or storm, he would never stay away from school. For the very young, school lasted half a day. As Ka Irbon had to go to the field almost every day, she made arrangements for U Kyuin to have his lunch with her neighbours.

On the first Christmas after he joined school, his teachers, seeing his intelligence, made him part of the choir group and even gave him a role in the Christmas play. The next year he was promoted to Class I. These were times when U Kyuin was most happy. His comprehension and his progress in his studies were such that his teachers even suggested that he should be given double promotion, but the headmaster considered it inappropriate to tax his proficiency too much.

Around this time, thirty year old U Sorju came to court Ka Irbon. U Sorju lived at Madan and was a carpenter by profession, earning as much as two rupees a day, a considerable sum at that time. For six months he was a constant visitor to her house, occasionally helping U Kyuin with his sums.

Sometimes, U Sorju would accompany Ka Irbon to the fields, although he had no idea whatsoever of working in the field. Noticing his inexperience, Ka Irbon remarked, "Bah Sorju, it seems you cannot work like us farmers."

"Why can't I?" he said, "It's simply because I haven't had the experience." But in his heart of hearts, U Sorju had already decided that he would not till land or clear bushes for jhum cultivation like these villagers. A trained carpenter, that's what he was.

Every time he called on the family he was polite and considerate, and Ka Irbon never saw any indication that he was a hard drinker, though she could not be sure whether he drank after leaving the house.

Not long afterwards, U Sorju came to live with Ka Irbon. U Kyuin started calling him Panah, stepfather. U Sorju continued to work as a carpenter in town while Ka Irbon went on with her work in the fields. A month later, U Sorju hinted that there were better prospects in carpentry than farming. If he could but secure a little capital, he said, he would be able to get a government contract in the PWD. When, as if to prove his word, he brought home six hundred rupees and gave it to her every week, Ka Irbon thought she had not made a mistake when she consented to be his wife.

Those pleasurable days were few. With every passing week, he brought home less and less money. He also started returning late at night quite drunk. Ka Irbon could not be sure whether this urge to drink started only after he came to live with her.

One morning, after he had returned home in a drunken stupor, Ka Irbon gave him a piece of her mind.

"Don't worry!" he said, "I'm not a habitual drinker. It's my friends who have somehow led me astray. I haven't wasted the money either. I've won a contract to build a new house in Laitumkhrah and had to pay the labourers. Naturally I am left with only a little."

His explanation sounded plausible, but Ka Irbon was still doubtful. But she said nothing more. Playing in the courtyard, U Kyuin overheard them, but to his young mind only his mother sounded right. From that day he stopped being friendly with U Sorju though the latter tried his best to be cordial with the boy.

A few months later, U Sorju again came home late, dead drunk. An argument ensued. U Kyuin looked on from a distance, a stick in hand, ready to go to his mother's help.

The following day U Sorju behaved as if nothing had happened. He was quite considerate to Ka Irbon, and soon when the conversation continued with no sign of irritation, he said, "Could you give me six hundred rupees? I have to pay my labourers, today being the big market day."

"Where would I get such a large sum of money?" Ka Irbon asked.

He said, "If I fail my workers, all the work, worth more than five thousand rupees, would go to waste, and whatever I've spent will be a total loss." His reasoning seemed sound. Ka Irbon went and took six hundred rupees out of the savings. In fact, out of all the money he had brought home, Ka Irbon had spent only sixteen rupees – for a coat for U Sorju and a set of clothes for U Kyuin. None of it had she spent on food. All the rice, vegetables, tubers, she got from the fields. Her groceries, meat and fish she bought with her own meagre savings. What startled Ka Irbon, and U Sorju too, was U Kyuin's reaction. He clung on to his mother's hand, shouting, "Mei, don't give!" It was only after much persuasion that he let go.

Months went by, but U Sorju's habits did not change. He was silent about his earnings. Ka Irbon had no means of knowing whether he had actually won the contract.

Ka Irbon gave birth to another son. She herself chose the name – U Kshuin, to rhyme with U Kyuin. No mother ever regrets bearing her children, and Ka Irbon was indeed more than happy that her two sons would keep each other company in the years to come. But the thought of U Sorju's wasteful ways, and the fact that from the time that he came to live with her she had been unable to work in her fields as regularly as she used to, made her despondent and anxious. She saw clearly enough that she could no longer depend on U Sorju's income. But this could only mean that all of them would starve and the very thought of her small children dying of starvation filled her with dread. Night and day, she would tell herself, "I must work hard this year. Only through my fields will I be able to feed my young ones."

She was only too aware how difficult it would be to work with a child on her back. What should she do about U Kshuin? To engage a girl to look after the baby required more money than she could afford. To pay in kind with paddy from her store was unthinkable – there might not be enough rice left for her children, the harvest having been poor that year for a number of reasons – the hailstorms just before harvest, the finches and other birds eating away the ripening grain, her inability to get anyone to watch over the fields ... Her recent pregnancy too had prevented her from doing her full share of work in the fields ... as a result, her granaries were woefully depleted.

She could see only one way out of her difficulties. She would have to take U Kyuin out of school and let him look after his little brother at home, leaving her free to work in the fields. This idea came to her one morning as U Kyuin was preparing to go to school. There he was, arranging his books happily, singing the various Christmas songs that he had been taught at school. He came up to her. She hurriedly wiped away the tears welling up in her eyes.

Although the traces of her tears had been removed, the look of sadness was there to see, and child though he was, U Kyuin sensed his mother's unhappiness, though he could not fathom why.

Countless times before, he had seen his stepfather as the cause of his mother's unhappiness, and his child's mind was filled with anger. Loving his mother as devotedly as he did, he grieved with her when he saw her sad face. "Why are you sad, Mei?" he asked her. Reluctant to explain, she changed the subject, feeling that this was not the time to tell U Kyuin that she had decided to discontinue his schooling once work on the fields began. Her jhum land on the higher part of the hill slope would be given to Ka Brin's father to grow potatoes and millet, and the brush would be burnt in time for the cultivation of these crops. She had put aside some money for that purpose.

At U Kyuin's school, arrangements were underway for the Christmas celebrations and children's entertainment. It was customary to stage the celebrations two days before the results of the final examination, after which the school would be closed for the winter vacation. U Kyuin would be singing the carol, "Away in a manger, no crib for his bed ..." He would join the other children later for more carols.

U Kyuin would sing these carols continuously – inside the house or out in the courtyard, sitting or walking around. He had a very pleasing voice, which was why the teachers had chosen him to give a solo performance. Soon, his mother also caught the tunes and the words of some of the songs.

U Kyuin asked his mother to attend the carol performance, the teachers having instructed the children to invite their parents. He felt some hesitation in inviting his stepfather because for some time they had not been on speaking terms, but his mother persuaded him that it would look odd if he didn't ask his stepfather to come as well.

"Ask him to come," she advised, "and if he refuses, it doesn't matter! You will have done your duty."

Thus urged, U Kyuin went to U Sorju one morning and asked him to come to the carol singing. U Sorju's reply was most unexpected, "What? I come to listen to your jackal howling? No way!"

When the great day arrived, U Kyuin went early for some last minute instructions from the teachers. Ka Irbon arrived later, carrying her younger son on her back. U Kshuin was then about eight or nine months old. She reached the school before the celebrations began, and saw U Kyuin running about on the stage, performing various chores with the other boys, everyone laughing excitedly.

Soon after a teacher announced, "We shall now begin." The function started with the teacher explaining why Christmas, a time for joy and happiness, was so important, to the little ones. Then came the first carol, "O come all ye faithful," with U Kyuin leading the song.

Then the curtain was briefly pulled together. When it was drawn aside again, Ka Irbon saw her son standing centrestage. Her heart was full and she felt as if it would burst with joy. All she heard, as the song rang out, was her son's voice. More carols followed, U Kyuin appearing with various groups. Then came another announcement from behind the curtain, "You will now hear a solo by U Kyuin of Class I." When the curtain drew back, Ka Irbon saw her son standing at the front of the stage, smiling confidently. In her eyes, he was by far the most good looking boy of them all. Her heart throbbed with pride. When he began to sing, "See in yonder manger low ..." she wept unashamedly. U Kshuin, the little one on her lap, looked up at his mother and also started crying, in a much louder voice. His howls brought her back to her senses, and somehow controlling herself, she tried desperately to quieten the child, before turning again to the stage to listen to her son as he came to the end of his song.

U Kshuin's howls had somewhat disrupted the audience's attention. Those who were sitting nearby turned their eyes to look at Ka Irbon, and wondered why she cried. If only they could look into her heart and see the feelings of pride and joy that stirred within! How proud she felt! What was there to regret on his behalf? More poignant still were the tears that welled up when she thought that very soon her son would have to discontinue his studies.

At the end of the show, U Kyuin ran down to where his mother sat and searched her face for signs of happiness ... or sorrow. He was glad when all he could make out on her face was a look of happiness. The teachers also went up to her to congratulate her, as she followed the others out. The headmaster commented that she must be proud to have a son like U Kyuin, and was surprised when she covered her face with her shawl and sobbed again.

"Why, what's the matter?" he asked, but she hurried away without replying.

Two days later the results were announced. When the headmaster entered to declare the results of Class I, all the children became quiet as mice, their hearts thumping with apprehension.

He then read out the names from the register. Some names were skipped over. Although U Kyuin's name was read out later, he was glad that he had passed. Then the headmaster made the final announcement, "Of those who have been promoted to Class II, U Kyuin comes first, the second is ..." and so on. U Kyuin was too excited even to sit, he wanted to run out and tell his mother the wonderful news that very moment, but he had to wait until school was dismissed.

As soon as school ended he ran home excitedly, as fast as his legs would carry him. "Mei!" he cried out even before entering the house, "I've been promoted to Class II, and I came first!"

He expected her to be delighted ... to smile, at least. But instead she stared at him for some time. "Very good!" was all she could bring herself to say. Tears welled in her eyes and rolled down her cheeks onto her knees. U Kyuin was bewildered, unable to grasp the reason behind the tears. The day before, his mother had wept at the school function. And today again she wept. Her tears seemed endless. Why?

Ka Irbon did not want U Kyuin to discontinue school until he had passed the higher examinations. But when she thought of the conditions at home, she could see no other way of saving her family from starvation than proceeding with her intended plan.

Meanwhile, U Sorju became more and more a slave to his habit. During the past weeks, not a night had passed without his coming home dead drunk. On Christmas eve, he was however in one of his more amicable moods and began telling Ka Irbon, of the work he had in hand – how he was negotiating for a contract with a certain person, how this man wanted to know if he had any capital to run the business, how he had explained to this man that his wife, Ka Irbon, had a paddy field that was worth five hundred rupees, as well as two upland fields worth the same amount, and how the man wanted these particulars in writing.

"To save time," her husband went on, "I have got it all written down here." He pulled out a sheet of paper from his pocket. "All you have to do is put your mark on it," he said, indicating the place where he wanted her to put her thumb impression as she could neither read nor write.

Ka Irbon grew uneasy and hesitated to do as told. While she was turning this business over in her mind, U Sorju held out some black soot he had been scraping away from a cooking pot. "Here," he said, "let me smear your thumb with this."

"Keep it aside for now," she said, "I shall put my mark later on."

"No," he replied, "do it now, so that I can take it with me when I leave for work." He tried hard to persuade her, but she would not consent, insisting that she would see to it only when she was free. U Sorju had no choice but to leave the paper with her, telling her to keep it safe. Then he left for work.

As soon as he left, Ka Irbon called her son who was in the garden. She showed him the paper and said, "Read loudly, I want to hear what's written." U Kyuin then read out slowly and clearly. Ka Irbon pricked up her ears, hearing something other than what U Sorju had told her. "I, Ka Irbon of the Myrdoh clan, am taking a loan of eight hundred rupees from you, Kaluram Mahajon ... I promise to repay the principal and interest within six months ... If I fail to do so, you may take possession of my paddy field and upland fields which I am mortgaging to you ..."

"Mei, when did you take out this loan?" asked U Kyuin, feeling very sorry for her.

"Alas, my child!" she exclaimed. "What should I borrow money for? This is the work of those who wish to destroy me. Good grief! A murderer, indeed!"

"Who, Mei?" said the boy, his inherited dread of professional killers newly enkindled.

Without replying, she took the paper from U Kyuin's hands and tore it into shreds. Her son looked on in surprise.

That evening, a carol party, with bamboo torches and lanterns, made its way towards U Kyuin's house. While they were still in the neighbouring courtyard, U Kyuin, recognizing the voices of his schoolmates, ran out to join them. Together they then entered the compound, calling out, "A merry Christmas to you, good lady!"

"We have come," said their leader, "to sing to you songs of joy and peace, that the Lord Jesus might bless you and your family. He will come indeed to those who receive him with faith, and his peace will reign in every such home!"

Ka Irbon said nothing. She could only smile, recalling the story often repeated to her about Jesus, and in her heart she longed for the peace that this person Jesus Christ was said to bring. The children sang carol after carol. They were about to begin their fifth song, "Who is he, in yonder stall ..." when suddenly they heard someone at the gate imitating the call of a jackal. "O-O-O-O, kya-kya-kya huwa ..." All turned to see who it was, both U Kyuin and Ka Irbon recognized the voice, and sure enough, U Sorju staggered into the courtyard, hopelessly drunk.

"Who is he, did you ask? It's me! I can howl like a jackal. You ... you know nothing, you're not like me!" He resumed his jackal imitation.

Enraged by his unseemly conduct, Ka Irbon, red with anger, strode to where U Sorju was standing and, seizing him by his arm, dragged him into the house. He was too drunk to offer any resistance. She pushed him inside, forced him into a seat and coming out, slammed the door shut.

U Kyuin was mortified at the spectacle happening in front of his schoolmates. But they, like small children everywhere, found the whole incident hugely entertaining. They went on with their singing, even as they could hear the drunken person howling away inside the house.

After the carol party left, Ka Irbon went back inside. U Sorju was lying spreadeagled. She did not try to wake him, but simply placed a blanket over him so that he would not die of cold.

When morning came, U Kyuin got up before anyone else and went to meet his school friends to make plans for the day's activities, it being Christmas. Ka Irbon also got up soon after and was immediately busy with her household duties, leaving U Kshuin to crawl around as he liked.

U Sorju got up last and went outside, perhaps out of a feeling of shame, or perhaps because he did not wish to be bothered by the baby. Eventually, he came back and sat down at his usual place, saying nothing. Ka Irbon also remained aloof, two plates in front of her, for herself and her small child. Both of them started eating.

After a while U Sorju went and sat down beside the hearth. "Could I have some food?" he asked. Ka Irbon put rice and curry on a plate and passed it on wordlessly.

After he had eaten he went out to wash his hands. Coming back, he pulled up a stool, apparently meaning to sit down for a smoke.

Not a word passed between the two for quite a while. At last Ka Irbon spoke. "Listen to me," she said, "it's time to be open about everything that has been going on. I can see quite clearly now what sort of a man you are. Last night you brought shame upon our family by your behaviour. With every day that passes, your drinking gets worse. There hasn't been a single night when you haven't returned home drunk. Whether we have food to eat or not is of no concern to you. I have had enough of your ill treatment. You've been lying to me all along. For months you've brought home not so much as a pie. Whatever little bit I've been saving, you have squandered ..."

U Sorju interrupted her. "That was what I intended doing yesterday. It was because you put off signing the paper that I could not do so. Is it signed now?"

He suddenly realized that what he was saying now was not what he had told her the previous day. He tried to cover up. "You see, it is

---

Pie: A standard currency used in British India and made for circulation at the end of 1831. One hundred and ninety two pie copper coins make up a rupee.

like this ..." But he was too late. Ka Irbon realized now the depth of his deceit. Her hopes that a heart-to-heart talk would make him see his mistakes and help him start a new life were dashed.

"Enough!" she said, "You planned to despoil me of everything I have, not only my savings but my property as well. It is my fields that have been feeding us, not you. Now you're trying to sell even those to some foreigner. All these months I've been accepting your lies in good faith. It is your belief, isn't it, that I shall ever remain a fool and that you will in time drag me and my children to ruin! But god, the dispenser and creator, will not permit it ..."

U Sorju, desperate, begged her to give him back the paper.

Ka Irbon paid no attention. She went on, recounting everything he had been doing. "You wanted me to put my mark on that paper. You said your man in town wanted to know that you had the capital to start work with, but your intention was to get me to put my mark on a paper prepared by thieves and murderers, to rob me of everything I have and to leave me and the children to starve. You want your paper? Go to the woodshed, collect all the pieces you can find there, and then get out. Go and build your new house elsewhere! You would ruin me, would you? Get out of house this instant. From today you are not to set foot in this house."

U Sorju could say nothing. Ka Irbon's words had touched him to the quick. He knew well enough what his intentions had been when he had asked her to sign the paper – to sell her property and get the money he needed for gambling and drinking. Without a word he got up and left the house. Ka Irbon watched until he had got clear of the yard and disappeared from sight.

She sat down to ponder on these events, then her thoughts turned to U Kyuin. If he had not been able to read, how would she have known of U Sorju's intentions? She was so proud of her son's learning. And yet ... she would have to take him away from school.

Just at that moment she heard U Kyuin calling out from the garden. "Mei! Our headmaster said he'd come here shortly. We came up together, but he's just gone into U Korti's house."

Five, six minutes later, the headmaster entered her courtyard and came straight up to where Ka Irbon was standing.

"Kong," he said, "I've come to offer my best wishes. May this day bring happiness and good fortune to your family."

"Thank you, Bah," she replied. "I don't know what I am to say, except that god may bless you."

"Nothing could be better than that!" the headmaster remarked, sitting down on the chair she offered. U Kyuin went outside with his little brother.

"I've been wanting to come and see you," he began, "but with the examinations and all the end-of-term functions I could not come earlier." Referring to her tears during the Christmas play, he gently enquired what troubled Ka Irbon. She told him everything that had been on her mind – her fears of want and hunger, her intention to discontinue U Kyuin's schooling so that she would be able to devote time to work in the fields.

"I know what you mean," he said. "There's, however, nothing to stop you from doing your work in the fields without taking your son out of school. You must know, Kong, that at school we are now teaching our pupils not only to read and write but also to work with their hands – at home and, yes, in the fields as well. Every season, whenever the occasion arises, we take our children to work in the fields of our villagers, particularly those who are sick and unable to work, or those who have no men to help them. Our children thereby get experience in every type of work, and the farmers also get the help they need. We have many youngsters who are quite proficient in farm work. Do not keep U Kyuin away from school. Whenever you need any assistance in your fields, our children are there to help. They'll finish the work in a day or two. You only have to tell them what to do."

In her embarrassment Ka Irbon could find no words to express her feelings. She could only tell the headmaster that she had already made an arrangement with Ka Brin's father to work in her upland fields.

"It doesn't matter," said the headmaster, "our boys will only take up what you have not given to anyone else to do." Then, rising, he took leave of her.

"Thank you, Bah!" she said, filled with gratitude and gladdened beyond words that U Kyuin would not have to leave school.

After his departure, U Kyuin came up and enquired why the headmaster had come and what he had said. She told him everything, even her intention to stop his schooling. U Kyuin was moved at his mother's decision, one that she had been forced to take in her desperate need to save her family from starvation, and he pitied her for it. In the manner of a grown up man, he said, "Mei, I'll be there to help you in the fields!"

Smiling, she replied, "Indeed, my son! And I shall take you out whenever I need your help!" What heartened U Kyuin was the look of happiness that was evident in her face.

"Mei," said U Kyuin, "this joy the two of us feel is our headmaster's Christmas gift to us."

Ka Irbon felt in her heart that what her son had said was very true. The joy and prosperity the headmaster had wished for her family might now be theirs.

S J DUNCAN wrote short stories, plays and poems. A bureaucrat with the Assam Civil Services, he started writing quite early. All his major works were however written after he retired from service as the Chairman of the Assam Public Services Commission. His most popular collection is *Phuit! Ka Sabuit!* (1968). He died in 1984.

IVAN M SIMON translates from Khasi to English. A linguist by profession, he has also taught at both school and university levels. Among his publications is *Folk Tales and Beliefs of the Khasis and Syntengs*, besides various guides to the languages of the North East.

A CHRISTMAS STORY was originally published in Khasi as "Ka Jingiathuh Khana Khrismas" in *Phuit! Ka Sabuit!*, 1968.

THE FINAL REQUEST

Nothing yields joy any more ... nothing inspires any longer.

Came back with Karel from the customary evening stroll at the park (fine weather today!) then fiddled with the switch of the tele-paper ... looked at it for a while, (books or newspapers no longer interest me) but no earthly event seems to kindle my curiosity.

Then to dinner – laid out by Friday, my robot helper (he is like one of your house robots of the late twentieth century, only technically more advanced) under instructions from Karel – eaten without relish, almost mechanically. Meanwhile, Friday sets up the whisky soda on the side table, along with my cigarettes, (both

Saurabh Kumar Chaliha
translated by Arup Kumar Dutta

permitted by my doctor) and then places the film projector's small, portable switchboard in my hand. I sit on the side table and run the film – a very old movie, an American musical from mid last century – on the whitened portion of the wall behind my desk (I prefer the wall to a screen or video monitor.) It fails to enthuse – no joy, no response.

Mechanically, I continue watching, occasionally sipping the whisky soda (artificial whisky, of course, an improved version of Japanese Suantory whisky, totally synthetic, but tastes like pure scotch, name Elixir-2) and puffing my cigarette (also synthetic, contains nicotine, but mixed with the anti-nicotine substance called Formulation 010, tastes like a real cigarette, but without the harmful effects of nicotine) but derive no enjoyment from these too. I switch off the movie. A vacuous, joyless existence mine – the sheer monotony of the same hackneyed routine ... morning to night, day after day. An ennui filled life liberated from all responsibilities, the intolerable weariness of mental lethargy – no, I cannot go on like this ... must end it all ... what's the point in continuing this pointless charade?

Contemplated calling Karel to banter with him a bit to while away time. Let everything end, but let it end with laughter – so what if the humour is forced. However, didn't feel like opening my mouth to summon Karel. Instead, pressed the blister on the back of my watch (the same communicating device is there on my desk, my bed, and my spectacles – to use at my own convenience.) Karel came silently (as if on all fours) and stood a metre and a half away (the specified distance for ordinary conversation.) A creaking sound and then a low, vibrating, thickly accented voice – obviously artificial, slightly nasal.

"Dada?"

"Listen, Karel. All this must end." I didn't know how to continue. Should I tease him a little? (Futile, really, because Karel has no emotion, at least not any that I have sensed.) "All this ... for instance, just now you addressed me as Dada ... elder brother ... is it appropriate?"

Karel remained silent for a few moments (a few moments imply some micro seconds – millionths of a second – Karel comprehends such minute units, for he is capable of carrying out millions of calculations in the matter of a second.) I've never been able to read his mind, since he does not have eyes or mouth. Only two tiny slits (having lenses most likely) on his upper portion and two more lower down where human beings do not have eyes. Below them a rectangular screen or membrane, somewhat like the radio loudspeakers of yore, from which the sound emerges. Otherwise, Karel is a limbless, long, flat box, nearly five feet tall, not disfigured – unlike twentieth century automatons – by antennae, sensors, et cetera. The box, meaning Karel's body, is not metal or plastic, but a kind of living membrane the colour of human flesh. He has neither legs nor small wheels, or anything else to help him move so effortlessly, quietly and smoothly. He glides over the floor, most likely upon a cushion of reflected air – I do not entirely understand the mechanism. Of course, the manual given to me by the Robotronix Corporation of Nebraska when I purchased Karel describes and explains everything in detail (along with illustrations) – but what is the use of bewildering myself with all those technical complexities? Karel does what I want of him, that's enough for me.

Another creaking sound – probably he had scanned his memory cells and found the answer to my question.

"According to B-001-01-B of my working manual, I have been instructed to address you as Dada, elder brother. You had submitted a number of alternatives – Dada, uncle, sir, gentleman, monsieur, yes?, and yes, sir? ... You finally chose Dada. Therefore, as per B-001-01-B, it was proper of me to call you Dada."

"You haven't developed a sense of humour yet!" I sighed. "I'm perfectly aware of what your B-001-01-B contains, but am I alluding to that? No, what I mean is that you were born after I had crossed sixty. Granted, you were wrought three years before your birth – but even then, taking into account the span of time, can you really be my younger brother?"

Silence. It was true. Karel's "birth" in Robotronix's laboratory in Sweden took almost three years. He was fitted out with neurons and electronic circuits simulating the human body after which the genetic configuration of his cells took on final shape – symbiosis does take a great deal of time. Added to that was his primary education under Professor Yamashita of Osaka in Sweden and then years of lessons and training in Nebraska under the strict supervision of their consultants, Dr Hans Levison and Dr Malini Seshadri of Cornell University.

Creak.

"Dada, according to L-C-010-00 of my working manual, I am your grandson, if we adopt human yardsticks."

"Right. In other words, I'm your koka, your grandfather. But we're neither grandfather and grandson, nor brothers. I'm a householder, citizen and taxpayer. You're my audience, companion, friend, philosopher and guide. You're not a commonplace twentieth century house robot, engaged in routine household chores. Your helper, your auxiliary robot, Friday, performs these chores under your supervision. These don't form a part of your duties. You're my companion, well wisher, friend and confidant. You understand my thoughts, you can analyze my facial expression and brain waves, you can tell whether I'm angry or amused, sad or happy, fatigued or perturbed. And yet I chose that you address me as Dada! Have you ever wondered why?"

Silence. Creak.

"I can find a possible cause in my file P-T-1101-C, the one containing all that I have been told about your personal life, tastes, and temperament. But it has been categorized under Sensitive Matters ... I have been instructed not to bring it up without your permission."

"No objection from my side, certainly!"

"I've also been instructed not to utter any word, sentence or sound which might hurt you."

"Oh, Karel ... I'm no longer of an age when old memories can hurt! Go ahead ... speak."

"In the year 20 ... on 11 August, at 14:15 hours your only younger brother died – the one who used to follow you around everywhere calling out, Dada, Dada. The circumstances of his death are documented in detail in my files. Whether his death was an accident or suicide remains inconclusive ... but for you it was an irredeemable loss and you considered yourself morally responsible for it, undergoing mental agony for the next two years."

I could not help laughing. "All right, all right, that's enough! Do you know how long ago all this was? Thirty, forty years – oh, these psychologists have been stuck in the same groove since the seventeenth, eighteenth century! It never occurs to them that I selected the words by which I was to be addressed by you at random and simply opted for one of them. But they can't rest unless they unearth some deep and hidden psychological significance in the most trivial stuff – when you were a child, a female cat stole a piece of fish from your plate, so you're a misogynist. Ha, ha, ha! Anyway, let it pass, now tell me, do you know why, out of so many possible names, I chose Karel for you?"

"Yes. You were an admirer of Karel Capek, a writer of the twentieth century from the country then known as Czechoslovakia, who first coined the word – Robot – to describe artificial automations like me ..."

"Ah, you have a fine memory! Of course, you're incapable of forgetting. Ha, ha, ha! Human beings like us occasionally suffer mental blocks, can't recall certain things, but not you. Your genes have been shaped in such a way that there's no chance of you misplacing something and then wracking your brain trying to find it! Anyway, Karel, let's see what you have in your databank on Capek – oh, haven't touched those books for so long ..."

"On the wall or the monitor?"

"The wall. I'll look at it from here."

Creak ... creak.

Letters appeared on the wall in bold, not much of a strain on the eyes.

> Capek, Karel: Czech Dramatist and Novelist. Born: Bohemia, 9 January 1890. Died: Prague, 25 December 1938. Education: Charles (Later Prague) University, Berlin, Sorbonne. Satirized contemporary society's mechanized "Modernity" in his drama *R-U-R* (*Rossum's Universal Robot*, 1920) and enriched the world's vocabulary with the word "robot." Among his other writings are ...

"Yes ... correct ... thank you, Karel." Creak. The letters vanish. "I think I once asked you to read Kapek's novel *Meteor*, didn't I, Karel?"

"Yes, Dada. And I have already transferred the text from the central databank to my contingency bank. But ... I am sorry, Dada, I have not read it yet."

"Never mind. Read it whenever you like, let me know your impressions. Oh, of course, it's likely you'll not get another opportunity to tell me ..."

"Dada?"

"Let it pass ... Now, what was I saying? Oh, yes, about Karel Capek – no doubt now you understand why I named you Karel. It's an utterance of affection, an address of love, a call for intimacy. One doesn't name one's pet animal or house boy after an individual one greatly respects and admires. In a word, I look upon you not as an obedient automaton but as a helpful companion ... a friend!"

That is a fact. Karel keeps a sharp watch on me. A flicker of my eyes, a crease on my forehead, pucker of my lips, my pulse, heartbeat, the adrenalin in my bloodstream – nothing escapes his "eyes." He can scan and analyze my brain waves, can read my thoughts even when I am silent.

Of course, we don't converse much, I have always been taciturn, but the little we do is in the nature of philosophical exchanges, rambling speculations about life and existence. Friday (another name chosen by me after the trusted servant of Robinson Crusoe, the fictional character created by the eighteenth century novelist Daniel Defoe) takes care of the household chores under Karel's supervision – keeping the house clean, controlling the room temperature, illumination and relative humidity, setting my papers in order, maintaining accounts of my income and expenditure, working out my income tax dues, catering to my palate, preparing my bath, making my bed ... My culinary preferences, of course, are not as demanding as they used to be – after the death of my first wife I developed heart trouble, after my second wife passed away I had to have a pacemaker inserted in my chest. I also suffer from kidney and liver malfunctions (thank heavens, no need for dialysis yet,) am hamstrung by a myriad restrictions on what I eat or how I live, have to deprive myself of countless pleasures, big and small, give up on many "tastes."

Karel is my ubiquitous watchdog – forever alert as to whether my pacemaker is working properly, whether the food prepared by Friday in his computerized kitchenette is fit for me. He "sleeps" (gives his neurons a rest, that is!) for four hours at night, but even then his auxiliary laser scanner continues to function, arousing him in case of a sudden emergency. Oh yes, although Karel (and Friday with him) had been ordered and acquired with my life's savings, he is no lowly item of purchase – Karel is my friend.

"Thank you, Dada. I am honoured."

"And in many other ways you're my helpmate, the beacon which guides me ..."

That too is true. In the evening, whenever the weather is fair, I take a stroll in the park and Karel accompanies me on my walk. I meet a few aged people there – physically debilitated, semi-crippled, accompanied, like myself, by robot companions. But there are other old timers who walk with dogs – who knows why, despite the inherent disadvantages, they prefer a living creature's company to that of a robot companion. Karel throws some kind of an invisible electromagnetic sheath around me that absorbs excess heat and sound, also keeps me unharmed from any accident (say, a sudden explosion) in my immediate vicinity, protects me from nails, thorns, potholes and collisions. Karel is truly my guardian, leading me on without faltering ...

"I perform my duties as best as I can ... if you are not dissatisfied, that is reward enough for me."

"In that case, let's return to what I'd proposed at the beginning – all this must end. I've arrived at this decision after deep reflection ... yes, all this must end."

"Dada?"

"I do not wish to go on like this. It must end."

"If you are bored with this pattern of life, my instruction manual contains two other alternative daily regimens. You too have studied the flow charts many times."

"You don't understand. The morning cup of tea at six thirty instead of seven – I'm not suggesting such superficial changes. They can't detract me from my primary decision. And this decision is that although, thanks to you, I continue to exist, there is no motivating force in my life, no interests, no enthusiasm – thus, there is no point in prolonging this life. You're my companion, no doubt, but your life is not the same as mine. Your existence is made possible – will continue to be made possible – by a configuration of chemical-electrical energy. But human existence is more than a mere transmutation of chemical-electrical energy. There is some imperceptible, microscopic entity, the cessation of whose flow will entail the cessation of life itself – what will remain is a mere metabolic functioning of the body and nothing else. Your case is simplistic, you continue to get your life force as long as electric pulses flow through your nerves – the wires of your circuit – you continue to function ..."

Creak. Silence. Creak.

"Dada, I understand what you're trying to convey. You've spoken of this a number of times (here Karel mentioned a few dates,) explained to me why water is not simply a combination of hydrogen and oxygen – it is something more. Why a conglomeration of tissue cells is not the body, mere endless conversion of energy not life. You've explained to me that we get our energy primarily from this planet's sun, a powerful source, one which sustains metabolism, drives machinery. Yet it is not the sole source, for there is some finer spark of energy which flows through disparate life forms from another source, no doubt in different forms and varying quantities (otherwise each life form would have had identical minds, identical emotions.) In our immediate environs, our neighbouring spaces, near the earth, its nature is crude, like dry, elementary solar radiation – but far off, high up above, this energy evolves from fine to finer, its pulsation fast to faster, imperceptible, beyond the sensory. Such a supposition is to be found in the yogic philosophy of ancient India – it was thought that a yogi, through deep contemplation, could direct himself into that micro-energy's path and disappear from the sight of ordinary mortals.

"As you said, it is difficult to prove the veracity of such a conjecture – but it is equally true that the fount of thought, intelligence and traits of divergent life forms is not the commonly used energy forms – not solar radiation, not the energy of food-chemistry, not sound-heart-magnetic-electric energy. Perhaps, as you suppose, from some distant galaxy in outer space an immanent or supreme intelligence is imparting in various quantities this micro-energy to all of you according to the toleration level of each life form. These are hypothetical matters, Dada. I cannot comment on them – my system does not contain the requisite programme which might enable me to pass judgement on these questions. But in all humility (Creak) I want to tell you something. Dada, perhaps I am not, as you think, animated solely by crude, conventional, comprehensible energy. Perhaps, contrary to what you suppose, my power does not come only as a flow of electricity or chemical energy through my nerves, my metal wire circuits. My respected teacher, Professor Yamashita, warned me not to be overcome by pride or self-praise at the thought that I have gained my power of reasoning and perception solely through my configuration or energy flow. Of course, my source of power is in my own control and absolutely assured (in fact, eternal, so to say, for it is supplied by a superconducting circuit.) He told me to remember that these were superficial and extraneous, that we do not know even today where true power or rationality – that too is a form of power – comes from ..."

"Meaning?"

"Professor Yamashita gave me just a hint, warning me not to brood on such things, for it might interfere with the purpose for which I was programmed and prevent me from performing my duties sincerely."

"What hint?"

"Poynting Vector."

"Poynting Vector?"

"Yes, an aspect of physics. Of course, along with physics, I was taught the essentials of chemistry, physiology, psychology and anthropology ... only as much as was required for my use – simple formulae, equations, theorems, charts, graphs, theories – just rudimentary knowledge. I was not taught anything in depth. But he asked me to remember that we still don't know where energy comes from – from the star of our planet, the sun, which is true in a utilitarian sense. But if we delve deeper we discover that the real source or direction of energy is yet unknown. Remember, he told me, none of us are omniscient, not even you ... none of us, in the ultimate analysis, have cause for self-congratulation."

"But this Poynting ... what is it?"

"I don't have it in my databank, but since you wish to know let me bring it from Central."

Creak. Silence. Creak.

Silence (of a longer span, around ten seconds,) and then bold letters on the white portion of the wall.

Poynting, John Henry: English Scientist. Born: Monton, Near Manchester, 9 September 1852. Died: Birmingham, 30 March 1914. Education: Manchester, London and Cambridge University, Degree from Cambridge in 1876. Fellow of Trinity College, 1897. Worked ten years in Cavendish Laboratory on experiments associated with earth's density. Adam's prize. Co-authored textbook of physics with J J Tomson, the discoverer of the electron (1902–14.) Opened up new horizons in the study of electricity through two research papers on electric current and energy transmission. Professor at Birmingham University till his death ...

The letters faded away. New letters appeared.

Poynting Vector: In phenomena such as electric current, elecromagnetic wave, et cetera, the amount of energy per unit surface area flowing through any point per second. A directed number or vector (*a mathematical formula just below this, which of course I cannot decipher.*) It can be seen that when electricity flows through a wire, the energy of electric flow comes in a perpendicular direction (from outside) to the wire, or, when a condenser is charged, energy flows from outside to create a field of energy between the two plates. Where this energy comes from is uncertain.

I waited in silent expectation as to what Karel might say next. Creak. "May I say something, Dada?"

"Certainly."

"I want to point out that contrary to our belief electric energy does not flow through an electric wire, the energy of electric flow comes from outside. In other words, even today scientists have not been able to determine the true source of energy, or its direction. You had explained to me about Yogashastra's kundalini force. When through unremitting contemplation the path of meditation is reached, a microscopic, powerful force, radiating from the muladhar chakra ascends through the sushumna artery lying between the ida and pingala and hits the sahasrar chakra of the brain, the yogi is infused with puissant, divine, imperceptible energy. But no one knows which part of the lower body holds the muladhar chakra, where in the brain does the sahasrar chakra lie – they do not exist in physiology. Can it be that this kundalini force is a supra-spiritual energy form emanating from a distant source to flow through the mediator?"

"Oh, I don't know, it's quite possible. You're talking of something probable ... at least, worth speculation." Perhaps my reply made Karel happy, for he let out a thin whistle, like air escaping through a tiny hole.

"I recall another thing – your fondness for American musicals. You had explained to me that what fascinates you about these movies is the stupendous explosion of life force in them. Dance, music, laughter, comedy, love, the pangs of separation ... everything is inspirited with overflowing vitality. As if the screen itself dances with excitement at the sheer explosion of unrestrained, youthful gaiety, the auditorium's air seems to pulsate with the joyous throb of life. (Dada, I've seen quite a few of these movies – *Singin' in the Rain, An American in Paris* – with you more than once.) Amazing, stunning! Where does this eruption of joyful vitality spring from? You told me that there is abundant power in other film genres as well – in westerns, gangster movies, thrillers, films dealing with war or adventure – bodily power, the power of guns and bullets, even intellectual power, but the power of Hollywood musicals is from another world, at another level altogether. No cruelty in them, no barbarism, malice, anger, no vulgarity – only an endless flow of pure, unsullied joy. Can it be, Dada, that the actors and actresses, the director and technicians, while making these films, were moved by some unknown force? Perhaps something lent them that power so they could portray a snippet of life's beauty before human eyes – an arousal of a collective stream of kundalini, as it were."

"Oh, perhaps yes. Perhaps something like that. I'm overwhelmed, Karel! Truly overwhelmed that you've given such deep thought to my words, endeavoured so earnestly to understand my mind and temperament." Another thin whistle. I do not know what string of joy in Karel's neuro-electronic heart had been plucked by my words. "And that's why, because you're a friend dearest to my heart, I want to make my final request to you. I'd spoken of it at the very beginning."

"Final request, Dada?"

"Yes. All this must be brought to an end. Surely you understand?

There is something ... call it a thirst for life, anything, which I no longer have. Even twentieth century musicals no longer give me pleasure. I've lost the desire to live, only my energy fuelled body-machine keeps functioning in a mechnical manner. Nothing more, not the least residue of lust for life. I thank you from the depth of my heart for your help ... your company. My request, terminate my life."

"Dada!"

"Painlessly, as far as possible, of course."

Creak. Silence. Creak.

"Dada, what kind of a request have you made? How can I carry it out? Everything I have been taught, my entire existence, the tenet central to the instructions given to me, is to provide you with company, to look after your needs and pleasure, to protect you from harm, as far as possible to shield you from the clutches of death. As per my central instruction manual F-01010-B-1001 ..."

"Oh, I'm aware of all that, Karel. But you'll also know of another central instruction – its number you no doubt remember, doesn't it say that you have to fulfil each request I make, do what my mind desires. Oh, the manual calls them Orders or Commands. I call them requests. That's because your relationship with me is not that of employer and employee. So will you fulfil all my requests? Tell me, isn't that what you've been programmed for, to satisfy whatever my mind desires?"

Creak. Silence. (A lengthy silence, about ten seconds.) Creak.

"That is true. And Dada, it is also true that I have been attempting to do my duty as best as I can – you've complimented me numerous times too on the fact that I can correctly read your wishes even though unvoiced, and thereby try to give you satisfaction. But, Dada, how can I simultaneously perform two contradictory tasks – protect your life, and at the same time, carry out your instruction to end it? If I were to attempt it my entire system would collapse – I will no longer be I.

When I was programmed, when my genes were configured, no one foresaw such a situation – thus I have not been empowered to resolve a dilemma of this kind. I will need a new set of instructions for it ... I will have to consult Central about this. I'm sorry, Dada, but till then I cannot take a final decision on whether to obey you or ignore your request ..."

"Karel, you've no need to consult Central about matters related to me. Central has nothing more to tell you. It's true that you were manufactured by Robotronix Corporation, modelled on their P-16 series, but after I selected you, you were made totally cognizant of my requirements. As far as I'm concerned you're the final arbiter of all thoughts and decisions ... you're all in all, an autonomous, self-motivated entity. They've placed me in your hands, absolutely, for my entire life. Whatever decision you make now, it must be your own, solely your own."

Creak. Silence. Creak.

"Dada, I too have a request – perhaps my final request to you, who knows – give me a little time. If, as you say, our perception of existence, our thirst for life, comes from some unknown source of micro-energy, perhaps from that same source might come an intuitive hint as to what one must do in a moment of existential crisis. Can I not make a plea in that direction, an entreaty, a prayer? Dada, just a few more moments?"

"All right."

Silently Karel altered his stance and began to rotate slowly upon his axis, coming to a stop in another position. I could not make out whether he had rotated on his own or had been turned round and round by some unseen force ... I could not tell what conflicts raged inside him, in which direction things oriented themselves – but I thought I heard a faint crackle like the sound of a pack of cards being shuffled. Then that familiar creak again ... once ... twice ... but a long drawn, nasal – creak, creak. And then utter silence. I waited in anticipation. Silence. I waited in ... Silence ... I waited ... Silence ...

SAURABH KUMAR CHALIHA is credited with having ushered the Asomiya short story into modernity with his short story, *Ashanta Electron* written around 1950. The bulk of his short stories are contained in five anthologies – *Ashanta Electron, Duporiya, Ehat Daba, Golam, Kavi* and *Swa-Nirbasito Golpo.* He won the Sahitya Akademi Award in 1974 for his short story collection, *Golam.*

ARUP KUMAR DUTTA has around seven non-fiction books for adults and fifteen novels for the young to his credit, longer fiction for younger readers being his specialty. Many of his books, including his debut adventure book for children, *The Kaziranga Trail,* have been translated into many languages. Some of his other works include *The Blind Witness, Smack, Revenge, The Lure of Zangrila, Chai Garam* and *The Brahmaputra.* He is the recipient of many awards including the Shankar's Award. He taught English at JB College, Jorhat for several years before taking up writing as a full-time career. A freelance columnist and journalist, he contributes to many of India's leading journals and newspapers.

THE FINAL REQUEST was first published in Asomiya as "Shesh Anurodh" in *Swanirbasito Sankalan,* 1994.

HE'S STILL ALIVE

It's still dark when Thamcha gets up, takes a bath, makes the viashnavite mark on her nose and forehead with black earth, and tucking her basket under an arm, goes to the keithel to sell vegetables. She is soon seated in the market as usual, hawking her wares. Brooding. How long has it been since she started coming out to the keithel?

Thamcha lost her husband at an early age and has had to eke out a living. When he was alive, they had led a peaceful, happy life. With him gone, she had somehow endured, gazing at her only son as if he were the sun and the moon. Today all that is no more.

For how long can she brood? Amidst the chaos of calling out to the shoppers, attempting to sell her wares – many a time

Bimabati Thiyam Ongbi
translated by Thingnam Anjulika

she forgets. Will he come? she thinks ever so often, suddenly. But he never does ... never reaches my side.

One day she had returned unusually late from the keithel. The moment she stepped into the house, she noticed anxiety writ all over her daughter's face. "What happened?" she asked, "Where's your brother?"

"Not back."

"Why? Even the sun has set. Who has he gone with?"

"Don't know, Ima. He left when I had gone to fetch water from the pond outside."

"Don't worry. You go and start the fire for the rice."

That night, waiting for his return, she and her daughter didn't eat. Their eyes didn't close for a second.

As soon as it was daybreak, she went asking to the houses of his friends. Not a single person had seen him, no one knew anything or had gone out with him.

Days passed into months, months turned to years. But not a word or a sign from him. Thoughts of her son become a malady for Thamcha.

"Ibemma, let me go out to the keithel. Otherwise you and I will die of starvation," she called out to her daughter one day, tightening the khwangchet at her waist.

"Ima, where could Dada be?"

"Who knows? No love for his mother, no love for his sister – that's him!"

"But we haven't searched for him either."

"Where do we search? Not one of his friends says they went out together. It's also not as if he's been captured or taken away."

"Ima, what unfulfilled wishes could Dada have had?"

"Unfulfilled wishes? Might have been many. But he is inconsiderate. Doesn't realize that I, his widowed mother, strives so hard so that the two of you stand on your feet. I ... I ..." Her voice quivered and fell. She didn't complete her sentence.

"I'm leaving. Be careful."

Tucking the basket at her side, she went out, down the narrow path winding through the yard overgrown with grass.

It must have been around four in the afternoon. Khwairamband bazaar was brimming with people. The air resounded with the cries of the women vendors hawking their wares.

The vegetables spread out in front of Thamcha since early morning had withered. Though she kept calling out, she had no takers.

"Daughter, come buy something at least from Ima. Is there nothing here that you want?"

"Your vegetables are not at all fresh, Ima."

No one bought anything. They merely glanced at her vegetables and passed on. But she did not stop calling out.

All of a sudden, Thamcha froze.

That – who was that? Was it ...?

"Tombi," she told the woman sitting next to her, "please look after my things. I'm just coming."

She started running, muttering to herself. That cheek and jawline ... didn't even see the face completely. Yet. Wasn't it the blue shirt that he usually wore? She ran through the crowd, searching. Her lips kept moving, The one I just saw ... yes, it was. Can he hide from me, his mother? Which way did he turn?

She searched and she searched. Then she gathered her withered vegetables into her basket and headed homewards.

Her daughter looked at her. "Ima, why are you so pale?"

Khwairamband: The main marketplace in the heart of Imphal. Only women vendors do business here. Men have a separate market called Nupa Keithel. This is true of most marketplaces in Manipur.

"Ibemma, I saw someone who looked so much like your brother."

"It must have been someone else."

"Maybe ... but he was so like him!"

Sighing deeply, her daughter said, "If he's alive, he'll surely come. Come Ima, let's eat. Thinking of Dada have affected your health. He must be alive. He will surely come home."

That night, Thamcha cannot close her eyes. She believes. Her child will return. He will stand at the door and call out, "Ima." Sharp-eared, she keeps vigil lest she misses the knock on the door. But passing time slowly sang a lullaby.

She wakes up with a start. Runs out and opens the door. Was that him knocking at the door? Saying, "Ima, open the door." I fell asleep, I didn't hear my child call. Leaning against the door, slowly she slides down to the floor. Tears stream from her eyes even as darkness and light are busy exchanging duties.

BIMABATI THIYAM ONGBI started writing lyrics and poems secretly while still in school, publishing them much later in higher secondary school and college magazines. She gained popularity after winning the best story award with her story "Numituma" (That Day) in a competition organized by Manipur University. She has two books to her credit – *Khongchat*, an anthology of short stories, and *Manipurgi Ningthoukon Amasung Chatna Lonchat,* a non-fiction book on the royalty in Manipur, besides several short stories published in various journals and newspapers. She is presently working on a children's volume. A teacher by profession, many of her short stories have been translated into English and published in national magazines.

THINGNAM ANJULIKA translates from Meiteilon to English. She has translated two plays by Sahitya Akademi awardee Arambam Somorendra, *Leipaklei* and *The Unrecognized Soldier,* besides a few short stories. She has worked as a journalist in Manipur and New Delhi, and as a researcher with the NCERT, New Delhi and the Centre De Sciences Humaines, New Delhi. Presently an assistant editor with Katha, she also writes short stories in English.

HE'S STILL ALIVE was first published in Meiteilon as "Mahak Hinglina" in *Wakhal*, 2002.

Unnatural deaths, deaths by drowning, during childbirth, in war and the like ran in his family. It was like the epileptic fever that plagued generations of Pulie's family. Genetically damned, each male child in Pulie's family grew up to adulthood only to be reduced to mere shadows.

It became a source of entertainment for the children in the village – those times when Pulie lay writhing on the ground, frothing at the mouth, helplessly struggling against the seizure. Giggling, they said to each other, "Look, the snake dances again." If their mothers came upon them they were pulled aside and severely reprimanded, "Never laugh at people like that lest you should become like them."

Easterine Iralu

But the children laughed nevertheless and waited eagerly for another seizure.

Pulie was Viu's friend. Was, because when it became evident that the family disease was beginning to manifest itself in Pulie after his initiation into manhood, his friends' parents cautioned them against playing with him lest they contract the dreaded disease.

Viu felt sorry for Pulie. And as he grew older, he often wondered which was more terrible – the epileptic strain in Pulie's family that robbed them of their manhood or the curse of apotia deaths in his own family that claimed the lives of the men when life was at its sweetest.

Viu had never known his grandfather, and memories of his father were faint. Viu's grandfather had married young and at twenty two, died younger than any of the men in his family. His great grandfather was blessed with seven sons. In the eighth year of their marriage, his wife bore him another son, and he was greatly content. On the fifth day of her confinement, he sharpened his spear and set out for the forest. His hand was good at the spear, in fact one of the best in the village, and his sight was on a young deer often seen feeding on the abundantly fruiting gooseberry. He didn't have to wait long. However, it was not the light footed deer but a heavier animal that came crashing through the undergrowth. He poised his spear and tensed himself to lunge it at the animal before it could retreat. It was a huge boar with magnificent tusks. His spear pierced its heart in a neat thrust. Blood spurting from the wound, the boar roared in pain and charged. Viu's great grandfather ran for the nearest tree but the animal bore down on him. The magnificent tusks thrust into the soft flesh of his thighs, tossed him in the air, and then ripped through his abdomen on his descent. The last thing his dying mind registered was the rage flushed, beady eyes of the boar as it gored him again and again. The next day, the villagers found both man and boar lying side by side, dead. The boar they quartered and buried in the forest because it was taboo to eat an animal that had taken human life, and the man, they bore home sadly. He was only thirty two.

The elders considered the incident carefully, going through the categories of deaths, and declared it an apotia death. The body would have to be buried beyond the village gate.

So, Viu's great grandfather was laid to rest in the graveyard that lay on the outskirts of the village, fenced by brambles. There were other graves as well – old, crumbling graves of the victims of apotia deaths made outcasts in death and denied a resting place within the village. To avenge their ostracism, their spirits returned to trouble the unwary.

Soon after the burial, whispers started going round the village. An old woman, filling her pot at the water source before dawn, had heard him cough. Two days later, a young man on his way back from a neighbouring village passed the graveyard well after the hens had roosted. It was a warm summer evening and his host had filled him with three day old brew, so potent that even the best drinkers had declared themselves defeated by it. As he staggered past the new grave, he felt a pair of hands at his neck, the grip tightening more and more as he struggled that he became stone sober. He desperately tried to shout. Even as his body started going limp, the village dogs came barking at the hostile presence and he was released as suddenly as he had been gripped. He ran home and pushing the chiekhe against the doorway, he vowed never to drink three day old brew again. The elders said, "Those who die apotia deaths do not really die. They live on begrudging the living their lives."

Viu's grandfather was six days old when his father was buried. "It's a curse," said one of the elders. The themoumia, the seer of the village, concurred, "The curse has to run its course through four generations before it can be expiated."

The seven sons grew up in the ever-present shadow of the curse. Was it any wonder then that four of them, grown to manhood, fell in battle? The fifth went hunting with his friends and, when a muzzle loading gun went off accidentally, a pellet went through his temple, killing him on the spot. The smell of freshly dug earth lingered in the fenced graveyard as it filled up with the graves of these young men.

When the sixth son's initiation into manhood was being done, the seer warned, "The initiation was not properly done. Don't let him go near water."

The sixth son was exceedingly careful. On the first morning of his peli's work his mother said, "It's not for me to hold you back from work. But I had a bad dream. I saw a great lake and you were on the other side of it, but I could not cross over to you nor could you return to me. Be very careful, Anuo, it is not for nothing that we're sent strange dreams."

"I won't take any unnecessary risks, Azuo," he told his mother.

The first day was always special. While the early part of the day was devoted to work, the elders usually relented in the late afternoon and allowed a good half day to go to waste while the young men engaged in boisterous mud play knowing they'd have to make up for this afternoon's play during the rest of the week. When the cicadas called, the elders announced, "Enough for the day, time to leave." And mud splattered youngsters trooped out of the fields to the river – arms around their friends' shoulders or singly – their laughter echoing down the path. The young men had their bathing spot further downstream.

It was summer. The bay where they went to bathe had been fed by rain water for a month now. They waded into the clear waters vying with each other to see who could dunk another first. The struggles of

---

Peli: A group of people sharing work, first working together in one field, then in another and so on until the work on the fields of the group is done.

one among them did not raise alarm at first. They were so full of life they never knew until too late how hard he'd struggled to cling to that sweetness, how loathe he had been to let go of life.

When they brought his body home, all the laughter of the day had set. The skies above were leaden, it being that time of the day when the sun has set and the stars have not yet risen to stud its length. There was no ambiguity, the elders declared it a clear apotia death. And so, the earth was dug up again in the fenced graveyard to add a fresh mound.

Viu's grandfather was seventeen when his elder brother died in the water. Viu's great grandmother was heartbroken. Grown old before her time from the shock of sudden pains that the apotia deaths always brought, she would not let her son – Viu's grandfather – out of her sight. At seventeen he was considered a grown man, matured beyond his years by the responsibilities of manhood his father's and brothers' absence had bequeathed him. He had no time for the play his friends indulged in. The field where he and his mother worked took up all his time.

"It is a good thing to marry," said his mother when he turned nineteen, "it tames a man." And she brought home a bride who was no stranger to the duties of a household.

Their son, Viu's father, was strong throated but weighed hardly five pounds and gave no trouble to his mother at his birth. He was a wiry little thing, making up in agility what he lacked in stature and weight. By the time the boy was two and a half, his mother was heavy with child again. "A girl would be nice," she said, leaning at the door, "I'm worn out chasing my son." This time, she felt different too, heavier, running out of breath when she carried water from the water source to the house.

Her labour began one late afternoon and they sent for the midwife before the evening meal. "It won't take long now," said the midwife confidently, seating herself on the bed beside her patient. But the labour became difficult and long drawn. As the pains came in quick succession, the woman tried hard not to cry out but was overcome by the intensity of the pain. It went on thus through the night. By midnight, everyone was anxious. She had developed high fever and the midwife sent the husband to fetch cold water to sponge her and bring the fever down. But the fever raged on, burning their hands through the cloth. At the first cockcrow, she let out a long breath, sighed and was still. Had the fever finally left her? But when they touched her forehead it was cold and clammy. Her husband was beside himself with grief. But the midwife said, "It is taboo to mourn an Ihaprie death." So he held a pillow to his mouth and screamed into it, muffling his pain the only way he knew.

"No mourning," the elders also said, "wrap the Ihaprie in a woven mat, take it out through a new opening in a wall of the house and toss it into the grave. Remember. No marker for the grave. No tomb. All these are taboos because an Ihaprie is the most abhorred of apotia deaths. Don't forget, the body is not to be taken out through the main entrance, be sure to make a new opening." So they buried her after sunset observing all the taboos regulating the burial of women who died at childbirth, unable to give birth.

Viu's grandfather did not die an apotia death. It was as though the curse had satiated itself with his wife. But he was so broken that he slowly began to die. Could it have anything to do with the fact that he was not allowed to mourn? His grief, unexpressed and permitted no external outlet, turned inward and ate away at him every day until one morning when they tried to rouse him from sleep, they found that he would never wake again.

Viu's father grew up with his grandmother – as only son and only grandson – fiercely protected by a woman who was so closely acquainted with the finality of death. She was both mother and father to him. A strong woman who understood that if life was hard, the key to survival was in becoming harder, the lad learnt not to insist when she said no.

But at times she would bring home a bird's nest carefully pilfered from an overhanging branch or a pfunuo, the green beetle that boys could play with for hours together, giving it to him with such a touch of uncharacteristic tenderness that the boy looked forward to her return from the fields, if only to catch a glimpse of that gentleness.

She dilly dallied on the matter of his initiation until his father's cousin impatiently burst out, "Are you trying to turn him into a woman? The boy is crossing the age for initiation." So he was initiated at the Festival of Sanctification a whole year later.

On his first day of peli work with his peers, he was pleasantly surprised to find his grandmother waiting for him on the path halfway to the village. She carried his hoe home in her basket. But after a few weeks, he grew resentful of her presence because it had become a joke. Now that they were all initiated, they were seen as responsible enough to complete the work allotted to them and make their own way home safely. But his grandmother was stubborn. And six months later, she still stood anxiously at the door of their hut peering at the path until she could see her grandson returning with his friends. Then she would quickly disappear into the house and busy herself with some task so he would never know how anxious she had been. She sensed that the more she bound him to her, the more the boy was likely to strain and withdraw altogether.

As she had done with Viu's grandfather, she sought a bride for Viu's father when he turned twenty. And she was almost unafraid of life when they gave her three great grandchildren – a fine strapping boy and two raven haired girls.

Viu's father buried his grandmother four and a half years after his marriage. She died content, no longer pursued by the feeling that life had defeated her. So she was mercifully spared the knowledge and the pain of the curse manifesting itself once more. Viu's father was the third generation of the cursed family but his grandmother had so resolutely stood between him and the curse that it had not dared touch him while she was still alive. In the months and weeks that followed her death, things that she had taught returned to him and he held fast to each lesson. "Be careful," she always advised, "carelessness was the undoing of your grandfather and uncles." At other times she would say, "Be strong. If your spirit is strong, you can master your destiny." He resolved to be strong and careful. Therefore he never took on any tasks that involved the slightest risk to life. He only wanted to be a father to his children and a husband to his wife, What could be so wrong in that?

The next year, he extended his field by another terrace because his wife was pregnant again and he felt the responsibility of another mouth to provide for. Since her time was near, one day he insisted that she went ahead, saying that he would come home before nightfall. She went home unwillingly. But when he did not return by night, she could wait no more. She pleaded with her neighbours to go and look for him. The field was not too far away but it was a slow and difficult trip, with only their bamboo torches to light their way. They found him at the crossroad where an old oak stood, struck down by the lightning that had chosen him instead of the tree. The elders were emphatic – it was an apotia death. He was buried beside his grandfather and because it was during the monsoons, the mound of earth was covered with fresh green moss in a week's time.

Viu had heard these stories, not from his tight lipped mother, but from his maternal grandmother in whose care he was left so often when his widowed mother went out alone in the fields. As a child he had wondered when his turn would come and if it might even be averred as his grandfather's was. But now he thought, why set so much store by these old wives' tales? Especially now when he was exchanging boyish pursuits for the sports of men, when women's eyes followed him and lingered where he stood, when he had newly thrown the village wrestler and mouths were full of his agility, when life bubbled up in his throat it with the sweetness of the festive brew — why think about it now? Tomorrow he was going to prove he was man enough to lead the stone pulling ceremony of his peers. There was no time to think of other things now.

Viu's age group headed for the appointed spot at the second cockcrow. The ritual stone was twice a man's height and about six feet in diameter. As instructed, the young men knotted their ropes around it and began pulling. They anticipated some difficulty up a brief incline but after that it was a downhill path all the way. It was fortunate, they agreed, that the incline was at the beginning of their journey when they had not expended their strength. The climb uphill was not easy but it was not too difficult either. After a quarter of a kilometre, their determination and combined strength had dragged the stone to the top of the slope. The older ones now positioned themselves at the back because they knew that the trip downhill would require a carefully balanced tugging on the stone by the men at the back to ensure a gradual pace so that the stone would not hurtle down and be damaged in the process. Viu, in front, was thinking of the intricate steps that he would display at his victory dance when they neared the village.

Later, no one could tell what went wrong or how. Everything seemed to happen all at once. Viu, trapped in the stone's path, heard his friends call out frantically. With the stone a hair's breadth from him he heard himself scream. Then it struck him down with such force that he felt himself becoming part of the stone and fragmenting as it and he bounced and crashed downwards like chaff.

Another apotia. They did not need the elders to tell them that. Viu was quietly buried beyond the village beside his father. And the curse, having run its course never returned to trouble the men of Viu's family or their children's children after that.

EASTERINE IRALU has two anthologies of poems and two short story collections to her credit. Her novel *A Naga Village Remembered* is the first novel to be written in English by a Naga writer. She teaches British Poetry and African Literature in English at the Nagaland University.

DEATH BY APOTIA was originally written in English as "Death by Apotia."

I sat facing the setting sun. Time flowed through me like water or wind through a pipe.

Occasionally, without being aware of it, I chanted a sentence over and over, like a mantra,

> In my head is a sun
> and in my heart, a storm.

The words weren't mine. I had probably read them somewhere and they had remained ingrained in my memory.

Suddenly, I heard footsteps behind me. There arose a mournful echo from the silence of my heart, like dried leaves crackling under the feet. Irritated, I turned. A man

Homen Borgohain
translated by Srutimala Duara

stood a few steps away, his face rendered unrecognizable by the last golden rays of the dying sun flashing momentarily on his face, creating a sheen over it like a dazzling net.

"Who are you?"

"Amal Barua," he replied hesitantly, as though he himself was uncertain of the truth of his own words. I felt that he actually wanted to say, "Perhaps I am Amal Barua."

The man was insane! Why else would he come to Amal Barua's house, stand before Amal Barua and say that *he* was Amal Barua? A moment ago I had been about to offer him a seat. But now I wanted him out of sight as quickly as possible. However, suppressing my amazement and irritation, I said calmly, "In this world there is just one Amal Barua and there can be *only* one. And he stands before you. Please leave."

I turned away, towards the setting sun. I pitied him, but did not want to waste precious time talking to a mad man.

After a while I realized that he was still standing there, motionless. A real nuisance! I turned and looked at him. This time, in the starlight, his face was a little more distinct than before. Surprisingly, he did not seem a total stranger now ... as if I had seen him somewhere, met him ...

I searched his face, like one trying hard to look through a dense mist. But the next moment I thought whoever he might be, he could never be me – Amal Barua. For a second, there was such chaos in my mind that I felt that I too had become insane. In as calm a voice as I could muster, I said, "Why haven't you gone? You must have made some mistake and come to the wrong place. I'm very busy with some urgent contemplation. If you could leave soon, I would be very grateful."

My words did not seem to have the slightest effect on him. Calmly, he said, "I haven't made any mistake, it is you who have done so. Try to

remember. A long time ago, you had put out an advertisement in the
Missing column of a newspaper –

> A man named Amal Barua is missing from his house
> since the last few days. He had left his home in search
> of a dream and has not returned. If any benevolent
> person can give any information about his whereabouts
> or can bring him home, the undersigned will remain
> ever grateful to him.

But you had made a great mistake. You did not give any description
of the missing person and your advertisement went in vain. Anyway,
here I am, finally. I've come back."

The boldness and self-confidence in his voice stunned me. Who
was the real Amal Barua – he or I? The answer to this question could
be decided later. But who was really insane – he or I? This now was
the question that posed a real problem in my mind. I tried hard to
remember if I had put out such an advertisement, but could not. Like
one doubting his own mental stability, I asked, "When did I give that
advertisement?"

"When?" I didn't quite understand whether he directed the question
at himself or at me. He appeared deeply confused. "When?" he repeated,
"Are you talking about time? To me time is something quite
incomprehensible and perplexing. I don't understand its mystery. A
person sitting on the bank of a river can say that the water is flowing
downstream. But can a man sitting by the sea tell the difference between
upstream and downstream? I don't exactly know when, but at one
point time had long stood still for me – just as at a press of the pause
button time stands still on the video screen, just as youth or old age, joy,
suffering, fear, sorrow, love or hate ... in short, a moment's experience of
life freezes forever in an instant immutably within the frame. Your *when*
has no meaning for me."

I was certain now that he was mad, and it seemed he would make me go mad too. I asked resignedly, "What did you say your name was?"

"Amal Barua."

"But my name is Amal Barua," I insisted impatiently.

"Then I am you." A pause. "And you are me."

How long the ensuing silence stretched I do not know, probably for just a few moments, but suddenly it seemed that many years had rolled by in the meantime. Perhaps I was already beginning to change my view about time. Without even being aware of it, I had started to become Him from I. An unknown fear began to engulf me slowly.

I stood up. "Wait, you're confusing me. How can two persons be one? Let's settle this now. " Lifting up my shirt, I pointed to my bare chest, "Look at this scar. Once I was badly hurt. The wound dried up long ago, but the huge scar has remained. Can you show a similar scar in the same place? Do you have this on your chest?"

He looked at my face and gave a doleful, enigmatic smile. Then, silently he lifted up his shirt. I was stunned. At exactly the same spot where my scar was, he had a big wound on his chest. The only difference was that his wound was not dry like mine. Blood oozed out of it like a vivid shaft of agony.

Mesmerized, I pulled down my shirt and said, "But my wound is merely a scar. Yours is still bleeding."

He too pulled down his shirt and said consolingly, "That doesn't matter. Time heals all wounds. But if you step out of time, the bleeding starts once again, so too the agony."

I was speechless. In truth, I myself had perhaps given up thinking on my own and was now thinking subconsciously with his mind. I tried to think of another way of proving my identity. I ran in and came out with a woman, holding her by her hand. His expression did not change. I said, "Look, this is my woman, absolutely my personal property. In her body I have bound countless days and nights of the past, darkness and light, the rolling of time, destruction and creation. In her mind I have written my life's history, a history that is absolutely personal ..."

"She is my woman," he interrupted calmly.

"Can you describe her body – the body that no one save I have seen?"

"Her breasts are two globes of moonbeams and two drops of curdled blood. On her thighs she has two sunsets. When she turns on the bed, a big tidal wave rises in the sea of passion. She is fair as the moon, clear as the sun and terrible as an army with banners."

A smile of victory broke over my face. Excitedly, I said, "You've lost. You're not me. Her breasts are actually two condensed globes of honey drops and perched on them are two small bees. On her thighs are two green paddy fields with the shadow of a cloudy sky over them. When she turns on the bed, then a storm of the primitive jungle vibrates ..."

"When one is imprisoned in the finite, one perceives things in this light. Look as I would and you'll perceive as I do."

About to shout out something, I stopped. His absolute self-confidence was evident in his serene expression. On the other hand, my restlessness and agitation was proving that my words lacked my previous conviction. Nevertheless, I gave a final try. "If you are I, then you ought to think whatever I'm thinking. So, tell me, what am I thinking at this very moment?"

"Your question itself is incorrect," he said, unruffled, "why do you feel that you think or can think of only one thing in one moment? Let me give you an example. One day, during sunset, at the time when the earth appeared unearthly, this woman gave an enigmatic smile. You wished to put your lips over hers and eat up that smile. But my wish was to hang that smile like the sunset in the evening sky forever and to sit till eternity with that light on my body. Actually, the same man was thinking about these two different things."

The moon rose at that precise moment. Taking a coin out of my pocket, I said, "There is just one way left. Come, let's toss. Whoever wins will be proven right, once and for all. Heads or tails?"

"Tails."

I tossed the coin. It flipped in the air and landed on my palm, the tail side glittering in the moonlight. A silent groan escaped my heart. Like a man reaching the nadir of despair, I stared at him blankly. I could not read the expression on his face. But I found him suddenly walking towards me with slow steps. My eyes riveted on his, I started moving backwards, step by step. Like a big and strong animal moving with absolute self-confidence towards its helpless and defenceless prey, he began to progress towards me, ready to pounce. He was very close ... he would swallow me now – suddenly I let out a scream. He stopped abruptly and said tenderly, "Don't be afraid. This fear is a part of each of us. Every man fears himself."

HOMEN BORGOHAIN is a poet, short story writer, novelist, essayist and journalist. He has been honoured with several awards including the Asom Valley Literary Award, the Sahitya Akademi Award, Asom Prakasan Parishad Award, besides many awards for journalism. His writings have been translated into several Indian languages.

SRUTIMALA DUARA is a translator and bilingual writer, with published works both in English and Asomiya. Her Asomiya works include two books of rhymes, four collections of children's stories, a novel and a collection of short stories. Her English works include three novels – *Travelling With Dreams, Ashes in the Seas* and *Maya's Party* and three short stories collections – *The Sunset Hour and Other Stories*, *Waiting for the Last Breath* and *The Jhoolan Evening*. Besides contributing regularly to various regional newspapers and magazines including *Dainik Asom* and *The Sentinel,* she is also a part-time announcer in Guwahati Doordarshan Kendra, a film, radio and stage actress and a full time lecturer in English in Handique Girls' College, Guwahati.

FEAR was first published in Asomiya as "Bhoy."

A bit of the leathery, rough skin of the litchis around the stalk had begun to redden, inviting the crows to sit on the tree during the day and the bats to hover around at night. Every year, around this time, Loknath would think of putting an end to this nightly vigil business to chase away the bats. He would sell the tree itself for a lumpsum to a fruit seller.

Whether the buyer chased the bats away or not, was not his headache. All he wanted was the cash and about five hundred litchis for himself and for some of his neighbours.

Keeping watch all night, picking the ripe litchis to sell in the market every day for thirty to forty days – all this was terribly tedious. But every year Loknath would

Bhabendranath Saikia
translated By D N Bezboruah

invariably be seen taking turns with his son Rajani, and daughter
Hemaprabha, at chasing crows and bats away from the tree, plucking
bunches of litchis with a long bamboo, split at one end, and in the
afternoon, sitting with a basket of litchis in the market.

This year too, the wholesale buyers had come – one, two, three of
them. There was a haggling over the price – the whole tree without
the litchis – forty, forty five, at the most fifty rupees. Fifty rupees?
Rather than let you have the tree for fifty rupees I would call ten
children from the neighbourhood and just give the fruits away. That
would at least earn me some virtue. Go away!

In reality, it is not any concern for virtue that makes him send away
the buyers ... Every time he talks to them he does the same calculation,
If he works a little harder he would get eighty rupees – thirty rupees
more than what the traders have offered him. How else would he get
thirty rupees? At least a month's expenses. Besides, losing sleep and
watching over the litchis for this one month every year has become a
sort of intoxication, a pleasure. Like the way they celebrate Durga
Puja every year at Saradindu Babu's house. Their fortunes had
dwindled, but the puja continued on a subdued scale.

This year, things were different for another reason. The litchi tree
had flowered as in any other year but the April storm had not brought
down quite as many blossoms from the tree. As a result, there were
more litchis, and bigger ones too! If they could be saved from the bats,
wouldn't they fetch at least a hundred rupees?

So once again Loknath made bamboo clappers. Their sounds
reverberated through the neighbourhood – khatep, khatep, khatep!
He got a leaky tin can for four annas, hung a couple of old iron bolts
inside, and got his son Rajani to hang the tin from a high branch
right in the middle of the tree. He then tied one end of a string to the
can and the other to one of the posts of the thatched veranda-like
shed near the courtyard. When the string was pulled, the sound

reverberated across three neighbourhoods – ghotong, ghotong, ghotong!

But these days the bats did not seem too scared of the clappers or tin cans. They would land on the tree at the first opportunity, and in spite of the roaring tin can, peel off the skin of the ripe fruits one by one. Hence the other unfailing prescription – Rajani repaired the catapult. The old, wooden fork was fitted with two bits of rubber bought from Rafiq's workshop and the tongue of an old shoe from Gokul's. Loknath got some clay from the bank of the stream, rolled it into pellets and dried them on the round bamboo platter. And the work of guarding the litchis began in right earnest.

In any case Loknath slept lightly in the small hours of the night. It was therefore settled that between midnight and the crack of dawn, Loknath would keep watch while Rajani would take care of the earlier part of the night. Some of Rajani's friends usually dropped in after supper. Together they would sit in the courtyard, with a lantern nearby, and play Ludo. On the other side of the Ludo board was Snakes and Ladders. Whenever they were bored with one, they played the other. From time to time, not only Rajani, but his friends as well, would beat the clappers, pull the string of the tin can, and whenever they suspected that bats have landed on the tree they would shoot the catapult at the probable location.

When it came to detailing the share of duties, Rajani's older sister Hemaprabha seemed to have been given hardly any work, but she was the one who had to keep awake practically all night. Rajani and his friends would take turns bringing bhujiya and roasted gram, and Hemaprabha had to brew them black tea around eleven. At one o'clock Loknath would come out to the courtyard. She would then have to make him a glass of strong, salty tea with ginger and bay leaves.

After drinking the tea, Loknath would say, "Go, get some sleep now." But the way he leaned on the wooden chair and stretched out his legs on the bench as he said this made Hemaprabha realize that the poor man, having had to shake himself out of deep slumber, could do with another hour's sleep.

At that moment, there would be a rustle of bats landing on the tree, and Hemaprabha would beat the clappers, drum the tin cans and, not hearing the sound of bats flying away, pick up the catapult. She would shoot with great care to ensure that the shots did not land on the corrugated iron roof of Sada's house nearby. Then she would tell her father, "Go and sleep a little longer. I'll wake you up when I feel sleepy."

Her father would ask, "What were you saying about a mekhela sador? Would you rather buy the cloth or shall I get you the yarn?"

"What made you remember that now?"

"No, I was thinking. As soon as I get the money for the litchis ..."

"Well, get it first. But then you said something about buying a sewing machine for Rajani."

That was true. If Rajani had a sewing machine, he could start earning a tidy bit on his own. Though he had already learnt quite a lot, he was working as an assistant just because he didn't have one. He did all the work from cutting to sewing buttonholes, but when it came to wages, all he got was eight annas today, nothing tomorrow and four annas, the day after – according to the mahajan's whims. Yes, it was time the sewing machine ...

"And you also wanted to cover the whole house with fresh straw."

True, that had to be kept in mind as well.

Actually, with the clappers, tin cans, catapult and her conversation, Hemaprabha had to keep Loknath company, only then could he keep watch. When there was no likelihood of Loknath falling asleep and her own eyelids drooped heavy with sleep, Hemaprabha would lie down sideways on the bench, her legs bent at the knees and sleep. Loknath would say, "Go in and get some sleep." Covering her feet with the hem of her mekhela, Hemaprabha would say, "It's all right."

The narrow bench of the loom was barely large enough for Hemaprabha's plump body. Loknath would gaze at the rise and fall of her body, and say to himself, The poor girl suffers so much.

They had guarded the litchis for three days, when one night the long drawn note of a whistle was heard. Phi-ri-ri-t. Hemaprabha was serving Rajani and the others their eleven o'clock tea. Almost in chorus they all asked her, "Whatever is that, Baideo?"

"God knows! A constable. I suppose."

"A constable? On this road?"

It *was* a constable. And he *was* walking down that road. The first time the policeman passed their house and went away. Returning a little later, he hesitated for a moment at the entrance, and then walked in. One of Rajani's friends had thrown the dice and got a six. He was pondering over which counter he should move forward to his best advantage, when the game stopped. Hemaprabha went inside.

Rajani got up from his chair and offered it to the constable. "Where have you come from? Was there anything you wanted to tell us?"

No, no. He had no business with them at all. He was on duty. The other day, there had been a theft at Doctor Manik's house. Quite steamed up, the doctor had gone to the SP's bungalow. After all, he was a man who had seen the war. Even now, three years after he had returned from the war, his hot temper was still something to reckon with. Nobody knew precisely what he said to the SP, but the outcome was that there was to be police patrolling henceforth on that street. That was how he was here – on duty. But what duty did he have? After all, how many houses were there in this neighbourhood that were fit to be burgled? The one that was, had already been. Why would any thief stick his neck out again in this area? Bored with pacing up and down the streets all alone without reason, he had come to find out what Rajani and the others were doing and to kill some time conversing with them.

The next day, the constable came again around midnight. When the game in progress came to an end, Rajani and his friends asked him to join them. He sat down to the game with the green counters to his lot. They were late in waking up Rajani's father. Actually they had been so amused at the policeman joining them that they had continued playing till the very end of the game. Rajani woke his father up only after the game was finished.

"The boys have been telling me about you," Loknath said to the constable as he emerged from the house, "do sit down." Then picking up the lantern, he inspected the patch of ground beneath the litchi tree to see if there were any rinds – the one unmistakable evidence of bats having fed on the litchis. Who knew what the bats might do while the boys were absorbed in their game!

The bats were very sly creatures. Loknath had noticed that whenever Hemaprabha and he were engaged in conversation or were inattentive for just a moment, there would be ten or twelve litchi seeds and rinds lying somewhere. What a shame ... seh, seh, seh!

Leaving the lantern with the constable, he went in. In the meantime, Hemaprabha had put some water to boil. Loknath asked, "A little tea for the constable also? Have you got milk? Salt will do for me. Actually I prefer salted tea at this hour, but a bit of sugar for our friend here ..."

At this unearthly midnight hour, Hemaprabha changed her sador and turned her mekhela around so that the torn patch was covered. Then she came out with the tea – a glass for Loknath and a cup for the constable. Leaving the tea on the bench she moved away from the light of the lantern and stood under the tree, wondering what she should do. But she didn't have to think for long.

Loknath took a sip and called out, "Go to bed." Hemaprabha went in at once.

Loknath drew his feet up on the bench. "Tell us everything – where you are from, and so on."

The constable's words were rather vague. Amid the occasional sound of clappers, the tugging of the tin can string and the shooting of the catapult, Loknath made out that his name was Mathura and that nothing was known of his true ancestral home. Apparently, his great grandfather was someone important from somewhere near the river island of Majuli, and had been an evacuee during the Burmese invasion to the foothills this side. And because the lifestyle there didn't suit him, his grandfather had migrated to the bank of the Bornoi. The floods drove them out from there to squat on the reserve land where they had to fight wild elephants. So his father had moved to Kadamguri village.

It was at Kadamguri that his parents had died. According to Mathura, the story that his great grandfather was someone big from around Majuli must have been all lies, but that his parents had died because they couldn't get enough to eat was absolutely true – something he himself had witnessed.

Who was there in his home in the village now?

None, no one at all. He no longer had a home in that village. Not just his home, he would be happy if the entire village disappeared.

Why, why?

That's a long story. Well, to put it in a few words, age, illness and hunger had taken their toll on his parents. This, he could try and understand. But he found it very hard to bear the way the villagers took the life of his young sister who had no reason to die.

One day a man had come to their house. At first he endeared himself to everyone in the family, then to Mathura's sister. After which, he ruined her. And then he endeared himself again to everyone else in the village, and the only one alienated was Mathura's sister.

Joining the police service had placed certain fetters on Mathura, or else he would have hunted that man down and made him see how heavy his sins were.

The narration over, Mathura took off his cap and put it on the stool. Eyes fixed on the ground, he started rubbing his scalp with his palm. There was no sound or indication of bats landing, but Loknath walked across once and took a turn around the tree shouting, "Hei! Hei!" and beating the clappers. Then he remained standing at one spot for a while – as though he was reluctant to go back to Mathura immediately.

A little later he came and sat on the bench again. After a moment's silence he asked very softly, "You haven't started a family?"

Mathura's "No, no," was uttered with the same rapidity with which Loknath would say "Hei, hei!" to chase away a flock of bats.

"Where do you live here?" Loknath asked after another brief silence.

"At the police lines. You need not address me so formally as Apuni, you can call me Tumi."

The following night, leaning back in the chair with his feet propped up on the stool, Loknath began, "You know, Mathura, it's the same for everyone."

Hemaprabha could guess what Loknath would say a little later when he started with, "It's the same for everyone." She lay awake in bed, ears cocked, worried that the bats would land on the tree while her father talked. There would be the rustling of bats landing and she would have to rush out at once. She was prepared for this.

The tone of his voice indicated that Loknath would revert to the same old story, "The two children and I were mere entities in the household. She was the real mistress of the house, Mathura. You've only seen fledglings sheltering beneath the wings of a bird, but have you seen a grown up man becoming a little fledgling and taking shelter under a woman's wings? I didn't even know what was happening in this world. And I couldn't even make out what happened in the end. But when the wing flapped shut, I discovered that my daughter was seventeen and my son, fourteen. Honestly, Mathura, if I had been the one to die, they would have been in no trouble at all. They wouldn't even have known who was there and who'd left. But when she left us ..."

Hemaprabha was worried. Perhaps Loknath would start sobbing uncontrollably. At such times it was very difficult to control the man. The sight of his grief stricken face, like that of an adolescent's, had taught Hemaprabha to be calm and composed even at the early age of seventeen. Just to keep him in control she had learnt to say that the loss of one's mother wasn't such a terrible calamity. She hadn't even had the opportunity to ponder over whether it was really a calamity or not. It had happened six years ago. Every single day during these six years Hemaprabha had tried to push her mother as far away as possible, but then, on certain occasions her father managed to resurrect her, so that she would seem to be sleeping right there in the courtyard.

Loknath was telling the policeman what he had been telling people these days, "You know, Mathura, now even my daughter has started spreading her wings over my head, but, as a father, ought I to take shelter under those wings?"

This kind of talk irritated Hemaprabha. Her father probably thought she was asleep.

She hurried out of bed and into the courtyard. Today she was dressed in slightly more decent clothes.

"What's the matter, Hema? You haven't gone to bed?" Loknath asked.

"I was asleep. I just came to see if you had fallen asleep by chance. I heard some sound, like that of bats coming."

"No, I'm quite awake and keeping watch. You go to sleep."

Hemaprabha went in again. At least she had changed the course of her father's conversation.

Such things really irritated her. The man would blurt out anything without rhyme or reason, or try to do something unexpected. One day he would ask out of the blue, "I say, Hema, this Manmohan had come. I believe you didn't talk to him properly?"

"Who told you such things?"

"I just heard."

"When people come to talk, one talks with them. But when they come just to make a noise and be a pest, does one talk with them? Don't let such things bother you."

Loknath would fall silent after that.

On some nights after supper, Loknath would say, "Sit down for a moment. I have something to tell you. Madan's mother gave me a lead. I think it might be a good idea to follow it up."

Hemaprabha would get up abruptly, saying, "Haven't I told you not to bother me with such talk?"

"Why don't you listen? I was thinking of something good for ..."

By then Hemaprabha would be at the main door of the house. With her back towards her father she would say, "I know what's best for me. Why do you rack your head unnecessarily?" On such occasions she would remain awake till midnight, thinking, "What great thoughts my father has! There's no telling when he will sob like an adolescent. This man, and serious concerns!" A firm conviction would take root within her before she fell asleep, No, no, if she went away leaving this man, her mother would curse her. And at such times her eyes would fill up.

After changing the course of her father's conversation and returning to bed, Hemaprabha realized that her father had got down to describing her mother's looks, In build and looks she was just like Hemaprabha. If people were to see them together now, they would think that mother and daughter were actually sisters. There was so much want and hardship, but the woman never lost her smile ...

Hemaprabha had fallen asleep briefly. The sound of the clappers woke her. She sat up. The constable must have left, her father must be alone.

But just then the strains of a line from the kirtan her father was singing reached her ears. It came from that part of the courtyard where they kept the stools and benches. Moving towards the doorstep, she looked out. Her father was leaning back in his chair, his feet propped up on a stool. At a little distance, constable Mathura was beating the clappers.

The next day, Rajani asked Loknath, "The litchis on the other side too have ripened well. Shall I pluck them?"

Loknath looked at the litchis. "Not today. Let them redden a little more. Pluck the ones on this side today."

"Why, only yesterday we picked some litchis like those!" Rajani spoke the truth.

"Well, the buyers at the market turn up their noses if the colour isn't good enough. Let them remain today," Loknath replied.

The litchis would be finished soon, and the job of keeping watch would come to an end. Loknath didn't relish the prospect.

At night, just as Hemaprabha was reentering the house after placing a glass and a cup of tea on the bench, Loknath began, "Are you going to bed? Are you really sleepy? If you aren't, sit down for a while. Let's chat. I say, Mathura, how do you like this tea without milk? As for me, when I have to go without sleep, I rather prefer plain black tea with salt. But are you used to black tea? Well, we'll have to get a little more milk tomorrow. By the way, Hema, is the bhujiya and the roasted gram meant only for Rajani's friends?"

The man never seems to shut his mouth. Doesn't even care about what he says. We take only a quarter litre of milk from the milkman and that too mixed with water. It gets over by the afternoon tea.

"I say, Hema, would they have goat's milk at Badan's house? I'll find out myself tomorrow."

Hemaprabha sat, gazing helplessly at the snakes and ladders on the board lying near the lantern.

The next night, even after Rajani and his friends had finished their game and Loknath had left his bed and come out, there was no sign of Mathura. Had there been a burglary somewhere? Had he suddenly been called away on duty? Or was it that something had ...

"Make the tea a little later, will you," Loknath told Hemaprabha. After a brief pause he continued, "I was thinking of this boy, Mathura. You know, he's very angry with people. Just like you — headstrong." He added, after another brief silence, "A simpleton." Then clapper in hand, he went out to the end of the courtyard on the pretext of chasing away the bats. Not being able to see anything further down the street, he returned after throwing a few glances this way and that.

A little later, he was quite ebullient. "There you are, Mathura! You know, we were wondering what could have happened to you today ..."

Actually Loknath had been carrying on a monologue, but now he gave the impression that everyone had been talking about Mathura.

At about three o'clock that night, he complained of an odd feeling in his chest — a sort of palpitation, a wild thumping. Hemaprabha was really worried.

"No, it's nothing serious. I'll be all right if I lie down for a while. Why don't you two sit down? Hema, keep watch till I return."

After Loknath lay down on his bed, the odd feeling in his chest was transformed into a mild ache. He had left Hemaprabha outside. Of course, he had immense faith in her. But how cataclysmic this faith was! And how agonizing it could be to continue trusting her in this manner!

He woke up at the crack of dawn. By then Mathura had left. Since the time for the bats' assault was over, Hemaprabha too had gone to bed.

Loknath went to the foot of the litchi tree. In the afternoons, Hemaprabha would sweep the ground around the tree. On the dust he now found rainbow shaped marks of the broom and numerous footprints, but not a single litchi seed or rind. Loknath could not quite analyze his feelings. Was he a little hurt or disappointed? Or was it that he felt pleased that Hemaprabha did not indulge in banter and Mathura knew what sin weighed how much?

Almost all the litchis were reddening beautifully, but Loknath was dismayed. If the plucking for the market kept pace with the reddening, there won't be many more days of chasing bats. Even if they were not plucked, they would drop off one by one with the weight of the juice in them. The ache in his chest grew worse. He felt that even Hemaprabha could hear the palpitations of his heart in some silent moments.

On the following nights, Loknath made it a practice to retire soon after his glass of tea. But every night, sleep eluded him though he tried to fall asleep without any worries. Alternately, he felt a certain warmth and a certain chill. At Hemaprabha's age, her mother's body ... how warm it had been! Was it then? Even long after that, both of them had kept watch over the litchis after putting the children to bed. In the mornings, sometimes thirty, forty litchi seeds and rinds would be littered around the tree. Loknath would scold his wife, "How did the bats get to eat the litchis?" His wife would narrow her eyes, and then, smile with soft embarrassment, a blush stealing over her face. He even asks me how the bats got to eat the litchis. How shameless!

At some point, Loknath was even disgusted. What had happened to the bats? They were indeed blind. They said bats raised some waves in the air, and that with the help of these waves they located the ripe litchis. But where were they? Here was this wide open sky, a sky filled with air. But where were the waves they had raised?

One day, soon after dawn, his eyes brightened. And like a Ludo counter going down the mouth of the snake in the game that the boys played, the ache in his chest descended.

At one spot, ten, twelve litchi seeds and several rinds lay scattered.

If the keepers were distracted even for a short while, ten, twelve telltale litchi seeds could be found beneath the tree. Good enough. For the time being, even ten, twelve would do.

BHABENDRANATH SAIKIA, apart from being a short story writer, novelist and playwright, was also a nuclear physicist, journalist and film director. He had to his credit around twenty works of fiction, numerous plays for both the radio and the Mobile Theatre of Assam, an autobiography and a collection of journal entries to his credit. He also edited a children's magazine *Sofura* and a fortnightly, *Prantik*. He was the recipient of many awards, including the Padma Shri, the Sahitya Akademi Award and the Srimanta Sankardeva Award, the highest award instituted by the Government of Assam, besides winning the Rajat Kamal Award seven times for his films. Many of his stories have been translated into English and various other Indian languages. His works include *Antareep, Ramyabhumi, Maramar Dewta, Ghobor* and *Srinkhol*.

D N BEZBORUAH has been the editor of *The Sentinel* since its inception in 1983. He studied literature at Banaras Hindu University and linguistics at Reading University, United Kingdom. A teacher for many years, he has also published several academic papers. He has translated many stories and poems from Asomiya and Bangla into English. He received the Katha Award for Translation, the Sadbhavana Award and the 1997 B D Goenka Award for excellence in journalism.

BATS was first publishedin Asomiya as "Baaduli" in *Asom Bani*, 1975.

THE RIVER WITHIN

My car broke down in the middle of a small town that boasted of just a single garage. The mechanic conducted a thorough scrutiny and announced that the spares were not available locally.

"Where can I get them?" my driver asked.

"At Uthoro Mile," he replied nonchalantly. This meant that one would have to travel by bus or truck to Uthoro Mile to get the parts.

"Saar, don't worry," my driver said to me, "I'll take a lift and be back in two hours. You can rest at the Inspection Bungalow."

This was the first time I had heard of an IB in this area. But when the driver guided

Harekrishna Deka
translated by Aditi Choudhury

me to it, I was rather dejected. It certainly didn't look as if anyone had stayed here recently.

The gates to the bungalow were wide open. Walking to the veranda, I noticed that both the rooms were locked. In a corner lay an old fashioned easy chair, the layer of dust on its armrests revealing that it had not had the opportunity of rendering its services to anyone for quite some time. A cat was comfortably ensconced in it, sound asleep. There was also a centre table, but even that looked uncared for. Two other dusty chairs were placed back to back, as if they had recently been engaged in a fierce quarrel and were absolutely out of sorts with each other. There was no one around, save a cow grazing in the lawn hinting at the presence of a chowkidar.

"Please wait, saar. I'll ask the chowkidar to open a room so that you can rest inside," my driver said, and went towards the backyard. I sat down on one of the chairs.

The driver was not gone for long, but to me even that short span of time dragged. The distance we had traversed and the time spent standing in the garage had exhausted me. I badly wanted to stretch out on a bed. So when he did not appear with the chowkidar, I went looking for them.

The chowkidar's house was an improvised shack at the farthest corner of the backyard. A thick bamboo partition around it gave it some privacy. My driver was standing outside, trying to explain our situation to someone inside. I could not hear his words from that distance, but could guess what he was saying.

"Konthi, what's the matter? Isn't the chowkidar home?" I asked.

"Saar, he has gone to the market. His wife has the keys but since we didn't reserve a room beforehand, she says she can give it only after he returns."

I asked him to come back. I had no choice but to remain in the veranda till the chowkidar returned. My driver said, "Saar, I must go and get the parts, or we'll be delayed further. Please rest here till I return," and left.

I sat in a chair, alone, cursing my luck. It was unusually hot. Added to it was the uncertainty. Tired and harassed, I dozed off, only to wake with a start. A boy about thirteen or fourteen years of age was standing nearby and calling insistently, "Saar, Saar." He held out a key, "Saar, my mother has sent this."

I opened one of the rooms and lay down on the unmade bed. There was a fan but no electricity. Uncomfortable, I went out to the veranda once again. The chowkidar's son returned with a bucket of water and a clean gamosa. He left them in the bathroom and told me that his mother had sent those too. I splashed some water on my face and felt refreshed. The gamosa looked clean but I didn't want to use it. So I wiped my face with my handkerchief and returned to the veranda.

After a long time, I saw a man enter through the gate, a jute shopping bag in hand – the chowkidar, middle aged or perhaps nearing retirement. When he noticed me, his face revealed his displeasure. I called out. But he kept walking towards his shack. Only when I called out a second time did he come towards me. I asked politely for a cup of tea. He replied reluctantly, "There is no provision for food here, saar. If you want tea, you can get it from the shop in the nearby market. For lunch, you'll have to go to the highway. You can get rice as well as chapattis from the roadside hotels there. But it is far, you'll need a car." Realizing that I would have to go without lunch till my driver returned, I gave him some money to get me a cup of tea. He headed towards his house to deposit his bag and get a kettle.

He was gone for a long time. I saw my chances for even a cup of tea dwindling. As it was, he had looked inefficient. Should I go looking for him? The only way to make such people act was to shout at them. But there he was, hurrying from his hut, carrying a brass goblet full of tea, two big bananas and a few biscuits on a brass platter. Wiping the table clean, he placed the kahi on it with care. He was a transformed man, the earlier irritation having given way to a beaming smile. With genuine warmth he offered the food and said, "Saar, have your tea. It was my wife who recognized you. I didn't, because I have never seen you before."

I was startled. How could his wife know me? I have never met this man before. "What do you mean?" I asked.

The chowkidar replied eagerly, "She lived in your house. Have you forgotten, saar? Ratani from Pathali Gaon!"

Bewildered, I looked at him. Then in a flash, I remembered. Ratani must be Radhika, I had forgotten her real name.

It was in our house that she was given the name Radhika. My mother had this habit of changing the names of the young people who came to work in our house. The name opened the floodgate of my memories and the past crowded in on me.

"Does Radhika, I mean, Ratani, live here? How long have you been married?" I asked.

"Saar, she's my second wife," he answered, "I'd married her elder sister. She died quite a few years ago, leaving behind a son. I'd thought I would never remarry, saar. Then Ratani came. She had no one to turn to after she left your house. How could I keep an unmarried girl in a household like mine, with no other woman? But she had nowhere else to go. I asked her if she wanted to marry me. She agreed and stayed on."

"How many children do you have?" I questioned.

"Just one. Ratani never had any. She has brought up her sister's son as her own."

Old memories stirred inside me. My mind winged back to the past. I remembered many things ... so many things ... about Radhika. From the day she arrived at our house till the day she left ...

Radhika was hardly nine or ten years old when she first came to our house. My father's overseer, Dina (whom we addressed as Kokai or elder brother, with respect,) had brought her. He told us she was distantly related to him. An orphan, her parents had died on the same day in an epidemic. Her elder sister who was married lived far away and in addition, was not well off.

My mother had wanted a help for a long time. So she was happy to have her. Ma was always kind to the younger domestic helps and she said, "Since she has no parents, let her stay with us. If her sister does not take her, we will look after her. When the time comes, we can even get her married to a good boy."

Radhika was a scrawny child, looking younger than her years. At first, my mother was sceptical about how useful she would be around the house. But soon she changed her mind. "Never mind! She will be company for me since all of you are out most of the time."

Her name was Ratani, but Ma did not like the name. I was staying at home after my Matric examinations. I suggested, "Ma, why don't you name her Radhika?" inspired by my recent reading of late Shri Suryya Kumar Bhuyan's *Buranjir Bani* and the saga of Rani Radhika Shanti who shone during the Moamoriya revolt against the Ahom rule in Assam during the middle of the eighteenth century. Ma also liked the name. That was how Ratani became Radhika.

My mother's assumption that the frail girl might be incapable of work proved wrong. Hardworking, sincere and tidy, within a few days Radhika became indispensable and Ma, left with a lot of free time, became increasingly fond of her.

The years went by and Radhika grew up in our house. I too entered college and then the university. Gradually, Radhika began to look after my personal needs as well whenever I came home for the holidays. It was she who gave me my cup of tea when I needed it, ironed my clothes, prepared my favourite dishes and made coconut laroos the day before I left. Somehow, such chores passed from my mother to her. She understood my finicky nature, knew how angry I could get when things were misplaced. From the time she started taking care of me, I could never find any fault in her work. There was always a clean gamosa in the bathroom, and my sandals were placed just outside. Both toothpaste and toothbrush were in the right place every morning and a cup of lemon tea was ready for me as soon as I woke up.

Radhika became an integral part of our family. My mother loved her like a daughter. She often told my father to look for a good boy for her, "She has been with us for so long. I'll be at peace only when I can get her married to a decent boy." Ma told Dina Kokai the same thing. People did bring information about one or two boys. But none of them met with Ma's approval. Radhika was illiterate, was just a domestic help. No one with a good job would want to marry her. The prospective boys my father and Dina Kokai found were peons, chaprasis, ward boys or the like. But my mother wanted a better match for Radhika.

Meanwhile, I passed out from university and took up a job. Ma now started looking for a bride for me besides searching for a groom for Radhika. Ma could not find a suitable boy for her, but I was luckier. She found a girl I approved of – an educated and beautiful girl. Soon after the marriage, I was transferred to a distant place. Ma suggested "Take Radhika with you. She can stay for a few days and settle your house." Although Ma didn't voice it, I knew she was worried that I would be neglected. My wife was absolutely inexperienced as well as uninterested in running a house. Ma repeatedly told my wife and me to treat Radhika as a family member. She still hoped that as soon as her bowari learnt to fend for herself Radhika could be married off.

So Radhika accompanied us to our new home. In the beginning everything went on smoothly. The fish tenga was as tangy as it should be, the khorisa cooked to perfection as at home. The gamosa was always in the bathroom, my slippers and clothes neatly placed and the bed tidily made. Radhika ran our household efficiently and stayed on.

As the days went by, it became obvious that my wife was totally disinclined towards housework. She also exhibited a marked desire to be ultramodern. The differences between us became more and more pronounced. She preferred the glamorous world outside the house, western food rather than "rustic" dishes like fish tenga, mati dali or khorisa. Since she had no interest in cooking, she often ordered food from restaurants. Though I was not happy with this and said so at times, mostly I remained silent for the sake of domestic harmony.

One day we were having lunch, Radhika serving us as usual. My wife looked up suddenly and said sharply, "Radhika, leave the room. You needn't remain here while we eat. There's no need to show so much affection."

I was stunned by the outburst. My wife's voice betrayed an anger which must have shocked Radhika also. She had never been treated like this before. Her face crimson, she left the room.

I asked my wife, "Why were you so rude?"

Turning to me, she said in the same strident tone, "I saw her staring at you as if she wants to devour you."

I never expected such a comment. Her innuendo made me lose my temper. I said heatedly, "Radhika's like a daughter of the house. You shouldn't cast such aspersions about her."

"You needn't be so soft. I know her intention," she replied with equal force, "she'd better not forget her position."

About to lose control, I calmed myself in order to preserve the veneer of civility. As I left the table, my food half-eaten, I noticed Radhika weeping in the kitchen. She must have overheard us.

From then on I noticed that my gamosa and sandals, my clothes and the glass of water I drank at bedtime were never in place. Radhika had looked after all these little details. Whenever I shouted, she had come and given me what I wanted. But now it was mostly my wife who answered.

One day I found a Turkish towel hanging carelessly in the bathroom instead of a gamosa. Angrily I called out to Radhika. My wife came in response, "Why are you shouting? What do you want? I'll look after your things from now on."

"Where's my gamosa? You know I don't like using towels ... and you've also placed it so inconveniently," I protested.

"The gamosa doesn't look good in the bathroom. Use the towel. I'll place it properly in future." I did not argue. After my bath, I found my slippers missing. Once again I called Radhika. This time too, my wife came and, dropping them carelessly, walked off. Her brusqueness angered me, but I silently slipped them on.

From the time my wife took on the task of looking after my needs, everything became disorderly. I tried to adjust as much as possible, but her social commitments far outweighed her domestic ones.

There was an old photograph of mine I was very fond of, taken during my college days. I was wearing a black coat and a tie for the occasion. Seeing it my mother had smiled and said, "You look like a foreigner." Radhika had chipped in, "Kokaideu looks like an advocate."

I had specially ordered an antique frame from Calcutta for it. When I was transferred, I brought the photograph along. It always stood on the dressing table and it became my habit to stand before the mirror, comparing the growing signs of age on my face with the youthful one in the photograph. One day, it disappeared and was replaced by one of my wife and me. I realized that the new photograph of us as a couple should rightfully be there but I felt that my favourite picture need not have been displaced.

I asked my wife, "Where did you keep my photograph?"

She pointed to an old wooden box where junk was usually dumped. "It's very old fashioned. No one puts up such pictures nowadays. I have kept it with the old things. I will store it in a trunk later."

The callous treatment meted out to one of my dearest possessions hurt me. But as usual, I kept quiet. After a few days I found the photograph missing from the box, and thought perhaps my wife had indeed stored it away.

One hot summer day I came back from office to find that my wife had gone out. Prickly heat had made my back itch terribly and, unable to reach the spot myself, I wanted someone to scratch it for me. Even if my wife had been at home, she would never have deigned to scratch my back for me. I sat under the fan, opened my shirt and called Radhika, used to having her do this for me in my school and college days.

While Radhika scratched my back, I relaxed and dozed off. My wife's raised voice woke me with a start. I had no idea when she came back and how long she had been watching us. Pouncing on Radhika, she dragged her by the hair into the kitchen. Soon after I heard the sound of slaps and Radhika's sobs. Anger rose in me, but I could not intervene. What was for me a harmless act had taken on a completely different meaning in my wife's eyes. I could not summon up enough courage to ask my wife but I knew Radhika went hungry that night.

When I returned from office the next day, Radhika was nowhere to be seen. When I asked my wife, she replied, "She decided to go away. Good riddance," and warned, "there's no need to look for her."

Her indifference made me suspect that she had turned Radhika out. The girl was an orphan. Her sister lived far away, we didn't even know where, since there was hardly any communication between them. I wanted to look for her, but gave up the idea, fearing my wife's reaction. My parents were long dead. My mother would have been heartbroken by this news for, till her dying breath, she had deeply regretted the fact that she was not able to find a husband for Radhika.

It was only after Radhika left that I realized how deeply she had touched my heart. I did not know if my wife had seen these emotions reflected in my eyes and face. Perhaps she did and that was why she took her anger out on the hapless girl. Maybe I myself did not go looking for her because I subconsciously felt that these nascent feelings might intensify. A niggling sense of guilt, however, persisted at the back of my mind.

And today I had discovered that same Radhika in this strange place ... in this middle aged chowkidar's house. As I brooded over this, he urged, "Saar, please have your tea. Your lunch is being cooked."

Did Radhika remember the gross injustice we had done her? Was she happy with this man? If not, was I not in some way responsible? Had I not been selfish in not trying to get her married? Perhaps it was the concern for my own wellbeing that had made me neglect her marriage. But she still bothered about my needs. She had even sent me the food I liked.

I told the chowkidar, "I haven't seen her for a long time. Do ask her to come here."

After a while she came and stood by me, gazing at me intently. Then suddenly the unshed tears gave way to her usual smile. Her eyes always crinkled when she smiled. My mother used to say that Radhika's smile was truly beautiful. I too felt the same today. A life of hardship had left its mark on her, but her smile still radiated a joy and vitality.

"Are you well, Radhika?" I asked. She started, hearing that name after so long. Once again her emotions seemed to overwhelm her. Controlling herself, she said, "I am well, Kokaideu. How are you all? How is Baideo?"

"We are fine. Please forgive us," I replied. This time the tears could not be stemmed. She covered her eyes and left. After a long time, I was eating a meal cooked by Radhika. Soon after, I left for home.

My life settled back into the old pattern. For a few days I did think frequently about Radhika but soon she faded from my mind. These days I had to spend a lot of time pampering my wife who was rising socially. She had become a member of a lot of organizations and went frequently to attend meetings in Delhi and other places.

Several years went by. I grew older. My hair began to grey. But my life continued in the same tenor. We had no children. If we had, perhaps there would have been some novelty and liveliness in our existence.

One day I was hurriedly preparing to leave for the airport. My wife, who had gone to Delhi for a conference held by a women's organization, had come to know there that she had been chosen to go abroad as a member of some delegation. There was no time for her to come home. So I had to send her passport to Delhi. I was going to the airport to see if I could find someone kind enough to carry her papers. These days, it was mainly such inane duties that took up most of my time.

I came out to the portico and saw a young man in his early twenties waiting there. At first, I could not recognize him. Then I realized he was the chowkidar's son, Radhika's nephew whom she had brought up as her own child.

"What's the matter? It's been a long time. Is there anything you need? You've really grown!" ... A host of questions tumbled out of me.

"My mother has sent me."

I realized that if Radhika had sent him, it must be important. She had never asked for help before. I looked at him questioningly.

"Aai is not well. She won't survive for long. Stomach cancer." The words hit me like a thunderbolt.

"Since when? How is your father?"

"Deuta is no more. He died last year in a riot. I am now the chowkidar of the Inspection Bungalow."

I was shocked by the news. "Have you left your ailing mother alone?"

"No, my wife's with her. I came because Aai insisted. She wants to see you before she dies."

I was torn. I had to go to the airport to send my wife's passport. On the other hand, Radhika's dying summons were equally compelling. My conscience finally asserted itself. We had treated Radhika very unfairly. I had to go and ask for her forgiveness before she died. My mind was made up. Instead of the airport, I headed for the IB where Radhika was waiting for me.

. It was already late when I reached the chowkidar's house. Radhika had breathed her last. We arrived to see her daughter-in-law weeping helplessly by her side. I went up to her body. She had become almost skeletal. But she appeared to be at peace in death, her eyes gently shut. Both her hands were placed on her chest, holding on to something. What could be so precious that she did not let go even while dying? Her son also noticed this. He went closer and prised the object away from his mother's inert hands. It was a moth-eaten, sepia tinted photograph in an old fashioned frame. The face of the man in the photograph had grown indistinct, just a vague outline remained. Her son and daughter-in-law looked at each other, completely at loss, but I recognized the photograph instantly. I had thought that my favourite photograph was lying neglected in an obscure corner of an old trunk. But it was being lovingly held by Radhika during her last hours.

Was my wife right in interpreting the message in Radhika's eyes? The photograph transmitted many silent messages to me, making me feel numb, an overwhelming emotional tide surging within me.

HAREKRISHNA DEKA writes short stories and poetry as well as critical essays. An officer of the Indian Police Service, he has received many awards in recognition of both his meritorious service as a policeman and as a littérateur, including the Katha Award for Creative Fiction and the Sahitya Akademi Award for his poetry. His works include *Adhunikotabad Aru Anyanya Probondho*, a collection of critical essays, *Nirbasit Rosona*, a collection of poems, stories and essays, *Sworbor, Ratir Xobhajaatra, Aan Ejon, Gaurav Chalihar Xoite Xakhat* and others.

ADITI CHOUDHURY enjoys translating short fiction from Asomiya to English, and has contributed to numerous journals, and to *Women*, a collection of women oriented short stories. She teaches English at Handique Girls College, Guwahati. Her areas of interest include Renaissance Drama and Twentieth Century poetry. She is keenly interested in the visual arts, and is an avid gardener. She is also involved with academic writing.

THE RIVER WITHIN was first published in Asomiya as "Antah Salila" in *Adhunik Asomiya Premor Golpo*, 1989.

The moment I stepped into the ward, the nurse said nervously, "Good morning, doctor, a serious case ..."

Paying little attention to her tension, I replied lightheartedly, "Every day you have some serious case. "

"No, doctor, this one is really serious. She's been in coma since yesterday." I could hear the panic in her voice.

Having seen innumerable patients and witnessed uncountable deaths, this was not a cause for panic for us doctors. I continued playfully, "If the coma has arrived, then at the full stop ..."

I had meant it as a joke, but couldn't complete the sentence. Though a doctor, I

Nongthongbam Kunjamohon
translated by P Biprachand

was a human being first – the softness natural to humans was in me as well. In a moment, my face changed and I asked, "Where's the patient? Who's it?"

"Bed number 12. A victim of the day before yesterday's incident."

"What incident?" So many incidents occurred every day, and this one could have been any one of the many.

"The one at Assembly Road."

Yes, a major incident that. It was being talked about hotly everywhere, its rightness and wrongness passionately debated. The day before, Akashvani Imphal had broadcasted the news in its evening bulletin –

> A group of people rallying along Assembly Road turned violent around dusk today. Police personnel had to resort to lathi charge and tear gas to control the mob. A number of people, including police personnel, are reported to have sustained injuries.

The mouthpiece of the Bampanthi Dal, *Anouba Mangal*, had carried a report with the bold headline, "Police lathi charge, tear gas, bullets for peaceful demonstrators – the terrible face of a fascist government."

But the ruling party's daily, *Achumba Paodam*, hadn't carried even a brief mention of the incident.

Nevertheless it was a big public issue. According to the *Anouba Mangal* report, the condition of three of the thirteen seriously injured was critical.

Two days ago, the opposition had led a big public demonstration against price hikes, unemployment, corruption and random allotment of public plots in the heart of Imphal town. The demonstrators, carrying placards and shouting slogans, had held a peaceful rally through the main routes of the capital before stopping in front of the Assembly Hall and shouting more slogans. Members of the Opposition had come out in the midst of the ongoing session to meet the demonstrators outside, and to make loud speeches. The demonstrators' demand to meet the chief minister was rejected outright. By four thirty, some of the younger lot were obviously furious and jumped over the outer wall of the Assembly compound. The police had resorted to lathi charge, trying to ward them off. However, like spark on dried straw, this could not be doused immediately, and within seconds a fire raged. The mob broke through the Assembly gate, compelling the police to use tear gas shells, and even bullets. The crowd ran helter skelter. It so happened that while retreating, some of the youths found themselves facing the huge plot behind the hospital which had been unfairly allotted to Terimal Merilaal. On seeing the building under construction – which some said would be later used to brew liquor – the anger of the youths was rekindled and they had started tearing it down with whatever they could lay hands on – stones, pieces of metal, just about anything. God knows why, but some of the police personnel suddenly joined in the frenzy. For quite some time, the place wore the look of a battlefield.

My assistant Dr Vinod came in, "Good morning, Tamo! Bed number 12 is very serious. Have you been there?"

"Not yet. I came in just now. Come, let's have a look." Both of us got up. The nurse followed us briskly, case diary in hand.

The woman, her head covered in bandage, looked old. Her eyes were closed, as though in sleep, her face swollen. The bandage at the back of her head was slightly wet, the wound still bleeding.

"When I came here in the morning she was shaking her head vigorously and incessantly. Seems she was like that the whole night. I didn't know what to do, and after consulting the doctor on duty at the Casualty ward, gave her some morphine," the nurse told me.

"Why didn't you ring me up earlier?" I asked, without really meaning it.

"But doctor, your phone was out of order yesterday."

"That's right, Tamo," said Dr Vinod, "we tried to contact you the whole of yesterday. But the exchange kept telling us that your line was out of order."

Yes, it was all due to the plan masterminded by my mother and my child's mother. A yagna had been performed to ward off misfortunes from my child's fate and had continued from sunrise to sunset. Some astrologer had warned that no member of the family should leave home during the yagna – that had been a real headache! Though I have no faith in such superstitions, I couldn't oppose the wishes of my child's mother and grandmother.

It was evident that the patient had received no other injury apart from that on her head. She was running a temperature.

Taking the case diary from the nurse, I glanced through it to see what they had done at Casualty — ATS injection, stitching, dicrostine injection, that's all. I thought it would be wise to ascertain the nature of the injury before further treatment. So I told my assistant and the nurse, "We need an X-ray of the head, urgently."

Both nodded their heads.

All this while, I hadn't noticed the quiet young woman dressed very simply and standing at the foot of the bed. Perhaps I had seen her somewhere ...

"Taibungo, my mother's condition ..." She stopped, a clear indication of her naiveté, especially in entreating people.

"Um, we're trying. We're doing what we can!" I gave the stock reply.

Back in my room, I checked the case diary. Till then I had not looked at the patient's name. I was stunned when I saw it. Name – Leipaklei Devi, Residence – Thangmeiband, Age – fifty five. A star in the blue sky of my memory gradually brightened. Could it be her?

"Nurse, call that young woman!" I said on an impulse, putting down the pen.

The nurse hesitated for a few moments and then went out. Within minutes she was back with the young woman in tow. The latter stood before me apprehensively, trying to compose herself.

"Ibemma, how many brothers and sisters are you?"

"We are two, my younger brother and I," she replied, head lowered.

"Your brother's name?"

"Manglem. He's also known as Jeevan."

Obviously, that boy named Jeevan ...

I must have been lost in my thoughts for a few moments, for when I came back to the present, I found the young woman still standing before me looking a little embarrassed.

"You can go now, Ibemma." Without asking any more questions, I let her go.

After she left, I finished the paperwork and passed it on to the nurse, "Send this immediately to the X-ray Department. Quick!"

"But doctor ..." She hesitated.

"But what?"

"Yesterday there was no X-ray film. I forgot to tell you about it."

Anger shot through me. What on earth is wrong with this hospital. Today no film, tomorrow no power, the day after the machine would have some problem and the following day ...

"I don't care whether there is film or not. Tell them it must be done."

I came to my senses the next moment. Why vent my anger on this poor nurse for the loopholes and wants in the hospital. I said softly, "Go, have a look. It's not you I'm angry with, but those self-styled experts in management, those big shots of the hospital."

At my extra seriousness about the case, Dr Vinod asked curiously, "Tamo, do you know this old woman?"

Before I could answer, the nurse asked, "Is she related to you?"

Um ... a relative ... Um ...!

I was a student then.

By the side of the road near our school stood a thatched shed that served as a teastall. In the absence of any other teastall nearby, it was our hangout. Teachers also dropped in sometimes. Ine Leipaklei, the tea vendor, was everyone's aunt, their Ine.

Ine had a rare quality, she never lost her temper. All the students took advantage of this. After having had tea, bora or pakora, if we left her teastall saying, "Ine, we'll pay you some other day," she'd merely say, "Yes, yes. Just don't forget." Who owed what, who was what – it was all committed to memory. Her largeheartedness made most students to pay up. She would admonish the students gently as if they were her own children. "Hai, don't behave like delinquents. This is not the time. Study hard, try to stand on your own feet. And keep away from bad company ..." Any student, however mischievous he might be, was sure to turn meek and docile in her presence.

It was the time when the movement for statehood was in full swing in Manipur. Some of us self-styled student leaders were jailed for campaigning. Soon after our release, Ine said, "Ibungokhoi, even if you involve yourself in politics, don't neglect your studies. If you enter politics without education, no one will respect you."

Her little son Jeevan would occasionally turn up at the teastall, and she'd say, "Don't you think my son will be good at studies? Even if I have to starve, I want to educate him up to the highest level."

The little boy, intelligent for his age, would memorize poems from his textbooks and recite them very nicely. An affable kid, all of us knew him. Ine told us that she also had a daughter. She was studying. But not once did we see her at the stall.

Long after completing our matriculation, some of us couldn't break the bond with Ine. Very often, we would get together and visit her

---

Ibungo: A term used to address a young boy lovingly. **Ibungokhoi** is the plural.

teastall. There we would spend a couple of hours over a cup of tea and a plate of pakoras.

The result of the Pre-University examination brought with it a baffling dilemma. Intriguingly, my results were far better than my expectations and as a result, I got the chance to make a choice between medicine and engineering. My parents opted for the latter so that I might own cars and buildings one day. But my political ambition was deep rooted, and I wanted to become a lawyer or a college lecturer. Neither of these two options would be a hindrance to my political ambition.

One day, over a cup of tea, I conveyed my predicament to Ine Leipaklei. She offered a simple solution, playfully, "Then let me draw lots for you, and you must choose accordingly. Agreed?"

An excellent idea. Then, the draw of lots. One of the two disagreeable options won the battle – medicine. The very prospect of my studying medicine excited Ine Leipaklei as if the lot had turned out in her favour. "This is exactly what I had wished for. A doctor's profession is the best, it means serving the sick and the suffering," she told me.

Noticing my disappointment, she reasoned, "Silly boy! Politics should be indulged in only by the rich and the affluent. Do you, a poor man's son, want to starve to death by joining politics?" Looking at me steadily for a few seconds, she continued, "Well, even if you are bent on joining politics, there's no harm in becoming a doctor. You need not look for a government job, you can treat the patients at home and then you'll never starve."

This is how I had gone for medical studies, motivated by Ine Leipaklei.

It was my third year at Medical College. During the summer vacation, I headed for Ine Leipaklei's teastall as soon as I got home. That part of the townscape was fast changing with many new buildings coming up. Ine's teastall had also altered immensely. However, while the change was from bad to good for the others, it was the other way round for her. The sight of the dilapidated teastall shocked me. The benches were dirty and dusty – an indication of dwindling customers. The corners were full of cobwebs. Obviously Ine did not bother much to clean up the teastall.

"What's all this, Ine?" I asked, as I stepped inside.

"What to do? It's the wheel of time in motion. Who can oppose it?" she said, pointing to a grand building across the road.

A grand building, a big signboard flashing the words – Modern Hotel and Restaurant. I realized instantly why Ine's teastall had so quickly deteriorated.

The following summer vacation again I lost no opportunity in visiting the teastall. This time Ine and her son were busy pulling down the shed, both drenched in sweat. Jeevan was then in his early teens.

Seeing me, she stopped her work and came up, "When did you come home, Ibungo?"

The face had become old so suddenly. There was no trace of the usual sparkling smile.

"Are you going to reconstruct the teastall, Ine? Be sure to make a better one this time," I counselled with the best of intentions.

"What a far cry from reality, Ibungo," said Ine. "Didn't you hear that I have been evicted? That's why we're pulling this down."

"But why?"

"So, you haven't heard, Ibungo? The government says it's going to develop and beautify the town, so they have given all these roadside plots for shops. That's why they are evicting us."

Quoting what I had once overheard some lawyers say, I pretended to know more than I did, and told Ine, "Why didn't you grab a plot for yourself, Ine? You have full rights to claim this place where you have sat for more than fourteen, fifteen years. No one has more right over this piece of land than you."

"Forget my fourteen, fifteen years, you know Inamma Ibecha who has been sitting at the foot of the banyan tree for the last twenty four, twenty five years ... even she has been evicted. This is it, Ibungo, all their shouts about eradicating poverty ..." After a pause, she continued, "Give ten thousand rupees, they said, imagine, ten thousand rupees ...!" A long and deep sigh escaped her lips.

Except for sighing in sympathy with Ine Leipaklei's sufferings, I wasn't able to do anything to help her. What a state of affairs! So this is the government's development programme for the state, this is its poverty eradication programme!

After a week or so, I saw Ine Leipaklei queuing before the wholesale cooperative store in Paona Bazar, along with numerous other women and children.

It was drizzling, but none of them seemed bothered by it. It was an intense battle to procure the two, three kilos of sugar at government controlled rates. Just as the rain could not break their line, nor could the sun. Around four or five in the evening they *might* get a few kilos of sugar, which they would then sell to big shops and traders for a few rupees more. With the two, three rupees they got as profit, they would buy rice and head home for the night.

One day, towards the end of my vacation I met Ine Leipaklei on the road. She was carrying something in a basket on her head. I stopped my bicycle and called out, "Ine, what're you carrying?"

She stopped. "Haima, it's you! I was collecting these empty bottles. But where are you going?"

Without replying to the question directed at me, and more eager to know about her condition, I asked, "Have you stopped going to the wholesaler's to collect sugar?"

Inamma: Sister-in-law, as a woman would address. Also used as a term of respect to address older women.

"No, Ibungo. It's not the job for an old woman like me, it's the young woman's contract."

I understood. People had not only been talking about the overt and covert malpractices regarding sugar rationing, it had also been regularly reported in newspapers. But the sad part is, the government which is supposed to listen to them, never cares to lend a ear to such things.

While we chatted, a motorcycle came up from nowhere and whizzed past, brushing against Ine. Fortunately, I caught her and she wasn't hurt. But all the bottles in her basket were smashed to smithereens on the concrete road. The three young men on the motorcycle drove away at breakneck speed without a backward glance. Anger and helplessness tormented me, but I could do nothing except hurl a volley of abuses at the unknown forefathers of those youths. But for Ine, she lost both her capital and profit for the day.

After that incident, I did not meet Ine Leipaklei for quite a long time. But around four years back, just before I was to depart for doing my postgraduate work in Surgery, I chanced to meet her at the construction site of the medical college at Lamphel – among the women working as manual labourers, carrying stones. I couldn't recognize her at first glance, she had changed a lot – she had grown darker, her cheeks sunken and face wrinkled.

"Isn't it Ine?" I asked.

She seemed startled to have a man dressed in a suit and tie addressing her. As soon as she recognized me, she said with a faint smile, "Yes, it's me. Aren't you Ibungo? Are you working now?"

"Yes. I'm employed ... here."

"I'm so happy. Now I needn't worry whenever I'm sick because you work here. Truly, I'm very happy."

Her face which hadn't reflected even the shadows of happiness for a long time seemed to relax for a brief moment.

The X-ray report confirmed my doubts. This was not the first time that careless doctors had closed the wounds, with pieces of stone or splinters of glass still embedded inside, provoking public indignation. We doctors are a strange lot, never cautious. Why are the injured and the ailing regarded as inanimate, lifeless objects!

In no time I took Ine inside the operation theatre. I cut the stitches and reopened the wound. After taking out two small particles that resembled stone chips, I stitched her up again.

I felt sorry for her. An innocent woman injured in a clash between demonstrators and the police. She must have been working at the Terimal Merilaal construction site. But why didn't she run away after realizing there was trouble? Was it that she didn't have time to do so?

Seeing my serious concern for Ine, the other doctors and nurses began to treat her a bit seriously. They searched high and low for those medicines which were normally denied to other patients on the pretext of nonavailability. As a result of this collective caring, Ine Leipaklei recovered in no time.

One day, after she was well enough to talk, I told her, "In future, if you even hear that there are demonstrations, run away from there."

"Why?" she asked, surprised.

"Idiots like them demonstrate and innocent people like you become the victims."

"You and people like you may be able to keep your distance, but not us. Forget keeping my distance, I've had to join in and lead the demonstration. In the face of changing conditions, poor people like us are not able to live. Prices skyrocket, sources of livelihood are rarer, have to lick someone's butt, pay five, ten thousand rupees – how can the poor survive? If starvation is death, so is death by joining demonstrations." Ine's words were the words of one heartbroken, her voice rose intermittently. I could not help being amazed at the way she had talked about topics as serious as these in such plain language. How much she'd changed! How did that happen?

Trying to change the topic, I asked, "I didn't see Ibungo Jeevan visiting even once. Where is he?"

"In jail. He was one of the few who was jailed for the incident that day," she replied without any sign of sadness. Just a strong ring of pride.

"Has he quit his studies?"

"What was the use, anyway? He completed his BA with great hardship, even forgoing meals at times. For three or four years he tried hard to get a job, no matter how small. Nothing works without the oblatory gifts to the ministers. Hoom! ... Five, ten thousand, from where do I catch hold of it, tell me, from where?" Shaking her head, gesturing wildly, she said, "Do you know, this government exists only for the rich – to give jobs to the rich, to safeguard the properties of the rich, to increase the earnings of the rich ... But it won't be for long ... The poor masses, unable to bear it any longer, will rise up as one, against this government of the rich. That day is not far off ..."

I could see it distinctly – the leipaklei flowers in full bloom at the head of our courtyard, pushing their way through the hard crust of earth in spite of the scorching summer heat. No one can keep them under their feet any longer. Be it tomorrow or the day after, the leipaklei will bloom, its petals widespread, and fill the courtyard.

"Doctor, phone!" The nurse's call roused me. Half-dreaming, half-awake, I rushed and picked up the phone.

The superintendent. Calling me.

I hurried to his room. A police officer was also seated there. As soon as I sat down, the superintendent said, "Is the patient named Leipaklei in your ward ready to be released, doctor?"

"That's right, sir. But it would be advisable to keep her for a couple of days more so that she can regain her strength," I said innocently.

"Let's release her. There's a warrant against her. He's come from the police." He turned towards the police officer. The latter nodded and turned towards me.

"I think it'll be good if she stays here for a couple of days more." I protested feebly.

"There is an array of charges against her – criminal trespassing, loot, arson, conspiracy ..." the officer recited. I felt like laughing! Charges like trespassing, looting properties, burning houses, rebelling against the government ... Against Ine Leipaklei? What a cruel joke!

"It's a question of law and order," the superintendent asserted authoritatively as if he was in sole charge of the law and order of the entire country. "Today, that is, immediately, they're taking away the other two patients being treated in separate wards."

It dawned upon me that the decision had been made beforehand. However hard and insistently I might object to the release, my boss, who would do anything to please the minister to gain his promotion, would comply. I signed the papers of her release much against my conscience.

Standing before her, I broke the news, "You are to leave now, Ine."

I was still wondering whether I should tell her everything, when she snapped, "So soon?" Then she continued, smiling, "Well, then, from today I will rest in jail."

Taken aback, I said, "How did you know, Ine?"

"Heard about it yesterday." There was no sign of remorse on her face. With every passing moment, the glow on her smiling face increased.

The formalities were completed in no time. Ine Leipaklei took leave of her fellow patients, and then, supported on one side by her daughter, walked out of the room slowly. She looked at me steadily and then said, "Farewell, Ibungo."

I said nothing in response. But within moments, I was suddenly on my feet and following Ine from a reasonable distance.

The police van was parked in front of the hospital. The other two patients were already near the gate. Seeing Ine Leipaklei coming out, they stopped and waited for her.

Scarcely had she reached their side when a party of two boys and a girl approached them from nowhere and garlanded each one of them. The next moment a chorus followed, echoing through the air, Inquilaab, Zindabaad ... Inquilaab, Zindabaad ...!

Goosebumps covered my entire body. My thinking, which had slumbered for so long, was finally resurrected by the cry from long ago which, as a student, I had so lovingly voiced. Inquilaab Zindabaad!

NONGTHONGBAM KUNJAMOHON is a short story writer, translator as well as travelogue writer. His major works include *Chenkhidraba Echel, Thawanmichak Amana Kenkhiba, Ilisha Amagee Mahao, Basanta Mameigi Kokil* and *Pairakhidre Cheklachado* (short story collections), *Sovietki Leibakta* and *GDR. Diary* (travelogues), *Sahityada Mityeng Ama* (a collection of essays), *Urubada Khara Ningsinglakpada Khara* (novel) and *Malemgi Mangal* (biography). He has also translated Rabindranath Tagore's *Gora*, Subash Mukhopadhyay's *Leirang Satlabasu Sattrabasu*, Jibananda Das's *Hallakhigani amuk Torbansida* and Tarunkumar Bhadhuri's *Sandhya Thaomeigi Meiree* into Meiteilon. He received the Sahitya Akademi Award (1974) for *Ilisha Amagee Mahao*. A teacher by profession, he retired as the secretary of the State Council of Higher Education, Manipur. He is presently the president of the Sahitya Parishad, Manipur.

P BIPRACHAND writes short stories and poems in Meiteilon, besides translating short stories and poems from English into Meiteilon and vice versa. He has also an anthology of children's poems to his credit. He teaches English at college level in Manipur.

INE LEIPAKLEI was first published in Meiteilon as "Ine Leipaklei."

THE ADVENTURES OF BAH TA EN

When Bah Ta En heard that the government and banks were advancing loans to landowners interested in agricultural expansion, he decided that he would also apply. So, one fine morning he set out for Shillong.

It was about one hundred and fifty kilometres from his village to Shillong. There, Bah Ta En went straight to the house of a fellow villager, one who worked as a peon in one of the offices, for he didn't know where to begin and how to go about his task. The peon, of course, knew exactly where to go, for he had been living in the city for more than eight years now. He took Bah Ta En to the right office and procured for him the loan form.

Wan Kharkrang
translated by Kynpham Sing Nongkynrih

But there was a problem. Bah Ta En was a simple farmer, a god fearing and conscientious man with a mind that was pure and innocent. But he could neither read nor write. His friend could not fill the form for him either. It was in English.

"Let's go to a friend of mine who's a BA. He's a clerk ... he'll have no problem doing it for you. Only thing is you'll have to give him a little tea money, for that is the custom. You know Bah Ta En," the peon advised, "nowadays it is not enough to just say, Thank you very much."

Bah Ta En nodded, gratitude welling up in his heart for his friend. "How much should we give this good friend of yours?" he enquired.

"I think twenty rupees should do," the peon suggested.

After filling in the loan form, the BA, because his palm was well greased, went out of his way to expound patiently to Bah Ta En, the necessity of acquiring various types of certificates. He named all of them and said, "It's not easy to secure these certificates. Of course, I have a friend who could get them for you. Only thing is you'll have to give him a little tea money, for that is the custom. But then, it's up to you," as though he couldn't care less.

Before Bah Ta En could say anything the peon interrupted, "We're depending on you entirely, sir. Please take care of those documents for us so that my poor friend could return home tomorrow morning." He then turned to Bah Ta En and said sotto voce, "It's better that you let him handle everything. You just give him the money that's needed, including his expenses, and leave it to him to arrange for the documents and submit the application for you. You can then come back next week to know the status."

"How much do you think is needed?" asked Bah Ta En.

Without a moment's hesitation the BA replied, "I think for my friend you'll have to give at least a hundred and fifty rupees. For me, fifty will do. I just want it for the taxi fare."

Bah Ta En winced. To his ears, the words were like the loud chirping of crickets. But what to do, he thought, when the work demands it. And the poor man took out the money. The peon winked at the clerk ... the fish had swallowed the bait.

The next week it was a hopeful and excited Bah Ta En who returned to the city and went to the loan-dispensing office to find out what they had done with his application.

The application had been submitted but the dealing assistant had gone on leave for two weeks. Nothing had been done about his application. And so Bah Ta En had to circle another one hundred and fifty kilometres homewards.

After two weeks had elapsed, Bah Ta En went back to the loan office. But he was told that the dealing assistant had extended his leave for another two weeks. Bah Ta En's face fell. But what to do, he told himself, when this is the way things are done.

It was only six weeks after his initial search for the elusive dealing assistant that Bah Ta En finally caught him at his desk. But the man was in a grumpy mood. In a peremptory tone he told Bah Ta En, "Come back after a week, I'm too busy right now."

Bah Ta En rushed out of the office in shame. No one had ever spoken to him like that. After all he was a respected village elder. As he stood cowering outside, feeling stupid and trying to make sense out of what had happened, the words of wisdom from his two friends repeated themselves to him, "You'll have to give him a little tea money, for that's the custom."

He headed back towards the office and approached the dealing assistant, "Babu," he pleaded, "please help me with my application. Please try to do it quickly, babu. Take this thirty rupees, buy a little something for yourself."

The babu's face underwent a cataclysmic change. It lit up and all at once assumed a benign expression. And then he said with feigned surprise, "Oh, why do you have to do this foolish thing? But thank you so much. You go now. Don't worry about it, I'll personally take care of it. Please come back tomorrow morning at ten." So saying, he heaved out of his armchair and escorted Bah Ta En outside. When they had said their goodbyes like old comrades, Bah Ta En's face blossomed into a triumphant smile. Now his work was truly on course. His brain was getting sharper and he was slowly but surely getting the hang of this loan seeking business.

"You will need two sureties," the babu announced the next morning. "These sureties will have to be well-known people ... and I think it will be of great help to you if these people are also known to this office."

"Babu, I'm only an ignorant peasant, where will I get these well-known people from?" asked Bah Ta En.

"I know some friends who would be willing to stand surety for you," the babu replied quickly, "only thing is you'll have to give them some tea money, for that is the custom. Or what do you think?"

What would Bah Ta En think, he had heard these words often enough to straightaway reach for his fast-depleting wallet and ask, "How much?"

"One hundred for each. Two of them – two hundred." The babu gave him the estimates.

Two months later, an inspector from the loan office arrived at Bah Ta En's village with the purpose of surveying and taking the measurements of Bah Ta En's farmland. But, he was a man who loved his drink. He headed straight for the local liquor shop. When he had had enough to contaminate the air several feet around him with the stench, he went to Bah Ta En's and without feeling a little bit embarrassed, bawled drunkenly at the poor man, "You, come here. Do you know ... do you know that the granting of your loan depends entirely upon my report? The moment I snap my fingers like this, everything will work like magic. Get me a deer within the next few days and I promise you'll get your stinking loan without fail ... without fail within the next few weeks. Do you understand? Why are you staring at me like a nincompoop?"

Bah Ta En was dazed by this unexpected harangue and the absurdity of the demand. He tried to cajole him out of it, but the drunken inspector stuck to his whim like a pampered brat. He must get his deer or else ...

Left with no choice, Bah Ta En enlisted the help of his brother-in-law and went hunting. After braving all sorts of hardships for three days and three nights in the nearby jungles, they eventually managed to track down and slay a deer on the fourth day.

"Well done! Well done!" the sodden official patted Bah Ta En on the back. "Your loan is as good as granted. Don't worry, I'll take care of it," he assured him. And for the second time since the day he applied for the loan, Bah Ta En's face blossomed into a triumphant smile.

This time it was with great expectation that Bah Ta En left his village for the city. It had been a full three weeks since the visit of his friend, the drunken inspector. He was sure that everything would have been processed by now. The loan must be waiting for him at the office, ready to be borne home like a trophy. The thought brought another happy smile to his face.

It was just after lunchtime when Bah Ta En arrived at the loan office. He entered it confidently and made a beeline for his babu's desk. But a terrible shock awaited him. The now indifferent dealing assistant told him that the government had issued an order recently to terminate all loan schemes. The reasons were unclear, but perhaps it had something to do with an unprecedented financial crunch.

Bah Ta En shook with rage as he listened to the sickening news imparted to him in a monotone. He had wasted around one thousand rupees and traversed more than one thousand and five hundred kilometres altogether for this thing, this ... this wild goose chase. But what could he do, he was only an ignorant peasant. Frustrated and helpless, he left the office, tears streaming down his face.

It was too late for Bah Ta En to return home that day. He set out in the direction of his fellow villager's residence, vowing to tell him everything...

The next morning, the fellow villager saw Bah Ta En off at the bus station. Looking at him, Bah Ta En thought, he is the only true friend I have in this city. But what to do, as he himself had admitted, he is only a peon. At that moment the bus rumbled to life. Bah Ta En climbed quickly inside. As the vehicle moved, his fellow villager waved and called out to him, "Bah Ta En, happy journey!"

WAN KHARKRANG writes short stories and plays in Khasi. His major works include the short story collections, *Shi Hali ki Khana* and *Ki Syntiew ha Ranab*, the play *Ka Khun Khatduh* and a collection of anecdotes, *Ka Pyrthei ki Shohkhleh*, besides several other short plays. Presently working as the Parliamentary Secretary at the office of the Khasi Hills Autonomous District Council, Shillong, he had also served as the honorary secretary of the Khasi Authors' Society.

KYNPHAM SING NONGKYNRIH translates from Khasi to English and vice versa. He also writes short stories and poems in both Khasi and English, which have been anthologized in two volumes, *Moments* (1992) and *The Sieve* (1992). His other works include a collection of folk-based short stories, *Death in a Hut and Other Stories from the Khasi Hills*, a book on understanding poetry *Ban Sngewthuh ia ka Poitri*, anthologies of Khasi poems *Ka Samoi Jong ka Lyer*, *Ki Mawsiang ka Sohra* and *Ki Jingkynmaw*. He also edits various literary journals in Meghalaya.

THE ADVENTURES OF BAH TA EN was originally published in Khasi as "Ki Jingiakynduh Jong u Bah Ta En" in *Shihali Ki Khana*.

To begin at the very beginning, I must concede that each one of us has, during our lifetimes, been through the capricious changes that only time can bring – times of difficulty, unease, joy and sorrow – in varying degrees.

I am known for being gentle, good tempered and rather laidback. I am the kind who has neither great name nor fame. But I am not ashamed of this, considering that a majority of the people in this vast world are like me. However, the incident that I am to narrate will always occupy a larger part of my mind.

It has been a long time, yet I recall everything vividly. The incident, the cause of my misery

C Thuamluaia
translated by Margaret Lalmuanpuii Pachuau

and lifelong tears, that dismal October night, at Hotel Odyana, Zolawn.

After my transfer from Sialton village, I, along with my family, was headed south of Mizoram to my place of posting. We bade tearful farewells to our friends, promising to keep in touch.

Enroute to my new posting I had to take a short detour to Aizawl for a couple of days. My wife and our two children – my seven year old son and nine year old daughter – stayed behind at Hotel Odyana, the best hotel in Zolawn, along with all our belongings, to await my return. Our reunion the next afternoon under the bright sunshine was a happy one. Sitting down to dine, I decided that even the mundane sound of my children squabbling over the cutlery was amongst the most joyous sounds in the world. We all looked at each other, and we knew we were happy.

As there wasn't a bed large enough to accommodate all of us, I decided to sleep in a separate room while my wife slept with the children. After dinner they left to pick flowers from the hotel's sprawling lawns, and I busied myself with some office work. It was then that it all started ...

On the bed beside me was a nondescript piece of paper. It was an old copy of the *Shillong Times*. I hadn't been able to read that particular newspaper for a long time. But I must also admit that I did not even desire to see one. There certainly was no love lost between Shillong and me.

I deliberately avoided reading the paper, but at the same time it held a strange allure for me, dated and old though it was. I opened its pages and came across the personal column, something that had not been there before. At once I saw the insertion –

D, if you could see my heart, it is bleeding now. – D.

I told myself, The world is still the same, and paying no more heed to it, I busied myself with the editorial.

However, another barely legible insertion on the right hand side of page three caught my eye, beseeching and beckoning me towards a bygone era. I read the insertion, my heart beating wildly,

> Dorothy and her little daughter, due to unfortunate
> circumstances, entered St Mary's Convent. It may
> be recalled in this connection that Dorothy married
> a handsome man, who later drank himself to death
> two years ago. Since then life has been a hard one for
> her. She was originally a tea girl of M locality here.

During my bachelor days, Dorothy was a name that was for me beautiful and profound, a name that had been embedded in my heart. "Dorothy," I cried aloud, "Dorothy, queen of the days I loved."

I read the item over and over again for I knew it was her ... it had to be her and none other ... it was her way of letting me know about her sad predicament.

A long forgotten milestone, incidents that had been relegated to the back of my mind came floating in front of my eyes – as fresh and alive as those days of spring when the allure of romance with my one and only Dorothy had played havoc with my mind. It was as if it had all happened yesterday. Time had not erased her memory. What was it about her that so appealed to me? I could remember every aspect of her being – her attire, her physical features, her personality and most of all, her delicate forehead fringed with the curly locks of hair that so suited her. I also recalled her lovely smile ... You must realize that I could perceive Shillong more clearly through my portrayal of Dorothy. I could not think of anything else, not even of my own family. Dorothy had implanted herself eternally in my heart and soul. A long time had indeed passed since we parted, but she seemed to grow more vividly beautiful with each passing moment. Unable to hide my emotions any longer I cried aloud, "Dorothy, I still love you the most."

I had never experienced such deep affection for anyone else. My knowledge of love and romance was gathered from the novels I had read. But being in love with Dorothy was a wonderful feeling, and because I had never had the experience of loving anyone, I committed myself to this affair with a vengeance. And reader, I must confess here that this was a grave aberration.

Dorothy was not from an affluent family. An ordinary girl but due to her, Shillong and its locales were like a pleasure dome for me. She made my loneliness and solitude a thing of the past. The romantic in me felt that she was even more exquisite than the loveliest of flowers. She had little occasion to dress up, as she had to earn her living as a tea girl. But when she did, she lent a new meaning to the term, "Perfection," the way she tied her hair with a yellow silk scarf, exposing her delicate forehead and the thick gold earrings. I can still recall the red and white shoes she wore on such days. She was contented with everything, so it was always a pleasure to be with her. Such was her impact on me, the most beautiful, the most marvellous Dorothy. Was it any wonder then that time failed to erase her memory?

Like any other couple, we made certain demands on each other during our courtship. For instance, if I didn't acknowledge her in public she would reprimand me. Why did you not greet me the other day? If I didn't go to her teastall she would ask, Why didn't you come over? Don't you know I wait for you? If I did go and spoke less she would chide, Why do you not speak when others are around? Why, o, why, so suited Dorothy.

One windy March day I saw her walking across the fields with a friend, kettle in hand. The fierce wind tugged at their garments till finally, unable to go any further, they sat down on the grass, laughing. I ran down and sat next to her. Her friend went away. We gazed at each other, she and I.

"What brings you here?" she asked.

I said, "There's someone whom I love dearly. Her name is Dorothy, she stays somewhere around here and I've come in search of her. Do you, by any chance, know her?"

She replied, "I certainly do. She's my best friend. What do you want of her?"

"I wish to know how long she intends to keep me waiting. Could she please confirm my status in the name of love?"

"In the name of love? Surely you must be joking. Anyway it's getting late, I'm only a poor girl who has to earn her living. Go ahead, study hard." She got up.

"Will you meet me at the cinema tomorrow?" I pleaded.

I had not expected her to come but Dorothy, as unpredictable as ever, was there. The sight of her from a distance made me ask myself, Is it a dream? Together we watched *Do You Love Me?* starring Maureen O'Hara.

I am not easy to please. And doubt, anger, pleasure, joy and even pain must have reigned in my mind. Yet I remember those little things not worthy of mention, that so pleased the ears of lovers.

That day, lying on the bed at Hotel Odyana, I recalled the letters that I had written – appeals befitting a lover's conscience. If she cared for me at all, I pleaded with her to tell me so and if not, to sever all connections.

D, if you could see my heart, it is bleeding now.

I recalled the line with profound intensity. Now seeing that very line again, various emotions rushed in, the memory bringing back haunting, troubled thoughts. In response to my letter we had met promptly.

Smiling, Dorothy had said, "I think I am much more anxious than you, D."

We went to a secluded place, and I recall pinning some flowers in her hair. She spoke first, "So you don't plan to ever return?"

"No, if you don't love me."

"Do you know how terrible it would be if you don't come back?"

"If you loved me, things would be different. To not return then would be even more painful for me. You know that."

She threw an indulgent look at me and tilting her head towards my face, laughed. "Listen D, even if I did love you, what would you propose to do with me?"

And I, in my utter innocence and lack of experience with women, had no suitable answer. Yet her coy challenge excited me and summoning all the courage I could muster I replied, "Why hoino, this is what I'd do," and took her in a long embrace.

Oh, the intensity of that spell, it was our one moment in time when the earth ceased to be and the pleasures of life turned ethereal and eternal. When I awoke from my stupor, Dorothy drew a long sigh, "Ah! If only fate decreed that I were a Mizo girl," she said.

She had greater foresight about the impending cloud that was to cast its shadow over our relationship. On my part, I had no inkling whatsoever of the phantom clouds that were to ruin it. When she was by my side there were none of those thoughts of darkness. My vision was blighted by her magical aura and I could foresee nothing else.

"Unless you tell me the truth I shall not go home," I declared purposefully, refusing to stand up.

She wanted to know how much clearer it could be, but what I wanted from her was some kind of affirmation, futile though it was. "Listen D, our final exams are almost here, after that I shall leave for Mizoram. Why are you detaining me like this without a real reason?

Your countenance does not seem cruel, why then is your heart so?" I beseeched, holding her hand and stroking the smoothness of her skin. "Tell me, D. Life seems impossible without you. I tell you, I'll die without you."

She avoided my gaze. And then suddenly, as if waking from her reverie, said, "Listen, you say that you cannot leave. Surely you're joking. Go ahead with your exams, do well and go home ..."

"Will you please wait for me?" I realized then that it was what she wanted of me.

"Certainly," she had replied.

That was enough to help me achieve my happiness. Dorothy had promised to wait for me. I knew then that I had no other rival. I alone occupied her heart. What bliss, what utter joy! But I also reminded myself that our world encompassed our parents and families as well. You know how these things are – the opinion of the family and such other things mattered, come what may. She gazed at me tenderly and from the look on my face she could decipher that my feelings for her were earnest and true. She was a clever woman, and from what I could make out from our relationship, my affection and love for her far exceeded hers for me. She was always in control of her emotions while I always took leave of my senses. I tried to reach for the stars without climbing, while she searched for the stars with the help of a ladder.

After those heady days of courtship, studies and my forthcoming exams took a backseat. But, much as I wanted to meet her, I could not. I met her friend though and asked about her. She was extremely loyal to her and did not respond truthfully. At last she said that Dorothy was to be married to a local khasi youth. Dorothy was reluctant to meet me. Anyway, it would have been difficult for both of us to know how to react, even if we did meet. I spent the rest of my academic session in Shillong with a heavy heart.

When I reached Mizoram, it was with a burdened, weary heart. My mind was scarred, filled as it was with the memories of Dorothy. However, I tried very hard to overcome my heartbreak and emphatically promised myself that I would never return to Shillong. Time passed slowly and painfully, and during this interval, I was offered a job at Sialton. I met my wife Nguri there and was reminded of Shakespeare, the wise bard's words. Men are April when they woo, December when they wed.

For me, I think it worked quite the opposite way for I was deeply in love and utterly happy. To tell you the truth, when I first courted Nguri, I was December or January or perhaps even February (all due to Dorothy.) But when we got married, Nguri brought out April, the fullest of seasons, in me. Nguri was responsible for making me forget all about Dorothy and my unhappy past. She was all that I could ever want. And as for my daughter, often I've thought that she'll put all other beauties to shame, so fine were her features and her countenance. Yes, I was as proud of my family as they were of me. In fact we would have no qualms about singing, "Wondrous beauties we claim not to be, our charming looks suffice for our village."

We were, as I stated earlier, a happy, contented family and Nguri and I were very much in love. With Nguri by my side I had nothing to fear, nothing to regret, for she was my strength and my inspiration. Even if Dorothy were to reappear in my life things would not change, I thought – so confident were we of our love for each other and of ourselves. Ah! If only one knew what the future held.

Reading the message in that hotel room, I realized that Dorothy still occupied a greater part of my thoughts and sensibilities. Reader, was it that fatal step towards doom? Yes, she who I thought I had forgotten was still etched upon my being. My mind raced back to the time when I was a carefree youth. Her memory revived a festering, yet long forgotten wound. My scarred heart and hurt pride, which I thought had healed, were still very much in the throes of passion. Deep down I knew that she was suffering. I pictured her in the convent chapel praying to Mother Mary for deliverance from her woes, and oh, how I pitied her. Where was I when she needed me most? I was at Hotel Odyana, at an obscure place called Zolawn, lying in bed with her memory for company.

The bustle of my family entering the room jolted me back to the present. Nguri and my son asked, "Why didn't you answer? We kept calling you." All three of them were there beside me and yet, so lost was I in thought that even though I registered their presence, I was unable to answer their queries.

Nguri went on, "Don't you like the sleeping arrangements that we've made? We'll spread the mattresses out on the floor so that all four of us can sleep together in one room."

This too did not elicit any response from me. "All right, if he refuses to talk to us let's leave him alone." Nguri walked off with the children.

I could hear my daughter saying, "Ka pa is being mean, isn't he, Ka nu? As it is we are the only guests here with just ourselves for company."

Nguri answered, "Go tell your father that your brother and I will sleep in the other room, and you could sleep with him." As always, my wife was afraid of upsetting me or making me unhappy.

My daughter, with her usual enthusiasm, happily agreed to her mother's suggestion and bounded back into my room. But I did not even glance at her. (My dear Mami, you whom I love more than anything else, was it not surprising that I did not even spare you a glance?) Deeply hurt and upset, she ran away from the room with tears in her eyes. I could hear her crying pitifully in the next room and being comforted by her mother. Dorothy had cast such a strange spell on me that nothing could wake me up from my reverie. All my thoughts veered towards her. I could picture myself waiting in anticipation for her in the parlour of St Mary's convent.

The receptionist would enquire, Who do you wish to meet? and I would state, Dorothy and her daughter.

She would then pass on the message to Dorothy. I could even imagine how tremulously Dorothy's heart would beat upon seeing my name. Suddenly I remembered that I had a photograph of her tucked away somewhere between the pages of an old notebook. The notebook itself was in an old suitcase in the other room where my wife and children were staying. I ran to the room, rummaged through the suitcase and grabbed the notebook. Back in my room, I gazed lovingly at the picture of a long gone, yet unforgotten love – Dorothy. As I looked at it, every aspect of her features and every strand of her hair which I had not stroked for the past nine years came to mind. Nothing had changed with the passage of time – her earrings, her eyes, her lips, ah, her lips ... lips I had spoken to, had caressed with mine.

Yes, I shall be as honest as possible. I called out to her time and again, yet from the haunting beauty of nature at twilight, no one responded.

Dusk gave way to the swift darkness of night. Moonlight streamed down and cast its magic, but none of this registered. I chided myself, for this was not the way things should be. I had to get away from the stifling confines of the hotel. Maybe take a walk. Without telling anyone I went out to the open courtyard of the hotel. Were it any other night my wife and I would have sat together, waiting for the children as they played, but all that was a thing of the past. For the present, and this evening in particular, Dorothy beckoned and I belonged to her.

Before we parted, Dorothy's friend had begged me to at least say my goodbyes. We did manage to meet, but as there was not much that could be undone, both of us said very little. Dorothy, I shall go away but there will always be a place for you in my heart. From Mizoram, I shall look towards the hills of the north and imagine you at the Khasi and Jaintia hills – I remember telling her all this and the words lingered in my soul. So this night too, under the soft moonlight, after nine long years, I gazed nostalgically towards the north.

As a youth I had indulged in alcohol sometimes, when anger at Dorothy overtook me. For a long time now I had been free of its clutches, but now temptation sneaked in. I was so firmly in the grip of the devil, wanting that contentment of the heart through alcohol that the famed lyricist Lalzova spoke of. I told myself that here is a man in trouble, his honour at stake. There was no one to drive away the evil thoughts. So I walked all the way to Zolawn village a little distance from the hotel, with the sole intention of getting totally drunk.

"Ka pi, do you have zu?"

"I have one pot of the sweetest zu."

"That's not enough, bring me another just as sweet."

I gave her a two rupee note and presently she was back with two pots of rice beer. She tried to ask me about myself, looking at me with wonder and embarrassment. I did not disclose much but brought out the photograph of Dorothy instead.

"Madam, have you ever seen anything like this before?" I asked her.

She peered at it in the firelight and asked, "Is she human?" I told her that she was perhaps too old to see it properly and that this was an angel who was pure and beautiful. Gazing at Dorothy's picture, I drank the night away.

Deep into the night, way past two in the morning, someone shook me awake, screaming, "Wake up! Wake up! Your family ... Odyana ... fire ..."

I heard loud, frenzied screams and panicked cries. The town crier was calling, "Wake up all you who sleep tonight ... Hotel Odyana is on fire!"

I leapt up and ran aimlessly towards the hotel, falling and stumbling along the rocky path, calling out, "Nguri, Nguri, don't fear. I'm coming."

How often I fell and in what state I reached the hotel I have no idea. It all happened in a flash and was over before I could decipher anything. When I regained consciousness I was told that a new day had begun. I was at the house of the village chief and was being treated by the village compounder. I did not answer the chief's queries, all I could do amidst these strangers was to call for my family – Mama, Mami, Nguri.

My hair was singed, my clothes and body badly burnt ... no, I will not go into details. I had tried in vain to rescue my wife and children. They were dead and I was alive ... alive to regret the fact that I had not been with them in death.

It was the nightmare of coming to terms with the reality of the present that haunted me. I am sure there were people who had tried to deter me from leaping into the flames though I cannot recall who they really were. All that I could piece together was that, as I had gone away without telling anyone of my whereabouts, my wife had faithfully waited for me after the children had gone to bed. She had sat up long into the night, forgetting to put off the lamp.

The fire had first been detected from their room, but because they had been so deeply asleep they were the last to wake. Oh, to think that I had lost the gift of a lifetime because of my own foolishness. Words could not really describe the way I felt ... the remorse, the shame. Oh my beloved family, you who were so pure and holy, how I do miss you even now!

I resigned from my job. I had to make a few representations in the court and after the legal proceedings were over, the full impact of how alone I was, finally hit home. I started wandering mindlessly. All I could hear was Mami's voice prompting me, "Ka pa, go ahead, just go on ahead," and I was unable to stay in one place. All I could do was go on and on. Sometimes I would ask, "Mami, do you forgive me? Where will I go? I don't know where to go anymore."

I wished that Nguri and Mama would say something too, but all I would hear was Mami's voice telling me, "Ka pa, go on ..."

I plodded on, ready to undergo every hardship. I came to know what it was like to be hungry and despairing, to wander in thirst, roam about like an animal in the wild and suffer alone the terror of the raw elements of wind and storm ... with no hand to hold on to, except a tree trunk out in the middle of the wilderness ... to suffer the biting cold of the deep forest, to hear the strange and eerie night sounds out in the solitude and loneliness of the wild ... Yes, it was my hope and prayer that somehow the wild beasts would take pity and devour me. Mami's plea to go ahead with life led me nowhere, and so I traversed the length and breadth of Mizoram.

Time went by slowly and painfully. Summer in the hills lost none of its beauty, with tender shoots and buds giving way to greenery everywhere. Birds flew amidst the haze engulfing the forests, their lonely calls echoing in the hills, filling me with utter loneliness. I managed to exist, yet I could no longer belong or even participate. I kept wandering for two years to be precise. Though my savings for my children's education gradually depleted, I still had some savings in the post office. It was for this reason that I went to Aizawl, and from there, in the month of April, to Zolawn. This is where I am now, writing this short but important saga of my life.

People were good to me, immensely compassionate after they understood the extent of my remorse and suffering. With the help of the Zolawn villagers and their chief, I was able to lay a tombstone for my family. It was made in the finest mould for I felt that they deserved the very best. I thought that even passersby who gave it a fleeting glance should feel the same. I laid a beautiful garden around the tombstone.

Hotel Odyana, which had been burnt to ashes, had been constructed anew on a much grander scale and life went on.

I still had no definite plans. One Friday evening I went and sat by the tombstones of my departed family. It was then that I realized that I had long ceased to hear the voice of my daughter. Not since I came to Zolawn. Her voice used to be a constant reminder of my terrible guilt, and there were times when I dreaded hearing it. But now ... I gazed eagerly at the names etched upon the tombstone and asked, "Mami, why is it that you don't speak anymore?"

Yes, since one cannot just die, I had to go on living, cross boundaries and broaden my horizons. I reasoned to myself that this was what my family would have wanted, going ahead meant living life to the best of one's abilities. I am well-educated. The world was cruel that was for sure, but its inhabitants too were just as sinful. Life was unfair. I decided that as one who could still have at least forty years more of life, I would devote it henceforth to the service of others. That very night, I went to the village chief's house to tell him about it.

He was delighted. "Ka fapa," he said, "it is indeed an honour for me to tell you that you've been forgiven your sins."

The chief and his wife had always been good to me. Ever since my life had taken a turn for the worse, they had implored me to become the headmaster of the village school hoping that though I was a sinner, the job would help reform me and perhaps bring me back on the right track. So this new turn of events made them truly glad.

The chief asked, "My son, your decision to teach is final, isn't it? Let me despatch the town crier to proclaim the good news."

And thus it came to pass that the person once referred to as "Sialton official" came to be known as the teacher of Zolawn.

A couple of years back, one terrible night, Zolawn had been awakened by the call, "Wake up all you who sleep tonight ... Hotel

Odyana is on fire ..." This time the call was, "Wake up all you who sleep tonight ... I bring tidings of great joy ..."

The chief's wife was the first to congratulate me. I stretched out my hand, smiling perhaps for the first time after the loss of my family. Then, at the suggestion of the chief, we all bowed our heads in prayer.

The entire village congregated at the church where I was assigned to preach a short sermon. There was enthusiasm all around. I was delivering the first sermon of my life. I looked around, raised my arms and gestured the crowd to come closer. Then walking towards the pulpit I began, "Come one, come all ... you who are sad and burdened ..."

C THUAMLUAIA wrote essays and short stories in both Mizo and English. His works in Mizo include the short stories "Leitlang Dingdi," "Sialton Official" and "Eng Tin Awm Ta Zel Ang Maw?" besides several essays. His works in English include the essays "The Disaster," "Christian Festival," "The Days That Followed." Many of his writings including *Chawngtinleri Puan Thin Tlang, Lakher Chanchin, Heavenly Sinner, Post War and Pre War of Assam*, and a play *Mizo Lalho Inkhawmpui* are lost. A teacher by profession, he was also elected as MLA for a tenure at the Assam Legislative Assembly. He died in 1959.

MARGARET LALMUANPUII PACHUAU translates from Mizo to English. A doctorate in English Literature from Jawaharlal Nehru University, New Delhi, she is a teacher by profession. She is presently translating and editing *Groundworks in Mizo Theology* for the Aizawl Theological College.

SIALTON OFFICIAL was first published in Mizo as "Sialton Official" in the *Mizo Students' Association Monthly Magazine*, Oct-Dec, 1973.

ITAMACHA

Itamacha left yesterday.

Laishram Megha took Itamacha, her father Mishralal and mother Kasturi in his truck till the North BOC bus stand. It didn't look like they would be coming back. Mishralal took with him all he could. The rest he had sold off cheaply. He even gave some away to his friends. He had gone around the neighbourhood, holding Itamacha by the hand, meeting everyone. He looked like he'd wept a great deal – his face was puffy, his eyes red. He'd said, "I'll be back. I'm just taking them to the homeland so they can stay there for some time." As for his wife Kasturi, it was hard to say whether she was happy or sad. Her head

M K Binodini
translated by L Somi Roy

covered, the little baby in her arms, she had seated herself properly on the truck. I had only a fleeting glimpse of her.

But, Itamacha? Poking her head out of the truck, she called out to everyone she saw. She said to her friend Ibemsana, Laishram Megha's daughter, "I'll come back at Yaosang, the Holi festival, Ita. I'll bring you a Jaipur sari. Abok, I'll bring you your namabali. Yes, I'll buy you, I'll buy ... and tell Bung Bung he's not to touch my dolls, I won't stand it ..."

Itamacha left very happily.

Mishralal was born in Manipur. His mother Suko used to regale us with stories whenever she brought in the laundry. The garrulous Suko often sat down for a while, indeed for quite a long while, to talk. She said a certain Chaonu Kamdar who served in the temple, had been very fond of Suko's father, Krishnaprasad when they were at Vrindavan. It was this Chaonu Kamdar who had brought the young Krishnaprasad over to Manipur.

"Though my grandfather was only a dhobi, he was quite well-to-do. He had four donkeys to carry the washing," she'd say. Since the Yamuna was far away, Suko's grandfather used to wash the laundry in the canals when the ploughing season was over. "The canal water is very clear and blue and pretty as it rushes," she said.

Krishnaprasad too had become a washerman, and when he came over to Manipur, he began to wash clothes for the Meiteis. His wife, daughter Suko and the rest had soon followed. Suko said, "I had a younger sister called Sari – as Suko-Sari we were celebrated for our beauty ... Sari died early, right here in Manipur ..."

"They say our baba was the very first dhobi to come from Gayadham, the homeland. The bara sahabs wouldn't wear any other cloth, save those washed by Baba," Suko would say proudly.

Abok: Grandmother. **Namabali**: Scarf with "Hare Ram Hare Krishna" printed all over.

Ine Suko had yet another trade – making leirangs. She often made these mud ovens at home. They did take some time to make but were very durable, and saved on firewood too. I had bought one for ten rupees. God knows what magic she wrought!

After Krishnaprasad died, Suko's husband, Biharilal, took over his father-in-law's trade and came to live in Manipur. He couldn't speak Meiteilon. He was not very bright either. Meek, if it came to quarrelling, it was Ine Suko who did the needful. Yet it was for Ine Suko that people brought khechree during Kang, the Rath Yatra festival.

Perhaps because they work so hard, dhobis don't live very long. Suko and her husband died quite early, in this very land. At that time Krishnaprasad's grandson and Suko's son, Mishralal, was young. His ten year old wife was still over at the homeland. It seems it is their custom. Mishralal had lived in this neighbourhood from the very day of his birth. Of course, every now and then he would visit his homeland but never in summer. "Too hot! Not like Manipur ..." Mishralal would report on his return.

Once, after Ine Suko had spent two or three months at Gayadham, she distributed some pieces of sweet pua rotis to all she knew saying that a granddaughter had been born to her. That granddaughter was Itamacha Ramdulali.

After Ine Suko's death, the mother and child were brought over. Mishralal found a larger house near Laishram Megha's teashop. It was not too good but it was spacious. There was also a small open ground nearby where the washing could be hung out to dry. We then knew Mishralal would settle down for good.

One day I said, "Mishralal, now that you have your wife and family here, I suppose you'll stay in Manipur for good."

"Where would I go, Iche, when all my ancestors have been left on the banks of the Imphal river, where could I go? Imphal river is my mother and father," he said with unexpected good grace.

And six year old Ramdulali was always at the Laishrams'. She was a great friend of Laishram Megha's daughter Ibemsana. People teased her, calling her "Itamacha," or little friend, and soon she became known as Itamacha, erasing out her given name, Ramdulali. For both the young and the old, she was Itamacha.

"Itamacha."

"Hao?"

"Have you eaten?"

"Yes."

"What did you eat?"

"Roti."

"Was it nice?"

"No, rice is nicer."

Another time ...

"Itamacha."

"Yes?"

"What did you have today?"

"Ima had roti. Baba and I had rice. She doesn't like rice. Isn't it funny?"

"And the curry?"

"Mashed vegetables with lots of chilli and utong nga. Baba is very fond of iromba, you know."

"So you put utong nga in it?"

"Of course."

"Then you are unclean. If you eat dry, fermented fish you can't come here," teased Ibemsana's elder sister. Itamacha burst into tears. We had quite a job calming her down.

As a rule, one tends to love all children. But there's also something called "a lovable child." Looking at Itamacha, one thought of a little deer. Of baby squirrels. The uchinau, the wagtail bird. A lively, talkative child, her tiny lips never resting – that was Ramdulali.

The six year old Ramdulali was often sent out by her mother Kasturi to gather cowdung.

"Just don't want to even look at this woman! Imagine sending her tiny child to gather cowdung. She might get run over, the road is so close by," Ibemsana's grandmother, the roadside vendor, would say.

But Ramdulali's mother was a regular memsahab. She wouldn't even deign to come out of the house. Not once did she help her husband with his work. She wasn't Ine Suko. She was terribly aloof. They said she came from a well-to-do family. And what with Mishralal being so timid ...

"Taking after that innocent father of his, that's why," those who had known Mishralal's father would say.

And a truly obnoxious thing about Kasturi was that whenever Itamacha got slightly late while playing in a Meitei house, she would invariably come, her head covered, and stand by the gate, never stepping inside.

" Ei, Ramdulali ... ao na," she would call out in Hindi.

"Don't you just hate her ways?" the other women would comment.

The child would drop her toys in a panic and rush out. Ramdulali was very scared of her mother.

This may not be generally known, but from the very day of her arrival Kasturi was never comfortable in this land. The flavour of life in this place was not to her taste. We knew right away, Kasturi could never love the Imphal river. She was an alien – in the saga of this ancient river she had no place. This woman of the burning sun, this mahua blossom of the sands – she was not a takhellei, the ginger lily, or the fragrant sangbrei blossom, whose leaves are used for garlands or in hair wash concoctions. Therefore, Ibemsana's grandmother would often croon to Itamacha, "My granddaughter, she's the beautiful daughter Radhika flower of her mother, the wild, prickly ikaithabi," and laugh heartily. She would give Itamacha a ball of heingal by her vendor's stall at Lamlong Bazaar. Ramdulali would flick her little braid and slurp at the candied fruit, her little nose ring sparkling in the sun. To tell you a secret – there was yet another reason for this intimacy between Itamacha and Ibemsana's grandmother. Whenever the old woman made dolls, and when customers were scarce, Itamacha would thread the needle for her. She'd bring cowdung for coating the oven and scraps of cloth from the tailors. And so Itamacha would get all her dolls for free.

Ramdulali loved eating khechree during Kang, she didn't eat even once in her own house during the festival. But what she liked best was collecting money from men going on the roads during Yaosang. Kasturi disapproved most this grabbing of strangers by their clothes. Ever so often she would call her in, and ever so often Itamacha would run out again.

Naakadheng lak-é ...
If you have rice, give rice,
If you have dal, give dal
Give me money ...

Ramdulali would run around, her pigtails flying in the air.

It was at the last Yaosang that Ramdulali joined the festivities. This year, with her Meitei friends, she ran absolutely crazy. She was out on the streets all the time. When Ibemsana's grandmother bought a phanek for her granddaughter, she had got a tiny inexpensive samjet phanek for Ramdulali as well. Bright scarlet, how it matched that dark, glistening complexion! Really I'm not being sarcastic. It truly became Itamacha. Her large, kohl smeared eyes darted over passersby ... whom should she catch hold of? She, along with her friends, ran even after big young men. She was always the first to grab the man's shirt.

"Hei, this one looks like a mayang, a non-Manipuri, doesn't she?" Giving her a twenty five paisa coin, the young man would free himself and run away. Ibemsana's grandmother, selling spicy singju and pakoras by the roadside, would rush to defend – "No, no ... don't you call my granddaughter a mayang ..."

Mishralal was popular with all the people in the neighbourhood. They were fond of him. He was of this land and good natured to boot. Many even asked him to join in their feasts and festivities. And he, for one, never missed pooling in his ten or twenty rupees for the leikai pali.

Once Mishralal was invited to the tarpon feast which the Laishram family was giving for their ancestors. With the Laishrams it was almost as though he was part of the family – also he never took any payment for ironing Megha's clothes. That day he brought his daughter Ramdulali along. I don't know who told him to do so but he had dressed her in a small muga phanek. For all you know he might have made her wear one given to him for ironing. As they say, a dhobi's family never runs short of clothes to wear.

Ramdulali sat down in the children's row. Most children love the uti dish made of green leafy vegetables or peas with a pinch of cooking soda. Well, so did Ramdulali. When the brahmin chef, came in with a brass pail to serve, Itamacha Ramdulali said, "Eiga, uti."

"Heima! I thought you were a mayang, what with the nose ring and all. But this isn't uti I have here, I'll get you some," and serving her a pakora, he went away.

Struck with shame, Itamacha lowered her head till her face was almost in her food. While washing their hands, Ibemsana told Mishralal, "Eiga said he thought Itamacha was a mayang and she almost cried."

The moment she heard this Ramdulali burst into tears. But instead of pacifying her, her father doubled up with laughter and carried her away in his arms.

It was at this point that things changed for Mishralal. It was as if mongba, the bird of ill fortune, had flown into his house. Munna, Kasturi's younger brother arrived from the homeland one day, as it was said, to look around Manipur. It was thought that he would go back after staying for a few days. He didn't. More than three months passed. There was no talk of his return.

Brothers-in-law couldn't just be asked to go. And Kasturi dominated over Mishralal. Munna would dress up very neatly and sit around in the teashop, a Hindi book in hand. Not once did he volunteer to help his brother-in-law. Lacked sense, that youth. And quite cocky too. Once Mishralal had said, "What can anyone do to me? I was born in this land ..." But this time round he too was in a fix.

One day Munna was seen at a cinema wearing a pair of pants that a boy had brought over for ironing, and was beaten up badly. Instead of being embarrassed Kasturi blew up. "It wasn't as if their clothes were stolen, so what if it is worn for a while ... What kind of a muluk is this anyway ... ?" The local boys said, "Ta Mishralal, don't get us wrong, but send that brother-in-law of yours away."

When Kasturi heard this, she said, "I'm not dying to stay here either. One shouldn't stay at a place where even our kinfolk can't visit us. Let's go home ..."

We'll go, we won't, let's go ... they discussed it endlessly. Kasturi said, "Let's go." Mishralal said, "Let's think it over, what would we do there to earn our living?" And Munna was hanging around the hotel, watching girls make their way to school, chewing a zarda eksobis paan. He was dressing up more smartly these days.

It finally got around that Mishralal would be going back to the homeland. Perhaps he was putting on a show so as to get rid of Munna – but it didn't look like it. He was packing his belongings. Maybe he could no longer put up with Kasturi's nagging, for, from the very day of her arrival, she had taken a step towards leaving.

Mishralal and his family left for their home Gayadham yesterday. Even now I can vividly see our Itamacha Ramdulali – how she went away laughing, riding on top of Laishram Megha's truck ... how she told everyone around the things she would bring for them, when she came back the next day ...

A day or so ago, people told me – Mishralal, holding his daughter Ramdulali by the hand, had stood at his washing place on the banks of the Imphal river. I hear he had wept. But Itamacha had gone ahead, skipping, in front of her father. There was but one regret – we never heard what Kasturi had to say ... we could never reach out to each other. She might also have had many things to say, many complaints. As she was veiled, the slight glimpse we had of her dark eyes didn't let us know. Her red sari was all we saw.

Itamacha left happily, our little friend of the Imphal river. She owed nothing, no, she owed nobody anything. She left very happily on top of Laishram Megha's truck ...

M K BINODINI is a short story writer, playwright, novelist and film scriptwriter. Her major works are the short story collection *Nung-gairakta Chandramukhi*, the play *Ashangba Ngongjabi* and the biographical novel *Bor Saheb Ongbee Sanatombi*. She has also translated Badal Sircar's famous play, *Evam Indrajit* into Meiteilon under the title, *Amasung Indrajit*. She has received various awards including the Padma Shri, the Jamini Sundar Guha Gold Medal and the Sahitya Akademi Award. A graduate of the Vishwabharati, she is the daughter of Late Sir Churachand Singh, KCSI CBE, Maharaja of Manipur. An active member of various councils and fora relating to literature, dance and films, she is presently the vice chairman of the Film Development Council, Manipur.

L SOMI ROY has translated many short stories and film scripts from Meiteilon to English. An independent film programmer, he has programmed over fifty film exhibitions, specializing in Asian and Asian American film and video. His film and video exhibitions have been presented at The Museum of Modern Art, The Film Society of Lincoln Center and the Whitney Museum of American Art, New York, among other sites. He is presently Executive Director of the International Film Seminar Inc (IFS), a New York based nonprofit organization dedicated to independent media and established in 1960 to present the annual Robert Flaherty Film Seminar under the Robert Flaherty Foundation.

ITAMACHA was first published in Meiteilon as "Imphal Turelgi Itamacha" in *Manipuri Ayibisinggi Khangatlaba Wari Macha*, 2001.

Ka nu, could you finish this portion with Thani? I have to go and fetch water," Lali called out to her mother. They were weaving a blanket and that day they had requested their neighbour, Thanmawii, to assist them.

"Why don't you wait till we finish weaving this section? Look ... your father has come back as well," her mother replied.

Lali turned around and saw her father, drunk as usual. Though theirs was a predominantly Christian area, Lali's father and several other village elders had stubbornly refused to convert. A confirmed alcoholic, that day too he had gone out early in the morning and was returning in time for the evening meal.

Biakliana
translated by Margaret Lalmuanpuii Pachuau

He walked towards them yelling, "Zovi, hurry up and give me my dinner. I'm starving."

"Wait will you? Let me finish this." Zovi usually did not argue with her husband especially when he was drunk, but this was a difficult patch of weaving that could not be dropped midway.

From the veranda he yelled again, startling her, making her lose her place in the weaving. But he was already mad with rage and, grabbing a piece of wood he began beating her.

Lali was disgusted. "Isn't that just like him ... here, I don't think we can weave any more. As it is we still have to cook dinner and fetch water."

Thani glanced at her friend, "I have to fetch water too." They put away their weaving and went downstream as if nothing had happened. Lali's elder brother, Taia, was due to return from the plains. He had gone to sell their hand pounded rice. Though Taia was a pet name, he was addressed by no other. "I hope my brother brings back the material I had asked for. Normally he's only concerned about his own clothes."

Thani asked, "What did you ask for? I had given him money to buy embroidery thread."

"I had wanted skeins of thread from the plains to weave a puanchei for myself. But as we are weaving this blanket I won't have time for that. So I asked him to get some of that lovely material like yours. If he doesn't then I'll have to go without a puan. Anyway, there's so much to do around the house these days, there's hardly any time to spare."

Thani replied thoughtfully, "Perhaps this is our fate."

They walked along in silence contemplating the pathetic state of affairs and the wretched condition of women.

Puanchei: Traditional handwoven lower garment of Mizo women with multi-coloured stripes on a white background.

Thani spoke up, "What is the lesson for tomorrow's Sunday School?" Before Lali could reply she said, "Oh, I forgot you're no longer in the primary section. You've been transferred to the junior."

Lali looked worried. "I haven't read the lesson yet. I don't have the new text and there's been too much work. Tomorrow's Sunday so I'll have to fetch water again after the service tonight. There's the rice to pound. My brother took all that I had pounded, and now I have to pound some more everyday. Do you have to fetch water again too?"

"I don't know. I can say I will. But Vani would have brought some. Only she cannot really carry very much."

"You're lucky to have a younger sister," Lali said smiling. "It's very difficult being an only girl ... I wish I had a younger sister too."

When they reached home Taia was back. "Have you bought me the cloth?" Lali asked eagerly.

"No. The grain prices had fallen. I couldn't get even a profit of two rupees ... and I wanted a pair of canvas shoes and some salt."

"How mean! You knew I desperately needed a puan!"

"You should have got her what she wanted instead of buying the shoes," his mother chipped in.

"All my friends have those shoes," Taia said.

By this time, the meal was ready. Lali ate quickly and then gathering the rice that she was to pound, headed towards the veranda. Their mother prepared some more food, and putting it on the stove she told her younger son, "Zualte, watch the fire. I'll go help your sister."

"Oh, no. I'm going out with my friends." Zualte said, quickly slipping out. His mother could only grumble and tend it herself.

Mother and daughter had finished pounding only a portion of the rice when the church bells rang. With the help of their boarders, they managed to wrap up the work in time for the service.

When they returned, Lali asked some of the boarders to help with the housework. Then, Thani and she headed for the river.

Lali was no dazzling beauty but she was very pleasant and exuded a certain charm, and was indeed one of the most popular girls in the village. She was of average height, slender, her oval shaped face accentuating her sharp nose and sparkling eyes. In the company of men she was all gentleness and feminine behaviour. Reader, bear in mind that Lali was highly dependable and could always rise to the occasion. She was different from other young women who often hung their heads, bit the edges of their puan nervously, or worse, rearranged it in public.

Sunday mornings were reserved for Bible study sessions. Lali rose early and as usual, read her Sunday school lessons while her mother cooked. Today, they were to study the message of God's love, For God so loved the world that He gave His only begotten Son ... Can God actually love someone like a father? And to think it was for the likes of us that Jesus died. If only there was a way to let my father see the light, she thought wistfully, but then we Sunday school teachers too are really no better.

Biakmawia, one of their boarders, walked in saying, "Why there, you must have read a lot by now. Why didn't you wake me up?"

"You were sleeping so soundly."

"Luckily, it's only a little after dawn."

Mawia got up to wash his face. He had been a boarder in their house since childhood and save when his father died or someone in his village, he had not shifted out. The two friends – Mawia and Lali – taught together at Sunday school, lending a distinct sense of respectability to their humble dwelling. However, their closeness was the cause of gossip and many a young man was often jealous of Mawia. Even Lali's father sometimes threatened to separate them. Lali and her mother's prayers alone kept the friendship going.

"Thank goodness, you've been transferred to the junior section. You always know a lot more and it'll save me a lot of trouble. Do you know we've stopped calling it junior? It's dubbed Jirniau instead, as they aren't a very serious lot. The girls are better than the others. In fact, I shall appoint you as some kind of a secretary," he said, a smile on his face.

Smiling became this fair young man. Though poor, he made a conscious effort to be neatly dressed. He was of average height, like most Mizo men, not much taller than Lali. But this often belied his strength.

"On the contrary," Lali said. "In fact, I'm highly absentminded. Today's lesson is on God's love, isn't it?"

"I think so."

"I think it's beyond my understanding."

"Hei! How do you expect to comprehend God's love when you can't even decipher the extent of a man's love?" he teased.

Lali smiled and went back to her reading. Mawia towelled himself dry, picked up his book and sat down too. Before opening it, he said seriously, "I've often wondered about God's love, and been amazed by it all, especially the verse, For God so loved the world ... To think His love prevails even when man is so sinful."

"I was thinking about all this too. I know that there are men a lot better than us, and yet prone to sins."

They fell into a companionable silence. Sitting by the fire, her mother listened with pride to their conversation. There were few youngsters like them who would seriously discuss the word of God. In her heart, she cherished the dream of marriage and family for these young people.

After the meal, they all went to church, and as her father was out, they fastened the door with a piece of split wood.

Sunday School began on time, but the adults started their session much later. Lali looked around and noticed that the attendance in the intermediate department was thin. Her cousin Mana too was not there. She didn't like the company he kept, and had told him so. He heeded her, so his parents too depended a lot on her support.

She kept thinking of him on her way home, fearing he might turn delinquent if he did not change his ways. She decided to go talk to him. The door was unlocked. Entering, she saw Mana and five other young boys. They stared at Lali as she walked in.

Putting down her books, she asked, "Mana, why didn't you come to church?"

She was greeted with silence, and then, a snigger.

As she sat down beside them, she caught a whiff of alcohol. "So you've been drinking on the sly. How could you! And why? And I thought you merely bunked for the sake of bunking. Don't ever do this again, for these are only for the wicked. You'll fall prey to gossip and hatred ... and everyone will mock you. Haven't you seen how alcohol has ravaged your uncle? Don't you see the evil of it? Drinking is a sin!"

The young men, on the verge of adolescence, had never seen her so angry before. They had the utmost respect for her ... and, as she was older, the fondness they felt for her was more like sibling affection rather than infatuation.

An incoherent Mana mumbled, "We were lured by them."

The others also started confessing sheepishly. Lali too felt embarrassed that she had allowed her emotions to get the better of her.

"You must never do such a thing again, no matter what. Drinking is only for wicked sinners ... it'll turn you into good for nothing rascals and cowards. You drank on the sly, taking advantage of your elders being in church. And that's sinful. In fact, some of these men who lured you have been stripped of their church membership."

The boys stood there, steeped in thought. Her words, spoken in hushed tones for fear of their secret being out, had made a deep impact much more than the words of their parents or the church elders.

That night, there was a guest speaker in the church and the service was packed. In the morning he had spoken on the love of God, choosing John 3:16, 1 Corinthians 13 and the latter half of Romans 8. Lali listened keenly.

"It is impossible for humans to coexist without love. But most of the younger generation are unaware of the biblical concept of love, for temptation has taken over ... Think. And judge for yourselves. Love can withstand many things for love is kind, it does not envy – these are biblical concepts but now our attitudes have changed. Our notion of love does not include patience anymore. It is envious and full of jealousy. It is given to anger, is selfish, and we often tell ourselves, I'd rather kill than lose anyone. Our warped notions of love are often laced with wicked thoughts. Love is prey to lust as well. Therefore, let us carefully scrutinize the notion of love."

Some of the young men chuckled in agreement. The speaker continued to speak of God's love and also of the sins of the world ... about the cruelty of the German soldiers, the increasing number of alcoholics, and kidnappers.

"When we were young, we were told that God abhors all liars, but tonight I want to speak of the love of God as realized through Jesus Christ, His Son. When you committed murder, when you bore unclean thoughts and every other conceivable act of sin, God still loved you, but when he deduced how far you had strayed, how his presence went unheeded, God was truly grieved. Think of the sorrow he must have endured. Perhaps his thoughts would have flowed this way – My child, to think I love you so, to think I endured sufferings for your sake. Know that your sins are hateful to me ... repent and come back to the fold. Why should you be cast off for eternal damnation? Look unto me ... are you still about to perish? I have redeemed you with my blood ... You must realize that nothing can ever separate us from the love of God. In conclusion, I want to add a few words of caution. The verse also states – Whosoever believes will not perish but have everlasting life. Let us reverse the situation for a while. The term, Whosoever believes, assumes that non-believers shall perish. Thus, if there are people who still refuse to believe in the love of God know that they shall perish. We do not know what the term perish implies here, but it signifies something abominable. Therefore, let us remember our fellow human beings, our loved ones who will perish forever without experiencing the love of God. We must strive harder, for we are but stewards of God. May the lord add his blessings upon us all. Amen."

His sermon touched the hearts of many. Lali's in particular. Her thoughts went back to the Sunday school and to her father, and she vowed to strive harder. She felt a deep burden for she wanted him to accept the love of God, but it all seemed too futile. The fact that God's myriad ways are unknown to man was to be proved very soon.

Hardly a month later Lali received a proposal of marriage. A love marriage is often the most desirable alliance, but as we all know, our tradition does not advocate this. For, finally, we remain but simple hillfolk, and our economic conditions are pathetic to say the least. Our women bear the brunt of it, for they are sold off like cattle, and cattle buyers buy the best and the most hardworking of them all. It is as if we auction them off. And even after we possess them, the adage – Women and fences are but disposables! – still holds good. We men beat them and leave them at a whim. In the olden days, the value of slaves was dependent on their health and strength. We look at our women today in much the same way ... The dreaded habit of slavery was abolished due to the painstaking efforts of Christians and other noble hearted men who invested time, labour, money and talent for the cause ... Who shall lead Mizoram's enslaved women into the light of freedom?

Lali too fell prey to the curse society had inflicted upon women. Rozika, the son of an influential man wanted to marry her. She had received other proposals before, but they had been refused for various reasons. This time, as the alliance was from a very well-to-do family, Lali's father considered himself fortunate.

The young man in question was handsome and virile, but arrogant and conceited. Lali did not want to marry him. She knew that Rozika was quite a scoundrel, he'd loiter around during church services. The leader of the local goons, he was the prime suspect in various anti-social activities (in fact, believed to be the ringleader.) However, it was difficult for anyone to confront him openly. Lali knew that he was all this and more.

But her parents didn't. What could Lali do, except share her dilemma with Thani? At first, everyone had tried to make light of the matter, but it was impossible for her parents to decipher her true emotions, for such are the ways of young women – they do not really convey their feelings. Lali and Thani continued to confide in each other, but the more they spoke about it the bleaker the prospects became. They resorted to prayer, but even this brought little solace. Eventually she was forced to discuss the proposal with her mother and her pu Manga. Her father had deliberately chosen her uncle for this purpose, and in her heart of hearts she was glad. Initially, all that she reiterated was that she was not keen on the match. But then, it was quite true that she was already twenty one and marriage beckoned furtively all the while. At this stage, it was impossible to say what she felt and, even if she did, it would be futile.

"He is an only son and the wealth will be yours. He's also from our village. You'll be able to visit your parents whenever you want, you lucky girl!" her uncle teased.

Lali was at a loss for words. "But you don't know how truly hateful and despicable he is," was all she could say, even though she wished to tell them that he was a drunk and a womanizer.

Her mother said, "That's a terribly childish of you. We're poor, we'll never get a better match. As for his ways, well, most young men are like that ... shall we announce the wedding banns then?"

"No, Ka nu, let's not put up the banns," she started weeping, much to their alarm.

Her uncle went away, and her mother said, "Why do you refuse? You'll never get a better match and you'll become an old, haggard spinster."

"You keep saying he's a good man without knowing how wicked he really is. Last Sunday, he induced Mana and his friends to drink ... and he has a reputation as a womanizer too. If you are so desperate, you can marry him yourself."

Her mother was silent for a while ... who knows what she thought. Women had, in any case, very little say in many matters. Her uncle sought out her father and said, "I really don't know what to make of it. Perhaps Rozika is simply not her type. But whatever it is, she's determined not to marry him. Lali won't argue with her elders unless there was a very good reason."

But her father declared, "We'll never find a match as good as this. Love at first sight doesn't happen to everyone."

Manga knew his brother-in-law's nature only too well. He felt that Lali would undoubtedly be forced to marry Rozika, but he didn't know whether he should rejoice or fret.

That night, at supper, Lali's father said, "How dare you refuse such a proposal, Lali? You'll never find such a good match, ever. Beggars cannot be choosers, remember. You must marry him and love will take its own course."

She sensed the finality of his words. "I will not marry him, ever," she declared.

But this protest was futile and she realized that her father would still have the final say. If she wanted a harmonious relationship with her family she would have to do as he bid.

Her mother chipped in. "Lali's right. It isn't good to force anyone into marriage. And he does have a terrible reputation."

"How dare you dub him wicked? Can anyone be as wicked as you? You should be rejoicing at your good fortune. The marriage will take place, even if I have to beat you into consent. You people don't realize what's good for you. Zuala, call your pu Manga after dinner. Let them put up the banns."

Zuala said, "I've got a headache."

"How dare you disobey my orders!" He hurled a piece of firewood at Zuala.

Zuala fell down, whimpering softly, not daring to cry out loud. Lali's mother said, "You could have hurt him, you wicked man."

She quickly walked over to her son, but in his anger, her husband was blind to everything else. No one dared address him so.

"How dare you! You're the wicked one, you've spoilt them all." He rained slaps and punches on his whole family.

Zuala hugged his mother crying, "Ka nu! Ka nu!"

Taia tried to restrain his father while Lali cradled Zuala, and cried, "Run, Ka nu!"

Taia was unable to restrain his father. Lali's mother was not the kind to run off anywhere though she often suffered at the hands of her husband. But this time she realized that if she didn't get away, her daughter would be in a worse predicament. She wanted to run off, but also realized that it was not proper for a woman of her status – with grown up children – to abandon the family. Hesitantly, she stood in the veranda, but her husband called out, "Don't ever come back! I'll hack you to pieces!'

Though the family never paid heed to his drunken ravings, she felt that she'd only upset things further by staying. So she decided to retreat to her brother's house till his anger abated.

The boarders came home as Lali was tending to her brother. Seeing the father sulking by the fireside, Biakmawia asked, "Zuala, why are you crying?" He looked at Lali for an answer.

Trying to act as normally as possible, she said, "He was a bit disobedient and was beaten. Come Zualte, sleep on my bed. Your head must ache."

She settled him on her bed and tried to deal with the others. But they hardly noticed that anything was wrong. Only Biakmawia did. He felt he knew the reason too.

"Lali, where has your mother gone?" teased his friends.

Lali tried to hide her tearstained face, and replied lightly, "Well, she must be around."

And they all laughed. Lali's father sat sulking, remorse eating into him. Lali grieved. Few could even understand her predicament. And, amidst the laughter, there was the solemn face of Biakmawia. Lali was to marry soon – he knew that this was the cause of the dispute.

The news of her marriage had ignited the fire of love Biakmawia felt for her. Neither of them had spoken about this before. He had never brought it up because he felt that Lali was not interested. But now, he suddenly fretted – did she even know how he felt? Not that he could ever be on par with Rozika. The sermon about love being unselfish should ring a warning bell in her head. But, as long as she agrees to it and is happy, who am I to stand in the way?

He tried not to think about it, but it remained embedded in his heart. God's will shall prevail, he told himself staunchly.

The entire household thought that Zuala had fallen asleep. Lali shushed the others to be quiet.

Everybody became silent. She asked after a while, "Zualte, did you call for me?"

"I am thirsty," he cried. As he drank some water she felt his forehead. He had a raging fever. Suddenly he started vomiting.

Biakmawia and his friends came hurrying at the sound.

"He'll be all right." Lali reassured them. "He's had a cold for the past three days, but we hardly paid any attention."

As some of them went off, Zuala clung to his sister, "Please don't leave me."

"Zualte, I have to finish my spinning."

"Where's Ka nu?"

"She must have gone to Pu Manga's house. She'll be back. Go to sleep, you'll soon be well," she said and went off. Their father had got over some of his anger, but he was too proud to speak. Gruffly he asked, "Where could your mother be?" Lali did not reply.

There was a gap of many years between Zuala and his other siblings. He was not yet ten while Lali was in her mid twenties. As such, he was greatly pampered. In fact it was his father who pampered him the most. Unfortunately that night his temper had got the better of him. He got up and went towards his son.

"Zualte, want something?"

"I don't know, Ka pa. My head aches and I feel cold." After a pause he asked, "Ka pa, where is Ka nu?"

"Let me send for her," he said, and called out, "Lali, where is your mother? Ask someone to fetch her."

Biakmawia said, "Let me go. Where is she?"

"No, let me go, you won't know where she is," Lali said.

Their boarders were amused. "Where on earth is she?"

Mawia said, "It's very dark. Wait for me, let me light a torch. I know where your mother is, I saw her borrow Thani's lantern. I'll bring her back."

He caught up with Lali at the veranda and both of them set off. They walked together but what was there to say? It was difficult for Mawia to say anything. And Lali was just not the same. She stole a glance at Mawia and realized that he was gazing at her ardently. Hastily she withdrew her eyes.

Lali noticed that Mawia's behaviour that night was different, and as they later parted for the night he called, "Lali."

Smiling, she turned towards him and though he smiled back in his usual manner she felt there was a certain ardour about him.

"Are you crying?" he asked. She knew that she could no longer hide her emotions. She looked at Mawia. In that split second, time stood still and an emotion that could not be conveyed by a thousand words dawned on them. She saw in his eyes affection, concern and love as if for the first time. And Biakmawia noted the longing and desire that replaced the laughter and carefree lightheartedness that he knew. Words failed Lali.

Mawia said, "It's all right. I understand everything."

And so it came to pass ... the night had brought a rare, special emotion to the two friends.

Zuala's condition worsened. The next day passed off in a frenzy of activity. Lali went to fetch wood and Taia on his usual jaunts. Their parents stayed by Zuala's side, and when she got back Lali hoped against hope that her brother would be able to eat a little food. But this was not to be. He was given all kinds of medicines. Dusk soon set in and gave way to night.

The boarders asked, "How is he? Did he eat?" before they went off to meet up with friends.

Lali sat at her loom, barely able to work. She was called often to bathe his forehead, give him water from time to time, clean up when he vomited. Mawia stayed with her. That night Zuala drank some milk. At last Zuala lapsed into silent sleep.

Mawia said, "Good, he'll be better soon."

Lali was about to heat some water. "Mana, Liana," she told the boarders who were back, "Please go to sleep. If there's any trouble, we'll send for you."

And finally they did go off to sleep. Lali said, "Mawia, you should sleep too."

Half in jest he said, "All right, but if you need my help, just give me a good kick."

Soon their gentle snores filled the air. Shortly afterwards Zuala started vomiting again.

Mawia sprang up, "What could be the matter? And to think that he had fallen asleep just now."

But Lali, feeling a little lighthearted, laughed, "Hei! There was no need to kick you after all."

"Well, this was nothing. There may come a time when kicking won't do any good."

Sleep was impossible that night. And the following nights. The neighbours too became concerned, and often came to help. Apart from their own relatives it was only Thani and Mawia who stayed up entire nights. Zuala's body had become frail and gaunt, but his fever had abated and he seemed to have recovered partially from his semi-comatose state. All of them were relieved but no one could really sleep at nights.

One midnight Lali told Mawia, "Why don't you sleep? You've been at his bedside all the while."

Her mother said, "That's right, Mawia, go rest." Her father joined in. "Yes, you must sleep."

Mawia however was determined. "If you want, you can sleep. I am as wide awake as the nghahrangchalpa fish."

Thani said, "As if you know what the fish that doesn't blink looks like. Perhaps it feels sleepy too."

"Of course, I know. They are wide-eyed all the time."

Thani teased, "So you don't even bat your eyelashes?" and both girls laughed.

Lali's mother said, "You a nghahrangchalpa of all the things!"

"There you two, stop now," Lali's father chided the girls.

Then, Zuala woke up. His mother's eyes lit up. He gazed at his parents and incoherently asked his father a question all men find difficult to answer. "Ka pa, if I die what will become of me?"

His father's face darkened, "There, Zualte, you mustn't talk of death. You'll get well soon."

Zuala's eyes closed, but he tossed and turned. Opening his eyes once more, he asked, "Ka pa, will I go to heaven if I die?"

His father realized that his son had, in his delirium, asked him a question he himself had always dreaded.

Mawai reassured Zuala. "Of course you'll go to heaven, we will all go there. Do you remember the memory verse we read together ... For God so loved the world ... but why are you talking of these things? You'll get well."

But the weak little boy could only murmur the verse softly. Then he looked at his troubled father, "Ka pa, will you come to heaven too?"

His father didn't quite know how to respond to such a question. He hid his face and turned the other way, weeping. Mawia too was at a loss. Silence prevailed all around, tears flowed. Zuala gazed at his family then shut his eyes. But his words left an indelible mark on his father, something that even the most convincing of speakers had not managed to do. And, reader, it must be said here that his acceptance of the faith at that moment became so complete that he never slipped ever again. Meanwhile, Zuala's condition deteriorated, the diarrhea that had started two days back worsened and he started vomiting blood.

He was unconscious for four days, causing much alarm. On the dawn of the fourth day the little boy passed away, to be with God his maker. The community gathered to mourn his death. His father was constantly reminded of his sins and his son's last words increased his burden all the more. He did not confide in anyone, seeking solace instead in the laments. Zuala's Sunday school classmates came to pay tribute and sang a beautiful hymn.

There is a friend of children in heavens high
Whose love and goodness know no bounds
Friends here on earth may change the while
This faithful friend above bears a name.
There is a resting place for children in heavens high
"Ka pa, Ka pa," his children cry
A place to rest our burdens and our woes
A place where all the saved shall dwell.

Grief rose anew in the father's heart. As they finished, Renga, Thani's father, got up to pray.

"Zuala has left us for his heavenly home, to be with Jesus, the friend of children," his voice choked. Lali's father sprang up and hiding his tear streaked face said, "My heart is saddened, dear children. How wicked I have been. How I wish I too could have a place where your friend Zuala has gone. Words fail me. But from now on I shall believe," and fell silent.

The children looked on, astonished, as some teachers and a few older children wept openly, bowing their heads. Lali shed tears of joy as well as sorrow, and so did her mother. Thani's father, who used to offer secret prayers for his neighbour's soul, wept openly. The humble home thus gave birth to a blessed altar of belief.

After service that night some of their boarders whispered conspiratorially by the hearth. Lali's mother asked, "Mana, what are you saying?"

"Rozika and Zami have been suspended for some time by the church for their immoral conduct," he replied.

As the news spread over the little home, two hearts in particular rejoiced and relief overcame their souls.

Throughout Zuala's illness, Lali's father discovered many things and one of these was the fact that Biakmawia was a gem of a person. Though penniless and the son of a poor widow, there were many things about him more precious than wealth.

Thus, nearly a year later, the banns were put up in church: "Biakmawia and Lalawmpuii are to be joined in holy matrimony on 15 January."

Thus, the biblical narrative about the temptation of Eve and consequently God's wrath upon all women, was realized in a number of ways ... but though Satan has often cast asunder the hearts of men and enslaved women in merciless bondage, reader, may it be inscribed here for posterity, that where the Word rules, darkness is cast aside and light sets all men free. "Abide by our nation, O Lord."

BIAKLIANA is credited with having written the first ever Mizo novel. The novel, entitled, *Hawilopari*, was written in 1936. He died in 1941 after contracting tuberculosis, regarded a dreaded, incurable disease at that time. He also wrote prose and composed over eighteen songs besides numerous translations from English into Mizo, most of which still remain untraced. One of his most enduring compositions still popularly sung for church weddings is "Inneihna Hla."

MARGARET LALMUANPUII PACHUAU translates from Mizo to English. A doctorate in English Literature from Jawaharlal Nehru University, New Delhi, she is a teacher by profession. She is presently translating and editing *Groundworks in Mizo Theology* for the Aizawl Theological College.

LALI was first published in Mizo as "Lali" in the *Mizo Students' Association Monthly Magazine*, February-October, 1962.

OJA DINACHANDRA'S DREAM

Oja Dinachandra woke up with a start.
He took out the watch kept under his
pillow. Eleven minutes past three thirty.
Just when the day is about to dawn. A
dream at this time of the day is certain to
come true.

Shaking himself out of his drowsiness,
he tried to recollect the dream – every
sequence of it. And as the dream replayed
itself, he joined his palms together and
prayed, turning towards the southwestern
corner of the house where Lainingdhou, the
household deity of the Meiteis, dwelt: Let
good tidings be the consequence.

Oja Dinachandra strongly believed in
Lainingdhou, though not openly. He never

Yumlembam Ibomcha
translated by Tayenjam Bijoykumar

failed to criticize his wife and children when they talked about other gods and performed puja. Once when his eldest son was seriously ill, his wife had run hither and thither and performed pujas to appease many gods. After consulting a panji, a feast was also arranged. Oja Dinachandra did not say anything then. He himself had stealthily gone to the Lainingdhou corner repeatedly and prayed. When the child's condition slowly improved, he took it as a blessing from Lainingdhou. His son is grown up now and studies in Class IX.

Now, numerous thoughts started playing in his head, keeping him awake. He remembered the birthday forecast given in a local Meiteilon daily a couple of days back. The forecast in yesterday's Sunday Magazine of an English daily also seemed to be in his favour. And then, today's dream at daybreak. My time seems to be coming, god. And why shouldn't I be blessed? To this day, I have done no wrong.

Nowadays, only wrongdoers become well-to-do and affluent. This made him think of Madhuchandra, his neighbour on the northern side. Madhuchandra was his student. He had failed twice in the matric examination. At the third attempt, he had failed in two subjects but had managed to get through after appearing in the compartmental examination. Soon after, he had joined service as a clerk amidst rumours about his not passing the BA examination.

Not long after, Oja Dinachandra too got "utilized" in the Inspector's office and since then had been working as a clerk. Oja Dinachandra, even though he receives his pay at the matriculate scale, was not just a BA, but an MA as well. No one seemed to know that he had passed the MA examination while working as a teacher. So, whenever Oja Dinachandra saw any new face, he always talked about it – how he had studied late into the night during the examinations. Even in the office he never lost the opportunity of letting others know that he was an MA. There were occasions when he was soundly scolded for making changes in the letter drafted by the inspector. But no one addressed him even as "Tamo" or "Dinachandra Babu." This hurt him.

Madhuchandra, on the other hand, was promoted as the Assistant Director soon after he joined service. Dinachandra was surprised. How had he, in spite of his dubious education, managed to get a job and supersede him to become the Assistant Director? But it was common knowledge that before Madhuchandra got his promotion, five acres of land that his father had left behind had been sold off. Oja Dinachandra weighed the matter – I have neither the means to sneak into such a post, nor any paddy field to dispose of. He felt like berating his dead parents.

His friend R K Basudeb, a clerk in the PWD, had constructed a brick house. Madhuchandra, a child till the other day, had his own pucca house too, built after dismantling the two storeyed wooden structure which his father had left behind and which would have lasted another thirty, forty years. In the neighbourhood, Madhuchandra's three storeyed house was the tallest and the most beautiful. Theirs was also the first family to own a colour television and the only one that owned a refrigerator.

Dinachandra's wife knew that Madhuchandra was once his student. So, every new development in Madhuchandra's house reached his ears. "We don't even have a tape recorder in our house, and your junior Madhuchandra has already installed a colour television." ... "Madhuchandra has purchased a refrigerator." ... "Madhuchandra has also bought a video player. They say he's going to buy a Maruti car." His wife's primary engagement at present was to record what was going on in Madhuchandra's family, what were the new things that had been purchased and report the same to him. Before this she used to submit many reports about the gold jewellery made and purchased by others in the neighbourhood. Tombi's wife has had a gold ring of three and half sul made, Biren's wife has purchased a gold necklace of eight mohor, also the costliest rani phi, the gossamery silk embroidered upper cloth for women – such reports had been reaching his ears for a long time.

With the news of Madhuchandra's family was added a cutting remark, "He whom you had taught, the youngster, is going to own a Maruti. Why can't you at least repair your rickety old Luna?" and a conclusion, "I shouldn't have married you."

The Luna he owned was usually with the mechanic for three to four months a year. Of late, it had been lying at home, unused.

The moped had been purchased at his wife's insistence. She even claimed that she had bought it for him. When Madhuchandra bought a new scooter, she had said, "You won't be able to change your old cycle, while even Madhuchandra buys a new scooter."

Around two months after that, he received the payoffs from a local chit fund scheme – one thousand, five hundred rupees. Around that time, Bamon Nimai had persuaded him to buy his Luna. Though Dinachandra himself hadn't been too interested, he had been compelled to buy it as his wife had handed over the whole of the chit fund amount to Nimai. He had paid off the remaining eight hundred in monthly instalments of two hundred rupees. The marup had been in his wife's name and so the assured amount was received in her name. However the instalments for it had been paid from his pocket. But still, his wife boasted as if she had bought the Luna for him.

During the first few months after buying the Luna, both husband and wife had enjoyed rides on the moped – going together to the market and sometimes to the cinema, without telling their children. But when the Luna started emitting unusual sounds, and his wife overheard the whispers of neighbourhood youths and saw too their smiles, she refused to go with him. Instead, she started pestering him, "Let's join a scheme

---

Sul and **mohor** are traditional measures of gold and silver used in Manipur, one *sul* being approximately 2.5 gm, and one *mohor* being approximately 10 gm.

Oja Dinachandra too had secretly wanted to own and drive a scooter! Not just a scooter – in reality he wanted to drive a car and stay in a neat and clean pucca house. All his days and nights, he pondered over ways and means of becoming wealthy. At least once in his life, he wished to rise above his neighbours. He had wanted to drive a car even before Madhuchandra had bought his. But, he didn't have the money to buy even a new shirt! With the kind of job he had, leave aside getting even petty sums as bribes, he had to pay for tea from his own pocket. Once in a while if someone paid for his tea and bought him a paan, the head clerk, sitting next to him, would tease, "Today's a big day for you. Tender grass has sprouted in the middle of the tar road!"

Sometimes he wanted to resign from the job and start a business. If he took voluntary retirement, he would get thirty, forty thousand rupees. But then, what business could he take up? Meiteis are neither suited for business nor skilled enough, and always suffer a loss. So, he couldn't just give up his job. In fact, he didn't really want to. He wanted to be an officer, by any means. Many had. He wanted to show off in front of his wife, wanted to spread the news in the neighbourhood that he had become an officer. His wife was there to do that too. All this would be possible if he had money.

It was not as if he had never tried his hand at becoming wealthy. Once, he had taken up some contract work with the five thousand rupees he had received as arrears. However, his partner, a con man, had vanished with the money. The next time he had started trading timber along with a younger cousin, his maternal aunt's son. The money had been raised with a loan of four thousand rupees from his General Provident Fund. In the first two trips, it had seemed that they would be earning a profit. Thinking that at this pace he would be able to construct a house within two years, he had even mentally prepared the estimate. Later on, his cousin had married a local woman and had stayed back at Moreh. The timber businesshad met an immature end and he had lost the money he had invested. Perhaps he was not fated to be rich.

One day the head clerk had told him, "Don't run after money, bondhu. Call it in instead. If you run after money, it'll run away." Taking another sip from the glass of tea on the table, he had continued, "Listen, a man may be able to live comfortably after labouring hard. But another man may get every comfort without putting in much labour. There are different kinds of people. My friend, you had tried very hard but didn't get any positive result. Stop trying. You're not destined to become rich through hard work. As you are not accustomed to cheating and bluffing, it might be written in your stars that you'd become rich without labour. Try lottery. Buy a ticket every month. If it's written in your stars, you'll win."

The head clerk's words had served as a mantra. It wasn't that he had never tried lottery before. Now his involvement was heartfelt. There was also a hope. At present, his rashi phal was in his favour. Moreover today's dream was not a simple one.

While such thoughts played in his mind, day broke. About to climb down from his bed, a thought struck him and he quickly pulled up his legs, before they touched the floor. He tried to see through which of the nostrils he could breathe more freely. The right one was blocked. After a while he found that he could breathe freely through both. No good! Inauspicious. He was restless. If he waited any longer, he was sure to wet his bed. Waiting to breathe more freely through the right nostril was becoming very difficult and tiresome.

Suddenly, by sheer chance the left nostril seemed to become slightly blocked. Immediately, he got down from the bed, placing his right foot on the floor first. Coming out of the house, he prayed to Surjadev, the sun god, with folded hands, then hurriedly headed towards the yenakha at the side of the house. His children smiled at their father's unusual action. He, an atheist, who spoke strongly against superstition, what was he doing today? But they were unaware that their father said his prayers to the sun every morning. Earlier, he prayed to Surjadev secretly. Today, his children had seen it with their own eyes. He was mortified. But since his mind was absorbed in thought, this did not last long.

Wanting to purify himself both in body and mind, he bathed and put on freshly washed clothes. He decided he'd observe a fast. He wanted to go to the Lainingdhou corner right then and prostrate himself on the floor in prayer, but couldn't do so openly for fear that his children might see him and mock him. He went in, prayed stealthily and came out swiftly. Then, checking again both his nostrils to see through which one he could breathe more freely, he took out the recently repaired Luna.

He roamed around Kwairamband Bazar, Paona Bazar, Thangal Bazar and BT Road. He went to the western side of Pologround and Khuyathong, and then moved on to RMC Road in search of a ticket bearing the number he wanted: 8. This came after adding the date, month and year of his birth to get a single digit. The astrologer had told him that it was his lucky number. Other tickets were available, but not a bumper lottery bearing his lucky number. He could not waste his luck on small one lakh rupee lotteries. If he won one lakh, he wouldn't actually get one lakh. Even if he got one lakh, it would not be enough.

He thought: If my wish is destined to be fulfilled then the ticket will surely be found. He was ready to go to Kongba Bazar, Singjamei, Thoubal, even to Moirang. But, he did not have to go far – god had blessed him. He found it at the corner of Nupa Keithel. Delhi Diwali Bumper, Ticket Number MI 09674. First prize one crore. The price of the ticket, ten rupees. If his hands were shaking when he took hold of the ticket, it was not because he was unwilling to pay the price. He could have paid even a hundred rupees for it!

After putting the ticket in his pocket, he returned home in a pleasant mood. His predawn dream kept coming back to mind. He was climbing up a hill, the peak of which was surrounded by snakes. Suddenly all the snakes vanished and he saw a bright shiny object lying near him. He had picked it up. Exactly at that moment he had opened his eyes.

Recollecting the dream made him restless. Such a good omen – climbing up a height, seeing snakes, getting a diamond! He forgot he was walking. His thought grew wings and flew up. Visions of mansions and delicacies floated before his eyes as he walked on. Twice he barely managed to escape being run over. The driver of the second vehicle, a jeep, shouted, "Didn't you hear the horn? If I drive over you, you'll lose your life." Then after belching out thick black smoke, the jeep sped away. Anger and shame mingled. Héhé, showing off since he drives a ramshackle jeep! Doesn't know that soon he, Dinachandra, would be driving a Maruti. Ehé, forgot to look at the draw date while buying the ticket. He moved to the side of the road and checked the ticket. The draw date was the seventeenth, the day after tomorrow. Then, on the nineteenth the result would be declared. Not very far off. Careful that no harm should befall him, he moved to the side of the road, and walked homewards slowly. He had come out early in the morning – when he reached home, it was already past eleven thirty. He decided to skip office. Instead he'd fast and pray the whole day.

Even before he could change his dress, his wife came in with the news, "Madhuchandra has been arrested this morning. They say it's a vigilance case."

She laughed soundlessly, but heartily. A sudden smile lit up Oja Dinachandra's face. At that moment, his eldest son entered and asked, "Baba, where have you left the Luna?"

"Luna?" Dinachandra asked. And without saying a word, he hurried back to the lottery stand.

YUMLEMBAM IBOMCHA is a poet, short story writer, columnist and teacher. There are only three published books to his credit, two anthologies of poems and one of short stories. Since, he uses many pennames while writing in journals and newspapers not many people are aware that he writes satirical pieces also. He has been awarded the Manipur State Kala Akademi Award in 1974 for his first anthology of poems *Sandrembi Thoraklo Nahum Ponjen Sabige* and the Sahitya Akademi Award in 1991 for his anthology of short stories, *Numitti Asum Thengjillaklee*.

TAYENJAM BIJOYKUMAR has translated several short stories and poems from Meiteilon into English, besides the script of a Manipuri film. He also writes short stories and poems in English and Meiteilon. He has to his credit a collection of Meiteilon short stories, *Turoi Ngamloiba Wagi Lanban*, besides various short stories and poems in both Meiteilon and English published in leading newspapers and literary journals in Manipur and outside. An electrical engineer, he is an active member of many literary fora.

OJA DINACHANDRA'S DREAM was first published in Meiteilon as "Oja Dinachandragi Mang" in *Numitti Asum Thengjillakli*, 1990.

THE HOSTEL SENTINEL

I wasn't feeling too well that night and so, had stayed back in the hostel. Alone. While all my friends had gone to Church for the Sunday Mass.

My roommate, Lalhluna, had offered to stay back to give me company but I had declined, saying that my condition was stable enough. In truth, I had also wanted to use the time to study. After everyone had left, there was only the haunting silence for company, and the only light in the whole building was from the bulb in my room. Through the window, the sight of the moon bathed in all its splendour made me nostalgic. I filled a glass of water from the bathroom and placed it on my table.

K C Lalvunga
translated by Margaret Lalmuanpuii Pachuau

I don't know why, but while in the bathroom, ancient tales about our hostel sentinel came rushing to my mind and my hair stood on end. Admonishing myself for letting such thoughts overpower me, I latched the door. Spreading a fresh sheet on the bed and placing a pillow, I lay down on it and began to read the chronicles of the Sepoy Mutiny.

The Sepoy Mutiny of 1857 ... also called the First Indian War of Independence. Undoubtedly, there has been a sea change in political thought, for during the British rule the event had been described as one that had done away with rebels, wicked murderers and thieves. Foreign authors had presented sordid tales of Indians and their atrocities. The present political powers, however, glorified those "rebels" as martyrs to the cause.

Just then the sound of people opening and entering the gate interrupted my thoughts – probably my friends returning.

Suddenly, I could hear someone running, and then a scuffle.

"Whatever could be the matter?" I thought, listening intently. The footsteps hastened, as others followed. It stopped outside my room. Suddenly, a cry pierced through the air, "Ka nu ... I can't take any more of this."

Another voice said, "Stab him ...!"

"No, no, please don't stab me ... please let me go," the first person said.

Silence. And then the sound of someone being stabbed. As I jumped up to intervene, full of anger, I heard a voice saying, "Let's put him in here." Then the sound of fleeing footsteps.

When I opened the door, a handsome youth stood before me – his sparkling eyes, aquiline nose and wavy hair enhancing his looks. I could not help noticing that the suit and the bow tie he had on were, however, a bit old fashioned.

"Who was stabbed?"

"Ah! It was me," he replied simply.

"Where did they stab you?"

He mumbled a reply indistinctly. I thought he said, "Right down my heart." I wasn't sure I heard it right.

He stood there seemingly without a trace of pain, but I could have sworn that it was a murder I had overheard. "Are you hurt?" I enquired.

"Well, yes." He quickly added, "Do you have any water?" Noticing the glass on my desk, he picked it up and gulped down the water.

"Why were you fighting?"

"Ah! It's a strange story, but if you want to know I'll tell you. I have a girlfriend, nay, let me call her wife ... her name is Laltinchhingi, and this is her photograph."

She was a sensuous young woman who seemed to epitomize feminine radiance. Her beauty had a magnetic appeal and I gazed at the photograph much longer than I had actually intended to. They made a fine pair indeed.

"Well, so, there she is ... my girl, whom I truly love. What's more, she loves me too. We were engaged last week. But there were a few others who desired her as well. Their love going unrequited, they plotted to kill me."

"Wait," I interrupted anxiously, "let's attend to your wounds, let's have a look at it ... Shouldn't we send for a doctor?"

"No, thank you, there's no need. But pardon me, I don't know your name as yet. What's your name?"

"Liankhuma," I replied.

"I see ... well, Khuma, sit down. What are you doing here?"

"I'm a student, and this building is a hostel."

"Oh! I know that. I stay here too. My room's just across the landing."

"Ah! Then you are a new resident, aren't you?"

"No, no, I've been staying here for quite a while. But I haven't really made many friends, so very few know me."

For a while we both gazed at each other silently. Then he said earnestly, "Khuma, the world is a terrible place to live in."

"Why do you say that? Young men like you and I should not have any such problem."

"Yes, it should be that way, but envy and malice make it appalling. Ah! Envy ... why is there so much of it in the human heart?" he brooded.

I had no answer.

He continued, "Khuma, allow me to confide in you."

"Yes, please do so ... A burden becomes lighter when shared," I urged.

Holding his handkerchief against his face he said, "Love is what gives pleasure to life, isn't it?"

"That's right," I said.

"Or rather, our loved ones are the source of our happiness. Greater than any other pleasure in the world is a life together with our loved ones. Every man's dream is to marry his beloved and live in idyllic splendour. To be pampered by them, to lean on them ... could any man wish for more? Is that not reason enough for love?"

"That is so," I replied. His words belied his youthful demeanour.

"Our parents shower us with love, eagerly waiting for the time when we will spread our wings. They make tremendous sacrifices, sending us to places such as this hostel by the sweat of their brow. They wait for us to mature and make a definite mark in this world. The tremendous anticipation that emerges from parental love is unparalleled in this world."

"That's right."

"Ah, to betray that hope ... that trust. Is it not the most disgraceful thing in the world?"

I was so engrossed in his words that all I could do was to stare at him in awe.

"What opinion would you have of those who have deprived me of such a love?"

228 The Hostel Sentinel

I was unable to comprehend what he was saying.

"I mean, what can you say about murderers?" he persisted.

"Well, they are abhorrent criminals who very often do not get the punishment they deserve."

"That's right. Very often they escape penalty."

We were silent for a while, then at length, "Khuma," he said weeping copiously, "I find it terrible that I've been snatched away from the company of my beloved. My fate has been most tragic and disheartening."

"Hei! Didn't you say she reciprocated your love?"

"Certainly, she loved me too and has endured many a hard time for my sake, shed many a tear for me. Khuma, no fate is as tragic as mine."

"Wait a minute ... why should your fate be as pathetic as that? Handsome men like you should not be prey to such a destiny."

"Ah! But fatal are the wounds of envy!" saying this, he clutched at his heart and doubled up in pain.

"Hei! Where is the wound? Why didn't you say so before?" I sprang up to hold him.

"Sit down, Khuma ... thank you for your concern, but now it's too late."

"Show me where they've stabbed you."

He then got up, took off his coat and unbuttoned his shirt, showing me the knife wound running down his chest. I winced at the ghastly sight. Panic seized me.

"Here, let's go to a doctor, why didn't you mention this before?"

"Khuma, doctors won't be able to help me. Don't trouble yourself." But I was determined and started getting ready to go to the doctor.

At that moment, I could hear the sound of my friends returning and my mind was more at ease.

"Anyway Khuma, let me go to my room briefly."

"All right," I said without looking at him, engrossed in dressing up. He left the room. Then I heard my friends thumping on the door.

"Come in," I called.

"Open up."

"Push."

Irritated, they yelled, "It's locked from inside."

I was still putting on my jacket when I glanced round and saw that the door was indeed locked from inside.

I opened the door and said, "Get ready, we've to go to the hospital."

Lalhluna replied in jest, "Why, aren't you well?"

"No, it's not about me. That young man there has been badly wounded. We've to take him to the doctor."

"Who?"

"The one who came out just now."

"From where?"

"From this room."

"We didn't see anyone."

Lalhluna grabbed hold of my arm and said, "What's the matter with you?"

I was annoyed. "I am telling you, this isn't about me."

"Then what is it?'

I could sense that some of them were a bit amused.

"That young man who came out from here just now was stabbed and we've to take him to a doctor."

They looked at each other in utter consternation. Then it dawned on me ... my door had been bolted from the inside all the while!

Horrified, I checked the glass of water, but it was still on the table, full to the brim. I rushed outside to where I had heard the sound of a scuffle but a vacant lot was all that awaited me. I was stupefied.

Alarmed, my friends hesitantly suggested summoning a doctor. It was then that I disclosed what had taken place. My tale was received with shock and astonishment. Some felt that a trick had been played on me. I realized that there was no way I could prove the reality of the incident. We made a thorough search of the entire hostel, going to the extent of checking out all the guests. Our search proved futile.

Our aged hostel chowkidar, whose quarters were located towards the main gate, appeared. We enquired if he had seen such a person.

Astounded, he looked at me. "You say he was in black?"

"Yes."

"A handsome, wavy haired youth?"

"Yes."

"Ah, that's him all right ... the hostel sentinel."

Then we learnt the whole story. As he had told me himself.

"What happened to the murderers?"

"Well, they were never caught. His body was found in the nearby well. It was a long time ago for, as you can see, the well too has dried up. I remember when we were young we could still draw water from there." Coughing loudly, he rasped, "When the body was discovered, it had decayed beyond recognition. Everyone, of course, had their suspects but nothing definite came out of it and no one was convicted."

We stared at him mutely.

"How long ago was this?'

"Ah! A long time ago. My father was a mere boy then and it was he who told me about it. They say that every twenty years he wanders about in this hostel trying to find his murderers."

And indeed, it must have been a long, long time ago, for our chowkidar himself was bent double with age ... his sideburns greying. Wearily, he sounded the gong, shut the main door and stooping, proceeded homewards.

That night, thoughts of the youth haunted me. Though nearly a century had elapsed, curses formed afresh in me ... in sheer condemnation of those who had snuffed out so cruelly the glory and splendour of youth.

K C LALVUNGA wrote under the pseudonym, Zikpuii Pa. He wrote both novels and short stories, besides myriad articles and essays, which he published in various journals and periodicals. He has fifteen poems and two songs to his credit, which have been compiled together in a volume entitled *Zozam Par*. He was the recipient of the Academy Award (Posthumous) by the Mizo Academy of Letters (MAL) in 1995 and the Writer of the Century award given by the Mizoram state government. The first Mizo to qualify for the Indian Foreign Service, he was the Indian Ambassador to Venezuela, Colombia, Oman, North Korea and Jamaica. He also taught at school, dabbled in politics and edited a newsletter *Zoram Thupuan*, before joining the civil services. He died in 1994.

MARGARET LALMUANPUII PACHUAU translates from Mizo to English. A doctorate in English Literature from Jawaharlal Nehru University, New Delhi, she is a teacher by profession. She is presently translating and editing *Groundworks in Mizo Theology* for the Aizawl Theological College.

THE HOSTEL SENTINEL was first published in Mizo as "Hostel Awmtu" in the *Mizo Students' Association Monthly Magazine*, March-April, 1960.

THUNDERBIRD

They must have really hated me.

I was standing in front of my house one evening when I was called aside and suddenly dragged into a waiting vehicle. Firmly blocking all exits, three of the men started pounding me heavily inside the moving vehicle. The reason? According to my tormentors, this was my punishment for speaking out against a certain person's corrupt practices. Unlike others who can either keep mum or speak in more respectable tones, I had opened my mouth – in a local bar, of all places.

Someone had warned, "Do keep quiet," but I had arrogantly continued my foolish tirade and brought my present predicament

---

Vanneihtluanga
translated by Margaret Chalthanluangi Zama

upon myself. My pleas for mercy only resulted in an increased show of strength. After some more of this beating, I was thrown out of the running vehicle on the outskirts of Aizawl and left for dead.

I was in my prime, thirty five years old, with a wife and children, and my health had always been sound. Hence I had never believed that a death blow would come easily to the likes of me. But when I heard my hipbones crack as they hit against the pointed corner of the stone pavement and darkness started enveloping my consciousness, I knew that I would never be the same.

To talk about such matters is irksome for me. Neither is my being alive today the reason that prompts me to do so. In fact I fear that what I have to say might offend. But after that night – six months to the day today – when a passing vehicle picked up what they thought was a dead body, something very extraordinary took place in my life ... which is why I have to bring up the past again.

The morning after my misadventure, my name, spelt incorrectly, appeared for the first time in my life in the newspapers in Aizawl. The relatives of my abductors turned up in full strength by my bedside, for a psuedo display of heartfelt pity and compassion, wiping their crocodile tears with my red hospital blanket. The eatables they brought along were exotic and unfamiliar while the huge amount of money they gave for the treatment was a secret. Some of them even threw in faith healers and spirituals in the bargain. They were certainly a sight to behold – though protesting that they were not worthy of absolution, they continued to plead forgiveness.

Even before I was in any fit state to forgive those who had nearly killed me, their families had already announced to the papers that I, a good Christian, had forgiven them. It must be true, for I am one of those who spend a month's salary on drinks alone, one whom religious counsellors see as "evil incarnate." In my full senses I don't recall forgiving anybody, unless, when lying half-dead by the roadside and well on my way to hell, I had metamorphosed into such a good Christian that I had perhaps forgiven my tormentors in a delirium. Unless such a thing had taken place, I don't ever recall being a good Christian.

But their emissaries politely said, "... they're moneyed and you'll never beat them in court. Therefore, forgive them while they ask for it. Besides, they intend to give you a large sum of money as well. Don't you think this will be better for your wife and children?" Of course no one said outright, "You'll be beaten black and blue if you don't comply." But I felt the implied threat nonetheless and so magnanimously gave my pardon.

So here I was, now a renowned "True Christian" who gave the other cheek even to those who hit him, still lying on the hospital bed and hoping for a cure. A month passed by thus and the doctors started losing hope of my recovery. So with the money earned by my *noble* act, I proceeded to bigger hospitals outside the state, but everywhere I went, the answer was the same, "You are too late." Determined to walk again, I shopped for every specialist I knew. And when I ran out of money, my wife Muani sent what I needed, though I did not know from where she procured the sum. But when that money too petered out, I finally realized that I was destined to spend the rest of my life in a wheelchair, never to stand or walk again.

Just as I was intending to leave for home, I received Muani's letter. "Dearest," she wrote, "we had run out of money, but since we wanted you to come home cured, we sold our house. We're now living on the ground floor of my uncle's house. The money I'm sending is from the sale of our house. Although I wanted to keep this from you, I feared you would be at a loss on your return. So I decided to inform you about it. Please don't be angry, I've done what I have only because I love you."

As I read the letter I thought, What a burden I had become for my family. Even if I returned, there was no hope for me in Aizawl. But the urge to set my eyes on those who loved me – my wife and children – once again, and the desire to be buried in our local cemetery were motivation enough to lead me back to Aizawl.

So I came home. One person took me out from the taxi and another carried what was to be my lifelong throne – my wheelchair. Two other persons carried me down the steep flight of steps leading from the road higher up on the hill slope to the ground floor. Aware that I would never see Aizawl and its beauty again, I longingly and regretfully drank in the sights. Dark and cramped, our house didn't offer much of a scenery. Inside, I sank back into my wheelchair. Muani put her arms around me while my two sons looked on, puzzled. Then the elder one spoke up, "Ka pa, can it turn around?" while the younger one piped in, "Ka pa, get up, I want to try it out." The future of our little family was something I couldn't bring myself to ponder upon at that moment.

I got more visitors than I had bargained for. They wanted to know how badly I had fared in the plains, whether the orthopaedic specialists were really good or not and whether I had given up the bottle. Then there were those, of course, who simply wanted to see me. They all came and closed ranks around me with their masks of pseudo compassion. And each time they prayed, I wondered why no one mentioned the milk I drank, but only chose to sermonize about my alcoholism and about the harsher trials that awaited me if I don't reform. The more they came, the more suffocated and depressed I felt.

There were others who tried to gain political mileage out of my misfortune by using me as a lever to topple what they called a "corrupt government." The weekly papers carried reports of the number of threat letters I supposedly received. Had it been possible, I might have left for good the Mizoram that I had come home to with so much difficulty.

But the passing of time brought on other news and other headlines more sensational than mine, and very soon, the vultures left to seek more interesting fields. Their sudden concern barely lasted three months, and by the fourth, the only people who knew I existed were my wife and children.

My younger son fell in love with my wheelchair. Unable to have it, he started demanding a new cycle, but we couldn't afford that either. We tried to repair his old one to make it look like new, but the efforts only made it worse. The front label on his cycle which proudly proclaimed, "Thunderbird" fell off and he started crying. It was only when I said, "Wait Valte, don't worry. I'll stick the label onto my wheelchair and the day I get well, you may have it," that he finally stopped crying. From then on my wheelchair was officially christened "Thunderbird."

My daily routine was simple. At sunrise, my wife would help me sit up on my bed and place me on Thunderbird. Then my children would push me around. The younger one would ask, "Ka pa, you will get well tomorrow and I will be able to sit on Thunderbird, won't I?" Sometimes I would answer "Yes," sometimes "No." What difference did it make? There wasn't even scope for privacy at the toilet. I had no choice but to submit to the humiliating ministrations of my family. Even a dog, I thought, must have more use for its family than I.

Muani proved a good wife and took care of my needs without complaint, while my children still held me very dear. Muani's salary took care of our needs and our two children were able to continue school. Each morning she would lead them by the hands out of the house and drop them off at school on her way to office. I would wheel myself up to the front door to see them off. From the top of the steps they would wave and call out, "Ka pa! Bye, bye!" and I would wave in return, gazing at them until they were out of sight. Then with tears in my eyes and a heavy heart, I would turn back to the room, to be by myself for the rest of the day.

It was during these lonely times that the realization of just how useless I was and how hopeless and bleak my future was would hit me all the more. Everyday I thought, "Today I will hang myself." But the memory of my children, waving at me and calling, "Ka pa! Bye, bye!" would always stop me. My deep desire to see their faces once more when they returned home in the evening was what kept me alive.

Trying to keep myself happy and occupied, I read books with a vengeance and tutored myself to listen to music, forcing myself to find ways in which to enjoy it. I would fashion bamboo slivers into toothpicks and little pins to clip the betel nut preparation together. Sometimes I would sketch, and at other times make the arched framework for the children's kites. Thus I passed my days.

But for one who had nothing to look forward to, the effort to be happy while remaining confined to a wheelchair the whole day was indeed a tedious one. The creator made a separate timekeeper for the dead and another for the living, but for me who was neither dead nor alive, there seemed to be no yardstick with which to measure my time. In reality, I belonged to neither world – for though I lived in the world of the living, I could not partake of it fully.

The daily news began to bore me because it no longer had any meaning or impact on my life. Songs began to annoy me for they spoke of a world I could not reach. All other sounds irritated me as well. Nothing that issues from man is worth close scrutiny when one has to sit the whole day in contemplation of it.

And so, with the greatest of efforts I opened a window and turning my back on all manmade efforts to keep me happy, looked out, my face towards the sky ... not knowing what to expect, yet knowing that I secretly did expect something.

There was nothing to see. Since the house was sandwiched between two concrete buildings, the only sight that was of some interest was that of the Zemabawk locality some distance away. A sickly looking mango tree grew on the slope below the house, one of its upper branches almost touching our window, a trail of ants moving steadily on it. Beyond this there was nothing else but the blue sky.

Counting the number of vehicles that entered Zemabawk was a convenient way to pass time. But to do this every day became much too trivial an occupation and soon I sought other ways to keep my mind busy. I observed carefully the nature of the caterpillars that steadily devoured the tender leaves of the mango tree below, then gazed at the gardens situated between Zemabawk and the Chite rivulet. This too bored me eventually and in despair, I again turned my face up to the silent blue sky.

Three martins flew by and went out of sight. When they returned they started flying in small circles within my range of vision. A fourth joined them. Softly calling out to each other, they flew high up into the sky playfully, then swooped down swiftly again without any fear. Just when I thought they would collide mid air, they would skilfully and speedily manoeuvre and pass each other by. Seemingly carefree and without a burden, the freedom they owned was one that was inexplicable to humans.

Watching these martins fly in the sky proved more interesting than watching the vehicles along Zemabawk road. But suddenly they ceased being a comfort and assumed a more tortuous role, that of compounding my frustration and misfortune with their provocative cries, "You are indeed in pain!"

I shouted at the top of my voice, "Fly away at once!"As though in compliance with my wish, they would be gone for a while and then return, infuriating me all the more. Scolding them was in vain. I had no catapult with me either, and when I tried closing my eyes the sound of their soft calls sounded in my ears even more. When they flew close by, I would stick out my tongue at them but of course, to no avail.

One morning as I sat by my window, gazing up at the sky, the martins failed to appear as before. Perhaps my scoldings had made them feel restrained and ill at ease. Their disappearance made me feel surprisingly lonely. I missed their presence and looking up at the blue sky, I waited for them to reappear. I thought of my life and I realized that ever since I started occupying myself with the martins, not once did the thought of taking my life ever occur to me. I now understood. I had been cursing the best friends that I had.

The next morning I sat waiting expectantly for them again, and sure enough the martins appeared at their usual time. "Oh you martins who are so pure of heart, I will never scold you again. Come closer and let's discuss Siamkima's *Zalenna Ram* and Keivawm's *Zoram Khawvel*," I jokingly called out to them. I felt as if my poor, heavy heart was eased of its burdens. The martins too appeared to be more excited than ever, their play and behaviour unduly pronounced and exaggerated. I teased them loudly about this and they laughed in reply.

I grew to learn their likes and dislikes and came to believe that they too learned to read my mind. They were ready to do anything to make me happy, and as we grew closer I confided all my problems to them. Sometimes they flew me and my Thunderbird high in the sky, and we would explore the length and breadth of Aizawl, looking at all that I wished to see. Had I felt up to it, I know they would have taken me on a tour around the world.

Siamkima: (1938-1992) Critic and essayist. *Zalenna Ram (World of Freedom*, 1986) is a collection of his essays and articles. **L Keivawm**: (1939-) Poet and prose writer. *Zoram Khawvel (The World of Zoram*, 1991) is a travelogue.

Every day I would fly with them, their small wings holding me up. The martins taught me freedom, and showed me how to be carefree. I grew to know each one of them individually and they never tired of what I had to say. Because of them I began to look forward to each new day.

But the more I ventured into this deep relationship with the martins, the more I withdrew from human beings, speaking very little to them. Muani began to worry, but as she understood how miserable my life was now, she let me be. The hopeful plea of my younger son, "Ka pa, can you get up? I want to sit on Thunderbird," grew louder in my ear day after day while my condition, instead of improving, deteriorated with each passing day.

With the passing of time – a month, a day, the batting of an eye was over in the ticking of a clock. But for me, noon and night dragged on and time was in no hurry whatsoever. I became more and more of a stranger to the rest of the world. I stopped talking to people altogether. But the martins and sparrows became more intimate, drawing me closer to them.

As the seasons changed, so did the birds. The martins disappeared and five months after my accident, the only bird that stayed back to be my companion was the humblest of the lot – the sparrow.

A few days back, after my family had left for the day, I opened the window to gaze out as was now my habit. Out of the flock, I had a favourite – a little sparrow which would immediately come near me to perch on the window curtain rod. Like a doctor examining his patient, the bird inclined its head and first carefully observed me, then my Thunderbird. Chirping loudly as though conveying something, it then hopped about on the mango tree below. I realized that the sparrow intended to build its nest on the most inconvenient spot, the branch that was closest to me.

The whole activity distressed me no end, for the bird was neither strong nor did it seem an expert in building a nest. Just watching its efforts made one believe that the task would never be accomplished. Without taking my eyes off the bird I wondered how it dared to carry out such a formidable task, and how it would put its little home together. Trying to think of some easier way, I would sometimes suggest, "Why don't you place the bigger twig below?"

The sparrow would fly off, come back with a twig in its beak, tuck it very carefully into the nest and then fly off swiftly again in search of more. Collecting dry leaves, broom twigs, random pieces of cotton wool and so on, it would arrange them together as best as it could. The result was the semblance of a nest that was unsteady and obviously not strong enough to withstand a gust of wind. Thus the day ended.

I could hardly sleep that night as plans for building the nest filled my mind. Both of us were busy again the next day and by evening, the nest was finally complete. But it was not firm. When the sparrow tested it, the nest almost dislocated from its perch. It needed more props and support for balance.

Today too, as soon as my family left home, I resumed my vigil. When I opened the window the bird was already busy at work, trying to strengthen its nest. After a while, it flew off into the distance and did not return for a long while. I wondered what it would bring home this time. It soon returned, a twig in its beak, flying unsteadily under the weight. It perched by the side of the nest for a while, breathing heavily, and then tried to place the twig between the fork of the branch that held its nest. Had it succeeded, the twig would have firmly held the nest in place. But no matter how careful it was, the twig fell.

The little sparrow retrieved it from the ground, perched on my windowsill, flew back to its nest and again tried to place the twig in the same place. It fell again. The sparrow retrieved it again, and the cycle continued for at least ten times, with no success. And each time it picked up the twig, the little bird would approach me with it in its beak.

This whole thing started affecting me in a strange way. This little bird was trying to teach me something. If it dared to attempt the impossible, why should I still be sitting? All right, I suddenly thought, even if I fail I must at least make ten attempts to stand up.

The sparrow was again perched by me, the twig in its beak, and this time it made no attempt to go to its nest. Rather, I felt that it waited for me. Without further thought, I tried to stand up.

Excruciating pain racked my lumbar region. I was drenched in sweat. The immediate thought that came to mind was that I had done something I was not supposed to do. Had there been anyone nearby I would have been told, Don't, you'll aggravate your condition. But my only witness was the humble little sparrow perched before me, unbudging, watching. Again, I held the armrests of my wheelchair with my hands and tried to push myself up. Breathing heavily from the exertion I managed to lift my hips up from the chair. As I tried to support myself on my feeble legs my hipbones felt like they were being pierced with a dagger – so great was the pain. My legs experienced pins and needles, and I shivered out of sheer fatigue. As my strength could no longer sustain me I slumped back despairingly into my chair.

But the bird was still waiting, twig in beak, challenging me.

Breathlessly, I tried to chase it away, "Go, don't wait for me. I just can't do it." But it refused to budge and kept looking at me as though spurring me on for another attempt.

Apprehensively, I tried to stand once again, and this time my body protested even more than before. I moaned aloud in pain, but steadfastly kept my eyes on the sparrow fearing I might not succeed if I shifted my attention elsewhere. I garnered my full strength once more and, despite the pain, forced myself to stand again on my feet. I had thought I would never stand again, hence I was so excited that there was no time to despair or faint. I would go through this terrible ordeal. Instead of being wheelchair bound and alive, I would much prefer dying on my feet, I thought, and again made several attempts until I finally stood up awkwardly, holding on to the windowsill for support.

I was giddy with the intense pain and my vision clouded so much that I could not see clearly the sparrow before me. But I stood! I was no longer seated on Thunderbird! How strange it was. I was not sure whether the tears that trickled down my face were tears of pain or of happiness. Were the sounds emanating from my throat that of pain or of laughter? I didn't know. Yet, I stood!

I recalled how I had been thrown out of the vehicle, and recalled too the sound of my hipbones breaking as I hit the parapet, and now, standing there with only the sparrow for an audience, I wondered whether I was dreaming it all.

Enthusiastic as I was my strength could not sustain me for long. I dropped back on Thunderbird. The sparrow meanwhile flew off with the twig and again tried to support the nest with it. But a gust of wind blew at that moment and down it fell once more.

Seemingly in despair this time, the sparrow gazed down from its perch at the fallen twig but eventually flew down to retrieve it. Having done this it again came and perched before me. It willed me to indulge in my crazy attempt once more.

My mind was filled with despair and dread. Even if I did stand I won't be able to do so for long. Afraid to make another attempt, I thought maybe I should rest now and perhaps try tomorrow.

But the sparrow compelled me, so despite my fear I took a deep breath and tried again. The pain seemed to increase with each renewed attempt. But when I did stand up with all my strength behind me, it eased a bit and I could stand for a longer period. Even when I did sit down again, it was slow and deliberate, not sudden and heavy like before. The sparrow too flew to its nest with the twig and this time, succeeded in placing it on the fork of the branch, making its home as firm and steady as it had desired. How overjoyed we both were!

In order to prove that this wondrous event of my life was a reality and not a dream, I had to prove it, not to the sparrow but to my fellow men. Although I looked forward to Muani and the children's homecoming, I was afraid to believe that I would be able to really stand before them. To prove that it was a reality I somehow repeatedly made myself stand up and despite my fatigue, managed to successfully stand up on my own six times.

Evening came and my family returned home. I was aware that no matter how convincingly I told them of my achievement, they would not believe me. I had to make them see the real thing. Weak as I was, I secretly took a deep breath and gathered all my strength. I knew that I would be able to do it.

"Muani, Mama, come here," I called. They all left whatever they were doing and came to me, surprise writ large on their faces. "I can stand up!" I announced, straining myself. They were at a loss for a reply. Muani thought that I had gone out of my mind, so with tears in her eyes she put her arms around me and tenderly caressed my forehead. I was a sight to behold as I prepared myself physically and mentally to stand up once again.

As I exclaimed, "Now then!" I tightly gripped the armrest of Thunderbird with all my might and determinedly pushed myself up, arranging my weak legs as best as I could, one hand on the windowsill. Muani put her hands under my arms and tried to help me, but I shouted, "Don't touch me!" I focused my eyes on the nest outside my window. My pain now seemed to multiply tenfold when compared with what I had suffered before, and I felt darkness clouding over me, but I was almost standing. That terrible second was overcome and I stood as before, holding on to the windowsill. Praise be to the sparrow!

My wife cried as she held me, trembling with surprise and shock. My elder son leapt up and down. "Ka pa ... Ka pa ... he stood ... he stood!" he shouted loudly to the world outside. The younger one said calmly, "There!

You said you could not get up, but you did!" and immediately started riding Thunderbird around like a cycle.

My elder son quickly rushed back into the house. His loud announcement had not succeeded in calling anyone in. He looked at me carefully and enquired hopefully, "Ka pa, can you only stand?"

"I don't know, Mama ..." I was silent for a long while.

"You will be able to walk tomorrow, won't you?"

"I don't know. It all depends on that sparrow down there."

VANNEIHTLUANGA has around four short stories, five plays and numerous articles and essays to his credit. He is presently working on a novel. *Keimah Leh Keimah* and *Neihfaka Rilbawm* are collections of his creative writings as well as autobiographical pieces which are both humourous and thought provoking. A businessman, he is the owner and editor of *Lengzem*, a monthly magazine on popular culture. He is also a social worker and social critic.

MARGARET CHALTHANTLUANGI ZAMA is a teacher by profession. Besides translating from Mizo to English, she has also written a short story, "Zoey," and some unpublished poems. She has been an active social worker closely associated with disabled children and their parents in Mizoram.

THUNDERBIRD was first published in Mizo as "Thunderbird" in *Khuarel*, 1992.

CHHINGPUII

It was the month of October and the full moon was clear and inviting. Dinner over, the children of Chief Buangtheuva's village Ruanzawl had gathered to play, one neighbourhood noisily pitting itself against the other. Their voices calling the young maidens to join in filled the air. The young men had lit a bonfire at the zawlbuk. This was the large dormitory where all bachelors slept at night, and, more crucially, were shaped into responsible adults. They were discussing their next elephant hunt. The older men sat on their haunches at the threshold, their handwoven puan pulled around their knees, talking about their battles with the Pawi tribe – those people who do

Kaphleia
translated by *Margaret Lalmuanpuii Pachuau*
and Mona Zote

not wear their hair knotted at the back of the head as the Lushais do – and the war between the north and the south.

It would soon be time for the young men to go courting. The older men stayed behind, chatting animatedly, puffing away at their pipes or tapping their feet in rhythm with the conversation.

The village boasted of five maidens whose beauty was much talked about. Chhingpuii with her dusky complexion, her rosy, oval face and lustrous hair was one of them. Coming from a well-to-do family, she was as charming as could be and was always well attired. Easily amongst the tallest women of the village, her good character and skill at weaving were more remarked upon than her beauty. Many young men would often pay court at her house, and on that bright moonlit night too there were many suitors.

Chhingpuii was spinning by the bedpost, close to the hearth. Her suitors lounged around a little further off, discussing an elephant hunt.

The children at play called out to Chhingpuii, "There are more of them than us. We won't be able to defeat them." But she refused to join. The young men admonished the children, "Run along, you reek of the stench of puppies." After a while, Kaptluanga, one of the suitors, rose and lit his pipe from the hearth. Chhingpuii invited him saying, "Warm yourself by the fire." Though he replied, "I don't particularly wish to," inwardly he was very pleased and sat there by the fireside.

More than a hundred tribal communities live in the northeastern states of India, the Eight Sisters. The tribes that live in Mizoram are commonly known as Mizos. A composite group of allied tribes, they have lived isolatedly because of the remote, inaccessible areas they inhabit. The three main Mizo sub groups are Lushai, Pawi and Lakher. The legendary love story about Chhingpuii and Kaptluanga, who belonged to the Lushai tribe, is commemorated by the Chhingpuii Memorial in the Aizawl Langlei Road and remains till today a popular tourist spot in Mizoram.

As the other young men rose to light their pipes, she invited them too, "Warm yourself by the fire." So at length, most of the young men sat closer to the fire while some reclined on the floor. She gave Kaptluanga a cloth to sit on, and he stretched himself out with his head on the seat in front of the hearth. Chhingpuii fetched more wood, stoked the fire and sat down again, shifting a little closer to Kaptluanga in the process. The young men narrated tales about their failures during their first hunting expedition and about how they met up with hunting parties from other villages as well. At regular intervals she would ask, "Do you want some light to kindle your pipes?" and pass around glowing embers of coal. Every time she fetched more wood and sat down again, she inched closer to Kaptluanga. She did this thrice and by then they were so close that he could have rested his head on the hem of her puan.

Though she hardly spoke to Kaptluanga Chhingpuii often stole a glance at him to see if he was looking at her. Pretending to be unaware of his proximity, she spun skilfully, puffing away at her tuibur and listening to the chatter around her. Kaptluanga, seemingly deep in conversation, stole glances at her in turn. One of the young men spoke up as Chhingpuii stoked the fire, "Ralte hearths are said to be warmer, so keep the fire blazing." She replied with a smile, "That's right. I'll put in more wood." Those close by the hearth said, "It's too hot," and scrambled away further off while those who sat far away edged closer and sat there, sweating profusely.

After stoking the fire, Chhingpuii sat down, but hardly had she begun spinning when the rotating band gave way. Kaptluanga rose hastily, only too eager to help, "Let me help you thicken the thread."

Aware of the other young men present she said bashfully, "Your help will be of little use," secretly hoping that he would help her. Kaptluanga asked, "Why?" and helped her thicken and fasten the thread. One of the young men by the hearth set fire to the broken thread, hanging it on the shelf over the fireplace, and said playfully, "We'll go home only after this thread smoulders completely." Another added, "Yes, we'll stay on longer than usual for we are to set out on a hunt tomorrow."

The young maiden said, "Then you definitely must stay." But scarcely had half the thread smouldered away when the first cock began to crow. Those reclining on the floor sat up, lit their pipes and made to leave. Chhingpuii cajoled, "Stay a while longer as promised."

Someone replied lightly, "If we do, you will not allow us to come calling next time."

"Why should I do that? It's up to you. If you break your promise how will I trust you anymore?"

Kaptluanga smiled and darting a glance at her, said softly, "You'll never trust us anyway. When have you ever done as we wished?"

As they got ready to leave, she asked, "So you'll be off hunting tomorrow?"

"Yes," they replied.

"Get me the soles of a tusker, one that I may use for a hand spindle. Take care and come home safely," she said.

"You must meet us when we return."

"Certainly."

"Good night," they called out.

As they were leaving they noticed that an eclipse was taking place and in fact was almost halfway through. "Ei, a lunar eclipse! Does bad luck await us?" one of them said.

Chhingpuii heard him and came out. "Ah, I think it heralds the fact that you will shoot a big elephant. You are in for a stroke of good luck," she said. She then brought out a bamboo tube of water and emptied its contents into the pig trough to see which way the moon's reflection goes. They peered at it and exclaimed, "There! It's rolling about, the poor thing! Will it get out from the bottom or from the side? They say if it goes towards the bottom there would be an outbreak of dysentery, and if it went out from the side there would be an outbreak of pleurisy."

They watched the reflection in the water for a while and then made their way home.

Chhingpuii lay awake in bed, fervently hoping that the eclipse would be a good omen. Deep down in her heart she feared that the hunters might meet with some calamity. Finally, resolving to be firm and optimistic, she slept, comforting herself with the thought that Kaptluanga would shoot a bull elephant.

Kaptluanga and Chhingpuii had secretly been in love since their early teens. However, their shy temperaments prevented them from conveying their feelings to one another. Kaptluanga would resolve, "The next time I meet her I shall surely convey my feelings," but the moment they met, all that was on his mind would take flight. Still, where words failed, their eyes gave them away. At times, unknown to others, they had their little quarrels, but these only served to draw them closer. For them the world was still young and it was a place filled with laughter and happiness. They had no major worries, no familial ties that cloistered nor the problems of old age. Lissome young girls and hunting game were all that mattered to the young men, while the maidens favoured chivalrous young men.

The next morning, the autumn sun lit up the Tawitlang slopes and struck aflame the hills of Darlawng. The morning mist hung low over the Tuirial river, enveloping it in white. At a glance it appeared as if one could walk on these soft clouds. From there, one could detect the shadow of Darlawng hills. The day sparkled clear and the hills loomed much closer. No wind blew, and so quiet and still was the air, as if the eastern sun had bid all of nature to be still and calm. The sky was a clear azure blue, save for a couple of dark shapes looming at the southern horizon like the pointed tips of a spear and a pipe. After a while these too vanished.

After the morning meal the young men of Chief Buangtheuva's village began to assemble at the village entrance, all set for their elephant hunt. They arranged a place to prop up their muskets and other equipment. A khiang tree, the wood of which is used for making mortars and stocks, grew nearby. A lizard perched on one of its branches. "The one who brings it down will shoot an elephant," they said, and the more agile young men tried to hit it. Kaptluanga not to be outdone said, "I'll be the one to shoot the elephant," but missed the tree completely. He put more force into his next throw but again missed his mark. A youth nearby advised, "This is the way to do it. Here goes!" and his shot landed near the lizard's head causing it to jerk its head upwards. But as it was pelted with stones right, left and centre, it did not know which way to run.

Kaptluanga, now quite apprehensive, aimed a well-timed shot and the lizard fell down. "Didn't I say I'd be the one to shoot the elephant!" Then seeing a bird on the tree, he shouted, "Wait, see that bird up there," and pelted another stone. But it flew away unharmed. Meanwhile, some of the others waiting by the roadside busied themselves whittling away pieces of wood, strewing the remnants around.

Soon, one of their leaders said, "Well, if we're all assembled, let's be on our way." They set out, a group of twenty, chanting, "All evil things, go back," to ward off evil spirits, and firing their guns They carried with them ten days' ration of rice. Kaptluanga himself carried a big brass cooking pot. He was one of the leaders.

They reached the hunting grounds on the third day, and were greatly excited to find recent spoors of elephants all over, some still fresh. Some of the first timers looked around eagerly, as though expecting to find elephants right there and then.

The next day, the scouts got ready, with Kaptluanga and an older man leading the way and the rest following behind at a slower pace. An elephant trail cutting through the bamboo groves was filled with huge gashes and torn leaves, and swarming with black flies.

It was late in the day when they heard the elephant. Tiptoeing towards the sound, they saw a herd at a distance. They waited for the rest to catch up. "There is a herd nearby," they informed the group as they made plans to camp there for the night.

Kaptluanga then took out his hunting knife from his bag, looked at it to check if it was sharp enough, rubbed its edge and went, along with four others, in search of white ants' nests which would be burnt to keep sand flies and mosquitoes away. The nests were scarce and one often had to wander around quite a while before finding it. They brought back some nests, and then caught some crabs from the stream. There was a flurry of activity in the camp – some setting up makeshift huts, some going in search of firewood and yet others collecting leaves. Near the camp a stream flowed gently by, making the task of fetching water a pleasant one. Firewood was piled high in front of their shelter. Some of the more diligent youngsters set about cooking a meal. In the meantime those who had gone foraging for food had returned, bringing with them tumbu – the flower and fruit bud of the plantain, hruizik – the tender, edible portion of wild cane, tortoises, large lizards and bamboo shoots.

After dinner the more assiduous set about cooking the food they were to pack for the next day while the elders lit their pipes and chatted. Kaptluanga and his friend dressed a large tortoise in the stream nearby for the morning meal. The tortoise was with eggs, and they laughed, "This would make a good gift for a maiden's younger sibling. Let's take one each," as they put them into the cooking pot.

"Would it be time to go courting?" wondered Kaptluanga.

His friend replied, "It probably would be."

"Will they remember us?"

"Of course, they will. There definitely will be a few who'll remember us. The one whose house I went to on the eve of our departure will definitely pine for me. I have dreamt of her two nights in a row and she brings out a yearning in me."

"Whose house is it?" Kaptluanga asked.

"I won't tell you."

"Tell me. Why are you being so secretive?"

"What about you, whose house did you call on?"

"I don't think she pines for me. I try to dream of her every night but fail to do so. I think it's a lost cause just pining for her, but had I been, like you, with a true cause for yearning then I would not hesitate to disclose her identity."

"I too was not serious when I said that. I don't merit a thought there for I have not even managed to brush the hem of her puan."

All this talk made them lovesick. They disclosed the identity of the maidens whom they had courted, making themselves out to be quite the fortunate lovers. The moon was brighter than before and they sighed, "Ah, how I long for that night! And to think they must be gazing at this very moon too." And they headed towards the camp, singing,

> We build our home in the wild,
> For our beloved's home, do our hearts yearn,
> Our hearts pining all the while.

Their huts were raised high above the ground, the floor made from whole bamboo stems rammed tightly together. Below their huts were placed as many as five white ants' nests for there were plenty of mosquitoes around. Another group of young men set about stewing the tortoise while the first group who had been cooking before took a break. The older men discussed their plans for the next day, while Kaptluanga and his friend tested the gunpowder by sprinkling it into the fire. Afterwards they emptied the gunpowder from their powder horns into bamboo tubes, using rags as stoppers. All preparations for the elephant hunt were complete. They then lit a roaring fire near their camp and went off to sleep.

The sound of night creatures, the tuitu nightbird's calls, the croaking of frogs and the varied cries of other animals resonated in the silent forest, keeping the younger men awake. Just as they were about to drift off to sleep, they heard the soft sound of a tiger walking briskly down the stream nearby. One of the older members listened attentively and declared, "It's definitely a wild animal." The others were aroused, "Wake up, there's something in the water down there, get your guns ready." The moon shone brightly but as the shadows of the foliage were thick and dense they could not make out anything. After a while the sounds receded and some of them fell asleep again. Some others kept vigil the whole night through. In the morning they went to inspect the area and saw the footprints of a large tiger.

After their morning meal, five men with the most gunpowder in the group were chosen to shoot the elephant. They walked ahead while the others followed behind in silence. If all went well we'll try for the bull, they agreed. As they reached the herd, they noted that there was a tusker as well as a padawp in ready line of fire. They fired and both the elephants ran amok causing the herd to stampede. The hills resounded with the noise of incessant gunfire.

By noon, the shots came from the other side of the hill. Kaptluanga and his friend wondered, "Hmm. Perhaps our friends have bagged the elephant." Afterwards more shots pierced the air in quick succession and most agreed, "They must have shot one by now."

Late in the afternoon, one of the leaders shot dead the padawp elephant. They set up makeshift huts at the spot and smoked the meat.

"What are the plans for tomorrow, should we return?" one of the elders asked. Some of them wanted to go home, and some of the married men declared, "We miss our children." But they also knew that the bull elephant was quite exhausted. They decided to track it down, there being no need to move camp.

Padawp: An imperfect male elephant incapable of reproducing.

The next morning they set out once more. One of the older men said, "I dreamt of a dead man last night." He seemed quite sure that he would be the one to down the elephant, and so walked ahead with renewed vigour.

Just as they expected, they sighted their quarry a little way off, trumpeting wildly in anger. Advancing, three of them fired at it from very close range. The elephant charged towards them and nearly caught up with the middle aged man, who had dreamt of a dead man. He ran for his life, turban askew, lamenting, "Why, O why did we suggest a second attack?" The animal was wounded and weak, and the bamboo entwined around its trunk prevented it from running faster. Kaptluanga fired, bringing it crashing to its knees. Fearing that it might stand up again, the others in the group positioned themselves, ready to shoot. Just then Kaptluanga's friend reached the place and aided his shot. The animal died instantly.

They carried the meat back to their camp. Cutting it up into big chunks, they placed it over the fire to smoke it.

Sleep was difficult for Kaptluanga that night for his thoughts were only of home. He broke out into a sweat several times. At times his thoughts strayed to Chhingpuii and he wondered if her feelings for him would still be the same. At other times, he thought about the other young maids and of nopui, the celebratory mug of traditional rice beer proffered to the hunter who shoots the game. And at yet other times, he wondered anxiously as to how he would raise the hunter's cry in Lalnawta's presence.

The next day they made preparations for their return. They set off homeward at a leisurely pace and did not reach their village even after a span of ten nights. After the eleventh night, they reached a convenient place at noon from where they could fire their guns. They halted there and began to fire their guns rapidly. And like the triumphant crowing of a powerful rooster they raised the hunter's cry in quick succession.

From the day that the young men had left, Chhingpuii had marked every passing day with a piece of charcoal on a wall. One night, feeling that they had been away for too long, she counted the marks and found that there were only five of them.

During all this time, Lalnawta courted her and tried to win her favour before the hunters returned. One night, after her other suitors had left, he tried to coax her into making a commitment, thinking that her family members were asleep. But as her thoughts were with the hunters she was oblivious to what he was saying. "Don't you even want to answer me?" he asked.

"What were you saying? I wasn't listening," she smiled.

He started to repeat himself but just then Chhingpuii's father spat out the nicotine water from his pipe by the head of the bed. Lalnawta sheepishly fiddled about with a pair of fire tongs and left soon after.

He would follow the maids into the forest when they went to gather firewood. But their thoughts were with those who had gone hunting, and the young men who stayed behind did not interest them. As soon as they reached a spot where they could place their em, the conical baskets carried looped across their head, they would chop some wood disinterestedly and sing,

> Beneath the mist I gaze,
> Is that where the tusked ones graze,
> Young men tease them, they tarry there.
>
> Beloved, fall not to the tusker's spell,
> Where death looms close at hand,
> Lest our offsprings chance not to frolic on the sand.
>
> To the spirits of great Lurh we appeal,
> And seek to appease them all,
> That, great elephants' heads they might bear home.

Chhingpuii felt that they had been gone for at least ten nights, but later that night she again counted the charcoal strokes on the wall and found that there were only eight. "What does this mean, could I have missed a night! If that isn't so, then these are the longest eight days I have ever known," she thought. She knew that she had not missed a single night. The next day her friend next door confirmed that only eight nights had indeed passed.

Meanwhile, Lalnawta was determined to win her before the hunters returned, but he never so much as got to brush the hem of her puan. He would make vows or brag about his family's high status. At other times he would say that Kaptluanga was courting another maid. Chhingpuii would only say politely, "There's no point speaking to me, it's my parents whom you should approach."

Finally at his wit's end, he thought, Come what may, I shall defame her, and set out with a friend one midnight. Reaching Chhingpuii's house, he bade his friend to stand guard. He was about to open the door when fear seized him and he trembled violently. She never did look at me with eyes of love, I'll surely be caught and made to pay a fine for nothing, he thought. His conscience thus awakened, he stood at the doorway a long while, thinking. He could not recall a single instance when the maid had ever spoken harshly to him or hurt him. He realized she had always been honest with him.

Unable to muster the courage to open the door, he called out to his friend, abashed, and both went home. His friend taunted, "So much for your bravado, why did you not go in? Were you afraid of a woman? She would never have caught you." Lalnawta then thought of going back but reasoned, "We would have gone only to run, nothing would have come of it," and so they returned home.

In bed he wondered, Why did I not go in? People would have simply thought that we were in love. At other times he would think, Ah, how does it matter, better leave the deed undone than pay a fine. Better judgment made him realize that the young woman was not in love with him, so he knew that he had no reason to repent or regret. She was not born to be mine! he told himself and tried to sleep contentedly, but could not come to terms with the fact that she should belong to someone else. Jealousy clouded his thoughts. That night he hardly slept a wink.

The hunters did not return the day they were expected to. The villagers speculated that perhaps they had shot game and the night would hopefully bring some sounds of gunfire from their shelters. They listened attentively but no sounds came forth.

The next day, Chhingpuii was at her loom in the front veranda, weaving a puan. Lalnawta was, as usual, paying court. Late in the afternoon they heard the sounds of gunfire and instantly Chhingpuii sprang up to listen. "Ah! It is indeed the hunters. We can even hear their hunting chants," she said.

The girl next door said, "Let's go and await our brothers."

"Yes, let's get ready" she agreed and rolled her weaving aside briskly. All this time Lalnawta was standing nearby, at a loss. Grinding his teeth, he swore to himself, As soon as there is another hunt I shall surely go, and with a heavy heart, went away.

Chhingpuii's elder brother had gone hunting too so she got ready to meet him, changing into a hmaram, the lower garment of the Hmar tribe, and a puanrin wrap. Then with a large gourd ladle full of rice beer, she hurried away. The children too ran along briskly.

When they reached the spot Chhingpuii spotted Kaptluanga even before she spotted her own brother. Kaptluanga's sister was about to pour her brother some zu to drink. Chhingpuii offered her brother some of her zu. He had only had a sip or two when another girl came up saying, "Though my zu is not very sweet, please have some."

Chhingpuii gladly took hers and went to Kaptluanga saying, "Though my zu is not very sweet, please drink some. Are you not well? How thin you look. Well! Is this what you have shot? Did I not tell you that the lunar eclipse would augur well for you? My predictions do come true." She removed the tusk from his pack and tried to measure it, exclaiming, "My, how big! My hands can't encircle it! Elephants have big tusks for sure! Did you get me what I had asked for?"

"Of course, but later when we reach home ... how sweet your zu is, I feel drunk already! I was sure you'd forgotten me," he replied.

"Go on, why do you talk about forgetting. Here's tuibur water, though it isn't salty enough ... and I thought you'd been away for such a long time!"

"How long did you think it was?" he asked.

Smiling, she said, "Seven years or thereabouts," and they both laughed.

"I tried to dream of you every night, but I never could. Last night however, I saw your eyes most clearly," he said.

"I too saw you in my dream last night," Chhingpuii replied.

Kaptluanga was glad to learn that what he had feared had not come to pass. They had pined to see each other all these lonely days, and absence only seemed to have made their hearts grow fonder. But everything they had wanted to say during the absence simply vanished, leaving them speechless. Occasionally they would steal glances at each other and laugh for no apparent reason, as the girls went around, saying, "My zu isn't so sweet, please have some anyway." The young men took out the pieces of dried meat that they had kept for the children and handed them out, the biggest shares going to the siblings of young maidens.

A round of tuibur water followed the zu. After a measure of time during which the nicotine would have lost its savour in the mouth, the leader said, "Let's go." The children led the way, noisily carrying the head of the game. Those who had come to welcome the hunters followed behind, carrying the loads of meat like charcoal bearers. Bringing up the rear were the hunters bearing their guns, their cloth bags slung to the left. They cut notches on their paths declaring, "As soon as we step on this we shall fire our guns," and shots thus rang out loudly and incessantly. Some of the young women screamed and stumbled, frightened by the gunshots.

Drawing near the outskirts of the village, they raised the hunter's cry and the guns went off once more. What with their shouts and the gunshots, no one in the village could have missed hearing them approach. People inside their houses leapt out and gazed at the hunting party from the platform of their homes. Children and grown ups bore the elephant's head to Kaptluanga's porch and gathered in big groups for a look. Kaptluanga then raised his voice long and loud in a hunter's cry again, ending it with shots from his gun, sending the children scuttling for cover. And thus, with an easy heart, he stepped inside his house.

When night fell, more people came to his house, carrying zu. Young men and women lined up on the floor across the fireplace. Kaptluanga's father rose to dance, chanting,

> A good hunt my son shouts from the hill,
> The god has sent this, our day of reunion.
> Unseemly to call so many to our modest home,
> Sound the drum loud, it is well ...

Thus they sang and danced the night away. Morning broke and the maids went home, their feet streaked with spilt zu which the young men secretly found enchanting. The following day, a mithun bull was sacrificed so that the slayer would gain power over the spirit of the slain, and would also be protected from evil consequences during this life. The night once again passed in revelry.

Time and again, Kaptluanga shot many more animals, becoming the most famous marksman in Chief Buangtheuva's village of Ruanzawl.

The walls of his front porch were covered with the heads of the
animals he killed, and every now and then folks would have occasion
to revel through the night. The blood-tinged waste water that seeped
from his house due to the constant feasting seemed but a natural
phenomenon.

But his fame as a hunter also roused the envy of many. There were
also those who tried to blacken his name. But he bore all their slander
and malice patiently, saying, "What's true does not rust." He was no
sweet talker, nor was he a man of many words. He was truthful and
resolute, and he thought deeply about things. On his social visits and
while courting the maids, he joined in everything that the others did.
He did not like to overreach himself and disliked the thought of
getting a good name by deceit. He always refused to be the first to
partake of the zu supplied to young men and women who husked
rice for the chawng feast, saying, "There are others before me who
deserve to have the first sip." But none dared to do so, for he was the
one who found favour in the eyes of the village elders.

Not long after, Kaptluanga's enemies cast a spell over him and made him
swallow a comb while he slept. That day on, his health worsened and a
cough racked his body. The ribs of his chest ached. He would feel unwell
in the afternoons and at night he would sweat profusely. He no longer
relished his meals and sleep was difficult. He grew thin rapidly and
walking even a short distance now tired him. The chief declared, "My
meat vessel has broken," and was filled with regret. The sounds of revelry
of the traditional salu men, who sat up at night with the head of an animal
killed in a hunt, feasting and drinking zu, now totally ceased and the
blood-tinged water that used to constantly seep out of his house had dried
up. Even the dogs that used to make a nuisance of themselves over the

---

Chawng: The first of a series of sacrifices and feasts to ensure an entry into pialral, the
Lushai paradise.

bones from the feasts no longer made their appearance. Those who called him, "Brother" in his heydays were now no longer in sight.

Yes, there are people who in times of prosperity call us, "Brother" but abandon us when we fall on hard times. A few even point at us behind our backs. The wise dog remains faithful to its master, but human beings are not like that. Those who want to share with us our good times but not our sorrows and troubles are worse than our known enemies. They are the ones who add to our unhappiness and heartache.

It was slack time at the jhum and while his friends went hunting, Kaptluanga would, in his loneliness, drag his elephant's tusk across the floor and chant tearfully,

> *Amidst my tears, my cherished tusk I caress,*
> *The gods have shielded me from death,*
> *Yet in a state between life and death do I tarry.*

Chhingpuii was sad for him. She would call on him secretly and comb out his hair. They still found happiness in each other's company and had no need for anyone else. Now that Kaptluanga's illness kept him indoors and he could no longer go to work at the jhum with her, none of the other young men could walk behind Chhingpuii to and from the fields. Lest she should hurt Kaptluanga's feelings, she would choose the company of old men. Their happy years of working together were now a thing of the past. Chhingpuii did not wish to continue this practice with others and she would follow her companions to work with a heavy heart.

Now, while Ruanzawl village and the deep love of Chhingpuii and Kaptluanga held our imagination, two other mighty tribes fought bitter battles on the Mizo hills. Sometime before this, there resided at the village of Chief Suakpuilala, a beautiful young woman – the daughter of a chief who had been humbled at war. Many eligible sons of chiefs courted her. One among them was Liankhama, the son of Vanhnuailiana and brother of Buangtheuva of Ruanzawl. His proposal of marriage was accepted, but when he was away arranging finance for the marriage, Suakpuilala's son, Kalkhama married her. The girl's family did not dare refuse the son of their chief and so gave their consent, but this enraged Liankhama and his family. On his deathbed, Vanhnuailiana proclaimed to his sons, "Even the mithun fights to death over a mate, so if you do not dare resent this act, I shall consider myself as having sired no sons." After his death the family migrated west. Liankhama wanted to wage a war just then, but his mother said, "Wait. Let's settle down first."

Soon after they settled down they realized that the villages that they had adopted were well populated, with enough men to go on a hunting expedition at any time. This made them eager to wage a war and scatter their enemies mercilessly. Whenever they went out of their province they displayed an aura of bravado and aggressiveness in an attempt to provoke their enemies, and lay in wait biding their time like a snake waiting for its victim. Loose talk floated around and it was clear that war would soon follow as those in the east too could tolerate only so much.

At that time Liankhama's younger brother, Buangtheuva, also held sway over Hmunpui, a village comprising six hundred houses, and some outlying villages. To the west and opposite the Tuirial river that flowed by Ruanzawl lay Tachhip, a small village bereft of a proper chief but under a person named Tulera. Thus the villages of Tualphei and Tachhip were arrayed one against the other.

The inhabitants of Tachhip wanted to cultivate this Tualphei region, so they had set about clearing the area. Tualphei was a very lush and even land, where Tualvungi, according to legend, sat weaving when the wood pigeon called out to her. The village supposedly belonged to

Phuntiha, her husband. Though Tualphei was not within their jurisdiction, the people of Hmunpui challenged the cultivation and so the area came under dispute. The villagers of Tachhip too refused to submit. "Don't you dare cross the Tuirial, or else we will shoot," they warned. Hmunpui was eager to attack for there were about four to five hundred houses in their village while Tachhip had only about eighty. Thus, paying no heed to the warning, a bamboo was put across the path. The Tachhip villagers warned Hmunpui again, "Don't cross over this area," but this too went unheeded. This occurred thrice and still those of Hmunpui paid no heed.

That year, however, Tachhip did not dare to cultivate Tualphei land and instead had jhums only towards the west. Hmunpui then tried to set fire to the shelters, and the bamboo and wood that Tachhip had piled for burning before starting the jhum cultivation.

At length one young man could not contain himself any longer. "What is this, why do you keep coming even after we warned you not to?" he said, and firing a shot at them, declared, "I am the man, Tulera." He shot dead Rokawlha Chhakchhuak, one of the forerunners of the Hmunpui raiding party.

As soon as the first shot was fired both parties ran helter skelter into the woods. There was one who was more cowardly than the rest and instead of running off to Tachhip he ran to Arthlawr village. His friends declared, "He is lost, they must have killed him," and went in search of him.

In the flight, one young man from Hmunpui fell down into a yam pit and some dry wood fell across him. At just that moment, a Tachhip warrior named Khuangluta had ventured nearby in search of his friend. As soon as the Hmunpui youth realized that it was Khuangluta he dared not stir, fearing that his end had arrived. Luckily, the other man did not see him and went his way. Only then did he dare to escape with the news of Rokawlha's death. When this news reached

Liankhama, he declared, "Let's strike at once." They went to take counsel from their mother who was at a Mate village. "All right, even if you were trees, you would have reached your full flowering by this time, so if you don't defeat them now you never will. If good fortune is with you, there is no one to fear."

And thus begun the war between the east and west, between Liankhama and Kalkhama the descendants of Lalsavunga and Manga, over a maiden and broken vows.

At that time Liankhama was at Tualbung, a village consisting of at least a thousand houses. Kalkhama was at Hmiuzawl, another village with nearly a thousand houses. Thus both villages seemed well-matched. The people of the east were more experienced in warfare and knew how to plan their strategies. Liankhama's advisors were a brave lot and as he encouraged and favoured men of valour, most of the young men of his village vied to outdo each other in terms of chivalry. The village boasted of five warriors, well-known for their bravery. The young men of Hmiuzawl were admittedly scared of them, and they declared, "We are no match against the young men of Tualbung. Why, there is a gulf between us even though we have all been trained in the zawlbuk." Tualbung, on the other hand, was very eager to go to war. It was an undisputed fact that everyone was ready to wage a war if it came to the question of saving the honour of their women and children.

Tualbung eventually raided Hmiuzawl with resounding success. They entered the village, set it afire and killed many in the process. This terrible deed shook the land but as the saying goes, "The gossip of a stranger and the pecked abscess of a chicken spreads speedily," so too was the version of the raid greatly exaggerated. They have burned down the whole village, only a handful have survived – was how the talk went.

After that incident many of the smaller villages merged with the bigger ones. The people of Tachhip too did not dare to stay on their own and so they summoned Lianphunga from Parvatui, saying, "If you don't lead us, we'll all be scattered, for the enemies from the east are gaining ground." Lianphunga arrived and banded together the smaller villages around Tachhip, and soon there were about a hundred of them. They rapidly began the task of fortifying their village.

That year, famine struck Tachhip. So just before the sowing season, the villagers decided to go to Sailianpuia's village to ask for help. They waited for each other at the entrance of the village. One of the elders, Darkunga, Chemchawia's father, said to his friends, "Let's go ahead, the youngsters will soon catch up with us." Three of the older men started walking ahead. Darkunga led the way. He had wrapped a striped turban around his head and also carried forty pieces of the chief's money with him. They offered each other nicotine water and conversed loudly as they proceeded on their way. Passing over the hillock at the outskirts of the village, they had hardly crossed a little gully when Lianlula, who had been walking behind, pointed ahead and exclaimed, "Look, it's the enemy!" The raiding party from Hmunpui who had been lying in wait began to shoot. Darkunga was hit and he rolled into the wild cardamom patch below. Their friend Thanghluma quickly took shelter down the side of the road and shouted to Lianlula to do the same. But Lianlula refused saying, "I will not die at the hands of some mere enemy," and was shot dead as he continued to run along the road.

As soon as they heard the gunshots, those gathered at the outskirts of the village cried, "Enemy! Enemy!" and ran back in confusion. The young men took up their guns and ran after the enemy, while women and children hurried inside the stockade. But as the Hmunpui raiding party were in a hurry they almost forgot to take Darkunga's head. One of the warriors, Pakunga, ran back and hurriedly severed the head, but as the money lay hidden beneath the body, it remained untouched.

As the ambushers fled homewards, they hacked at the grazing mithuns that belonged to the Tachhip people. The mithuns ran wild, spurting blood and bellowing loudly in pain. Those working at the jhums ran into the jungles for safety. The raiding party gathered to wait for each other at Sibuta Memorial pass. The young men of Tachhip nearly caught up with them and even exchanged fire but as spikes had been strewn in their path they could not run very fast. They pursued them till the Darnghaki pass and then turned back.

The raiding party climbed Muallungthu hill, crossed Tuirial river at Darkhuang and passed over Hmunpui hill just a little before sunset. They raised the warrior's cry at the outskirts of their village and fired their guns. Those at home heard the firing and crowded out to welcome them. Little boys not yet of warring age were handed hunting knives and made to hack at the severed heads of the enemy. Mothers carried their infant sons in their arms, helping them hold hunting knives to slash at the heads. Then they said, "He has killed the enemy."

The next morning they gathered at the chief's courtyard in celebration of the heads of the enemy taken in the raid.

> *Will all this ever pass?*
> *The village of Tachhip where our people dwell,*
> *We've piled eightfold with graves galore.*

Thus, they sang and danced and fired their guns at random into the air. Pakunga then continued,

> *Who exalts my name in song?*
> *Tachhip, that dwells beneath the hills,*
> *Is not the striped headgear too your due?*

They composed many other songs of a similar nature.

When Chemchawia's mother went out to her jhum, she saw the shoot of the khuangthli tree that her husband had peeled. It had not even dried but was beginning to wilt now. She sat next to it and wept.

Talk about war did the rounds of the hills. Villages doubled and trebled their existing stockades and young men kept guard the entire night. In fact, it was as if the watchposts were more crowded than the zawlbuk, so frequented were they. Armed young men guarded the maidens on their way to fetch water in the morning, singing,

> *Ka nu, does the enemy clamour?*
> *Pristine white waters do I seek to draw,*
> *Shielded by men and thrice ringed walls.*

Everyone lived in constant fear of the enemy.

Soon after, the people of Tachhip requested Lungliana, the chief of Hmawngkawn village, to help them raid Buangtheuva's Ruanzawl. Thus both the villages of Tachhip and Hmawngkawn allied together. Thangzika Hauhnar and Tumtawia led the party from Tachhip. Some of the young men of Tachhip had been injured while chasing the Hmunpui people so they did not go.

In Ruanzawl, Chhingpuii was visiting Kaptluanga after dinner. "We'll try to finish sowing the paddy tomorrow. Had you been well we would have been so happy," she told him.

"Sow the rice and be happy while at it," he urged.

"These days, there is talk only of raiding parties and we live in constant fear of the enemy. I fear we won't be able to work the jhums properly. In fact, we won't be able to venture out to work without the men. Had you been well, I'd have been at peace."

He gave a faint smile, "Even if I'd been well, there would have been little that I could have done. Why, there're plenty of young men braver than me ... there's nothing to fear. No one will ever want to invade our village anyway, we are small and few in number."

"That's not the point. In fact, the smaller the village, the better the prospect. Women and helpless children are often the main target. It would be proper if men only fought men," she replied, smiling back.

"Do light my pipe," he said.

"I don't know how to," she said, already rising to her feet.

"Put in some embers and give it a few puffs, that's all."

"How good your tobacco smells."

"It's the one you gave me the other day. Your family must be wondering where you are, you'd better go home ... Should you find some hogplum in the jhum tomorrow, do bring me some."

"I will, if I find any. Don't you want some khuangthli stems too?"

"Yes, anything you find," he answered.

The next morning, the villagers going out to the jhums waited at the village entrance. Without pausing, Chhingpuii called out, "Come, Pu Ren, let's go on ahead slowly," and walked away with Rena, an old man.

The young men called out, "Wait a while, let's all go together." They longed to accompany Chhingpuii, but not wanting to hurt Kaptluanga's sentiments, she declined to go with them and went off with the old man. She carried the grain which had to be sown, and in her hands spun the spindle made from the soles of the elephant Kaptluanga had shot. Rena joked and they laughed along the way.

"My pipe's gone out again. They do say that a chatterbox's pipe and a consumptive always die, my pipe keeps dying," said the old man.

Chhingpuii said, "Wait, I'll blow it." She blew into the pipe bowl, put in one end of her spindle and gave it a few pokes. Having finished lighting it they looked up to find the muzzle of a gun trained at them. They shouted, "Enemy," and turned to run. Shots rang out and Rena fell to the ground.

Chhingpuii flung her basket and ran down the road. Thangzika of Tachhip grabbed her by the arm, his sword landing on her shoulder. She pleaded, "Spare my life, my father will give you whatever ransom you demand." Even as she spoke, blood flowed freely from her shoulder. But he declared, "You are as good as dead," and hacked her to death. He severed her head and took away her belongings. He and the others then proceeded to chase away those who were at the jhum and shot at the barricaded village. After this they returned home. The young men of Ruanzawl came in pursuit but failed to overtake them.

The Tachhip men raised the warriors' cry at the outskirts of their village and fired their guns. At the sound, the entire village turned out to receive them. Those who had gone ahead met them at the grassland near the edge of the forest. There they rested awhile. Then the Tachhip warriors grabbed Chhingpuii's head by the hair and pulled it out of the bag it had been thrust in, and the children were made to hack at it. Soon her smooth face was all disfigured even before they entered their village.

Zakhama had captured two young maids. Fortunately they turned out to be from the same clan as he, the Chawngthu, and therefore he guarded them all the way home. The other men persisted in trying to kill them but he adamantly stood against them. He took them to his house, from where they were later released after a settlement was reached.

The next day, they held a celebration in the meadow by the chief's house. They erected a platform, placed the heads upon it and left rice and cooked meat beside them as an offering to the spirit of the deceased. As was the practice, only the men who had killed enemies at war stuck plumes and tufts of red-dyed goat's hair in their heads, and fired random shots in the air.

Chhingpuii's beau from the west,
At Tachhip village square,
Is heady on wine, fair damsel.

Youth of the east you boast, Brave are we.
Yet the Chhinghermawii you adored,
Was dropped like feathers, unto the enemy.

Thus they sang and danced. Late in the day they bound the heads tightly with palm leaves and hung them high on the zuang tree at the southernmost tip of the village. After they finished the task, they fired another round of shots and headed home.

As Chhingpuii was a beautiful young woman in the prime of her youth, many songs were composed in her memory. Her fate touched and grieved many. Many too were the songs composed in her honour.

Did suitors woo you then?
Alas! Chhinghermawii,
Crows woo you now atop the trees.
We have done her to death amidst the stones,
Valiant warriors we cast our swords,
We have made her loved ones weep.

Her parents also lamented,

I dare not glance towards Tachhip,
Where my beloved child's head hangs,
Amidst frolicking crows the whole day through.
The crow will now and forevermore,
Claim Chhingpuii as its fruit,
We her loved ones cannot cease to weep.

After Chhingpuii's death, Kaptluanga's life was no longer the same. He felt like a wanderer in the arid desert, thirsting and crying out in vain for the water of life. The shady grove that once gave shelter became a thing of the past and he was bereft of all hope.

Though there had been none to claim him as their own, while Chhingpuii was alive she had been like the winter sun to him. Grief and despair wracked him. The days of happiness were now bedimmed by the clouds of sorrow and there was now never enough sunshine to give him warmth. Instead of living in such a manner, he longed to depart for pialral to be with his beloved.

One morning, as he was sunning himself along with a group of others, the talk came round to the songs that the west had composed in memory of Chhingpuii. Such talk sent a sharp pang through his heart and gnashing his teeth he went home.

Kicking at the wall with a vengeance, he lamented,

> *Like feathered plumes*
> *You yielded unto the enemy,*
> *Yielded unto the enemy.*

"Ah! We did indeed yield her," he cried, and in anguish sat down heavily at the back door of the house. He shut his eyes and pondered deeply. Soon his anger flared up and he looked at his gun on the wall. It hung there levelly. He took it down and gently stroked it, singing,

> *Muskets as these are good for game and foe,*
> *Holding it now I aim not at my foes,*
> *But towards the hereafter Mother!*

And saying so, he shot himself dead.

KAPHLEIA was a short story writer, poet, lyricist, essayist and a meticulous diarist, but most of his works are yet to be traced. He has to his credit three essays, nine songs and the short story "Chhingpuii." His essay "Thlirtu" (The Onlooker) written in 1931 is considered to be the first full-fledged essay written in Mizo. His songs reflect on various themes chief amongst which is the wonder of a mother's love as seen in "Ka Nu Hmangaihna," and his nationalistic spirit reflected in songs like "Zoram Nuam" and "Zoram! Ka Ram!" A good sportsman who participated in various indoor as well as outdoor games while in school and college, he contracted tuberculosis while in college in Calcutta during the early thirties and was confined to isolation in an outhouse, where he died in 1940.

MARGARET LALMUANPUII PACHUAU translates from Mizo to English. A doctorate in English Literature from Jawaharlal Nehru University, New Delhi, she is a teacher by profession. She is presently translating and editing *Groundworks in Mizo Theology* for the Aizawl Theological College.

MONA ZOTE translates from Mizo to English. An officer at the Taxation Department, Mizoram, she is also a poet and a scriptwriter. Some of her poems have been included in the *Anthology of North East Poetry* published by the North East Hills University Publication Board, Shillong.

CHHINGPUII was first published in Mizo as "Chhingpuii" in *Zonun*, 1963.

SON OF THE SOIL

I am twenty five, but still a teen at heart, still the young man I never was. Heaven knows what I was meant to be, but I am what I am because of my upbringing and circumstances. Society moulded me, and good or bad, society must accept me for what I am because I am its product. Given the right opportunities I could have made the right contributions to society. I am no less an individual than the next person. I am not yet decided if one's fate determines one's destiny, or if one's nature determines one's fate. Perhaps, dear readers, you can shed some light on it for me.

I am Neiu. I was born in Kezekevira of Kohima district one cold wintry night of

---

Sebastian Zümvü

1972. My kith and kin, I am told, were overjoyed at the birth of a son. "He's got a manly voice," they had said, "he'll be a man."

But my parents took it too far and produced six more boys. My mother was a legend of sorts in the village. They say that for my mother childbirth was as easy as rolling off a log. Indeed, the gap between any two of us boys is not even fourteen months.

After my sixth brother, thank god, they decided to rest.

I was barely five months old when my mother had to flee with me to the forest.

A few days earlier, an Indian army convoy was ambushed a kilometre or so from our village. A captain and several other soldiers were killed, and a large amount of ammunition looted by unknown armed youths, believed to be NNC cadres. The villagers were told through local informers that security forces were planning to conduct a combing operation in the area. That meant only one thing – we had to flee. That night, all the villagers – men, women, children and the aged – went to the forest carrying a few days' ration of rice and other essentials.

The next morning, a column of deadly looking soldiers from the Punjab Light Infantry approached the village, surrounded it and set fire to the first house they came across. In a matter of minutes, the whole village was ablaze. And by nightfall, Kezekevira was wiped out from the face of the earth. We had no home. The soldiers were hunting us. We had become fugitives in our own land!

NNC: The Naga National Council. Formed in 1946 to unite the sixteen major Naga tribes to avoid incorporation of tribal areas into the Indian Union and to press for regional self-determination, the NNC is the first public movement of the Nagas.

Shillong Accord: An agreement signed between the NNC and the Government of India in Shillong, Meghalaya, on 11 November, 1975. The main terms of the agreement were (a) unconditional acceptance of the Indian Constitution of their own volition, and (b) the surrender of arms.

For three months, we scoured the forest, not unlike the wild animals hunting furtively for food. The district administration then imposed a fine and allowed us to return to the village. I still haven't figured out until this day why we had to pay the fine.

When the Shillong Accord was signed the villagers breathed a sigh of relief – they could now work in their fields without fear. Army operations were thankfully suspended. The Army went back to the barracks and the Naga army were fenced inside the perimeters of peace camps. The man from Kohima, however, told us that the Naga people had surrendered their birthright and that they are now subjects of Hindu Raj, power having been transferred from the British Empire to the Indians.

But for once, gunshots ceased to echo in these hills.

I studied in the local government primary school and it took me only four years to master the English alphabets – all twenty six of them. By the time I reached Class III, I already knew how to write 1, 2, 3, 4 ... What's more, I knew how to count them aloud as well. I was becoming too smart for my age. I was, at one time, convinced that the teachers had hardly anything more to teach me! The following year, I earned another laurel – I was elected the class monitor for one whole year. My duty was to chase away the cows taking shelter in the classrooms. I was also to do away with the cowdung. My joy knew no bounds that whole year!

Looking back, I suspect I was elected to the post by virtue of the fact that my father owned the largest herd of cattle in the neighbourhood.

My alma mater had convenient timings – convenient for the students, for the parents and most of all, for the teachers. Classes started a few minutes before our parents left for the fields, and were over an hour or two after. The teachers too had their fields to attend to, and no one could ever argue with that. The rest of the day, we were left to our own devices.

School was fun. Now, come on, why won't it be fun when about forty of us were packed into a room several times smaller than the students' capacity? Think of a zoo ...

I went to school one fine day and came back home with a broken thigh. A classmate had climbed up to the ceiling of the classroom and jumped down. How did that break my thigh? Well, I was lying all quiet and obedient on the desk, my feet resting on the shoulders of a younger boy in front and my head on the chest of another boy in the row behind me, when this fellow jumped down on my legs. I howled with pain, but the din in the room was such that it took a good quarter of an hour – an excruciating century for me! – for the teacher to realize something was amiss.

Both Azuo and Apuo, my mother and my father, had their say in the matter when they came back from the fields in the evening. (Heaven knows I did not deserve rebuke from them. But by nightfall they were all sympathy and I was touched nice and proper.) That night, the mother of the boy who jumped on me came to my house. She apologized profusely on behalf of her son who, she said, was very naughty. I quite agreed with her – the boy was very, very naughty. You know how naughty boys are these days. I felt the matter was of such grave implications that none but the village council was competent enough to decide who was right or wrong and how the wrong party should be penalized. A leg for a leg, I reasoned, for the picture of the old pastor of our church floated across my mind, shouting down the pulpit that god will smite our transgressors. And as far as I was concerned the boy who broke my leg was my deadliest enemy. I wasn't ready to forgive him, but wanted to bash him up even if we met in heaven.

But at that moment, something happened that turned the tables, or plates if you please. The woman took out a cute, healthy puppy.

Puppy meat mends broken bones, she said. I agreed, and nodded my head vigorously in the dim light even as my mother vehemently declined the "gift." Finally, she relented and accepted the puppy ... I suspect, as a result of the mental messages I sent her. I knew for a fact that dog meat mends broken bones, and at that moment, I realized it also mends broken fences.

I forgave her son then and there, for I relish dog meat. Now, isn't it said that a way to a boy's heart is through his stomach? I never argue with the maxim.

The village bonesetter was called for. He was a wise old man with a cure for everything. He could castrate piglets, cure a stomachache, set broken bones and prick and bleed people with bad blood, among other accomplishments.

He came, saw me and patched me up. I mean, he pasted some herbs on the injured area and declared everything would be all right. He said I would have to eat a lot of dog meat. And I did. In about six months I was my big self again – as sprightly as a ten year old boy can ever be. The dog meat did it, I swear. No thanks to any of those so-called doctors and their much-hyped about wonders. Give me the bonesetter anytime. No fancy tablets or such dreadful things as sticking a needle into your body.

Anyway, the nearest health centre run by the government is located five kilometres from Kezekevira in another village atop a hill. None in the vicinity knew for sure whether the doctor and nurses will be there. Or if there were any medicine in the health centre, for that matter.

By the time I completed Class VI, I had achieved a great many things. However, I daren't say I passed Class VI. It somehow makes me uncomfortable. So, let's say I completed the sixth standard. Among the great things I achieved, one remarkable achievement was that I learned to write with a fountain pen. I developed a writing style that paid no heed to trivial cursive lines. And it is with a certain degree of pride that I announced that I alone could read my handwriting. My teacher couldn't, and I felt that I was better than my teacher in some respects. Come to think of it, the jealous teacher said my handwriting was like dogshit scattered all over by a hen.

But I felt I had to do something about the way my writing sloped. I start from the left hand corner of the paper like most people of the world do, but I ended up on the right side somewhere down the middle of the paper. I tell you, it really didn't look good.

One memorable experience of school is helping out the teachers in their paddy fields. There are different seasons in a year, and there are different kinds of chores to be done. Come spring, and it is time to hoe. Summer is wet and hectic with the task of rice planting. Autumn brings along its due share, such as harvesting and bringing home the paddy.

One fine summer, due to the late onset of the monsoon, most of the teachers in our school could not finish all the work in their fields during the school holidays. I don't really know how or why, but by a general consensus it was decided that we students help them out. So we left our pens and books home, took up spades and headed for the fields. There is more to education, someone once told me, than classrooms. But I am still not convinced why we should work in the fields of our teachers when our own fields were left unattended.

The eighties were years of peace, progress and prosperity. Drug culture took firm root in the society, corruption assumed alarming proportions, the unemployment rate multiplied yearly, insurgency abounded and morality took to the gutters.

Development came to the village. Pipe water was to be provided. A huge sum of money meant for the development of the village through its Village Development Board paid for the pipes. Water pipes were laid all the way to the source, and water tanks and taps were constructed. We boys and girls sang and danced. The days of fetching water from the springs down the valley were over. We only had to walk a few steps to the water taps with our jars and hey presto! we would get water. We praised the chairman of the village council for initiating such a noble scheme. A friend of mine, whose widowed mother sells zutho, the beer made from sticky rice, and mekhie, ordinary rice beer, says that the chairman and his colleagues were praised best as the nights grew and the jars of zutho or mekhie were brought forth for refills for the umpteenth time.

Weeks turned to months and months to years, but still we had to fetch water from the springs. Only after spending several lakhs of rupees did the contractors and engineers realize that the source was lower than the village. The traditional law of gravity did not allow us water. The solution? Easy. A water pump was required. The image and integrity of the village council was somehow redeemed. But not entirely.

When the village received its annual allocation of funds the following year, it was diverted to purchase a water pump. Alas, after things appeared to be proceeding smoothly, the villagers found out that they would need a large reservoir. That meant we – young and old alike – had to wait for another fund allocation by the state administration. Kezekevira, being small in size as well as in population, received a meagre sum as compared to bigger villages like Viswema, Kewhira and Chiechama. This was because there are just a few households in the village and the annual house tax of five rupees per house was a pittance. However, rumours were doing the rounds in the village – our ingenious leaders had already devised a scheme so that the village could get more money – house tax would be paid for fictitious households, and in the names of dead persons. A friend, whose mother sells liquor, told us that this is a way of honouring the dead as well as the living in the sense that the dead are made to live on, and the living could get more funds!

The reservoir took about a year to be completed, and we suspected from the very beginning that this was because the contractors too had to make a living. And by the time the contractor finished, there were no water pipes. All the pipes had been stolen! The pipes made very good hearth bars especially during marriages and Christmas when feasts were prepared for multitudes. The Christian Revival Church in our village is said to have purchased four pieces of these stolen pipes, and the very next day the church expelled from its community two orphans who stole a fistful of rice from a neighbour's house. The pastor stated the church wouldn't have anything to do with sinners. A visitor from Kohima, however, pointed out that Jesus Christ came to this world to save sinners. But the pastor replied that he wasn't Christ.

Anyway, the result of this water scheme was that one of my uncles built his house on a water tank. He broke down one of the walls of the RCC water tank for the doors and windows of his storeyed house. And to this day, the idea of supplying pipe water to the village remains a pipe dream.

Another development which came to the village was electrification, and this was prominently aired by the All India Radio, Kohima. Our small and isolated village was the last Angami village to be electrified. And electrified the villagers were. After being wired for lights, we found out what it's like to have electricity – power goes off when darkness falls and comes back when everybody goes to sleep. Matters improved later on when power went off for weeks altogether. It was an improvement because by then we did not have to bother about electricity at all.

However, we children experienced a different world of electricity. Once, the earthing in our house developed a short circuit, and one and all who touched the exposed wire received electric shocks. It was a rainy day when the neighbourhood kids gathered around the wire. Someone said that those who touched it and got the shock of their lives are manly, and those of us who were afraid to touch it are kids. And it so happened that there amidst us was one boy who had the habit of stealing. There was always some sort of bad electricity between him and our crowd. And when an older fellow told us that electricity doesn't go through rubber, we became on-the-spot smart alecs. We told this boy that a person doesn't get electric shocks if he is wearing anything rubber. I handed my slippers to him, and for good measure, pretended to touch the wire. He fell for it hook, line and sinker. He held my slipper – so worn out of shape that it hardly resembled slippers, but rubber nonetheless – in one hand, and with the other hand reached for the wire.

Thunder, I tell you, is but a faint whisper compared to the cries of a boy who has just held a live wire. But thank god and the powers that be, electricity is not much of a threat to careless children in the villages even these days for the simple reason that there never is much power in the rural areas.

We had started feeling we did not need any more development in this world when a sub-health centre was constructed and inaugurated in our village just before the elections. The building was constructed in a hurry because the local MLA, who desired to run for the post again, wanted to inaugurate it before the elections, so that he could make a few votes out of the whole thing. A ceremony therefore was called for, and the villagers set about organizing one.

The day was fixed and the budget for the feast prepared. The gift for the chief guest – who else but the MLA! – was thoroughly deliberated upon. The election agent of the MLA was asked how much the chief guest was expected to donate. The gift was arranged accordingly and the cost of the feast was conveniently covered by the donation expected. All the peli age groups and women groups wanted to present songs and dances during the MLA's visit because usually the chief guests donate handsomely to all those groups who take the trouble of composing paeans, songs and dances.

The day dawned fine and clear, and the function went on smoothly. The singers sang their paeans to the MLA, and the superlatives and qualities extolled in their songs spoke of demigods, for no one in the village knew the person concerned was so good and had such royal ancestors. Words like "He is our dream ... our hope ... our tomorrow ... our everything ..." did liberal rounds that day in the songs.

But it paid off – the MLA was liberal too.

The monsoon set in, and more and more people got ill. This was when we realized the health centre was without proper staff and medicines. The building too threatened to collapse when the rains set in, having been constructed in a hurry by a local contractor.

The health centre, however, did some good – it provided a place for the Romeos and Juliets of the village. These, in turn, provided us little boys and girls some very good live peepshows almost every night.

When I passed the Class VIII examination from the local government middle school in 1990, I did not know what I was studying, or what I was supposed to do or become. Heaven knows how I ever passed at all, for none but I know how much I have studied. So far, I always did what Apuo told me to do. He was illiterate but he had been to Kohima and had seen how people were clean and wore clean clothes. He was given to understand by some kind souls that one has to study to become like townspeople. And ever since, his one ambition was to get one or more of his children properly educated. He was always there, breathing down my neck, and I sort of grew used to him telling me what to do or what not. But being illiterate, he had his own shortcomings which became more obvious once I began to get older, and, as I fondly believed, more erudite.

Apuo gave me a choice – study and pass, or go with him to the fields every single day of my sweet life. I assured him I would study, but study I always did not. When examination time came I was seized by panic. The night, when the choir sang "Hallelujah" I caught a roosting fowl from our coop and furtively made my way to our headmaster's house. The headmaster – a man of this world, but is no more in it – gave me some "suggestions." I memorized these suggestions like there was no tomorrow, and passed the examination.

I had passed out from the school in the village and that meant I had also passed out from the village. I had to get admission in some other school. The nearest one was in Kohima. Come to think of it, I was getting too smart for the village, anyway.

Searching for admission in the Kohima schools was a trying experience, to say the least. No school was willing to admit a student from a village government school. This opened my eyes to my rustic background. I had depended on one of my uncles, a peon in the Secretariat, for the admission. But much to my dismay, I discovered that a peon does not have much weight in these matters. I was helpless and had no one to turn to. It was at this juncture that someone suggested I should meet a certain headmistress who had a weakness for venison. So I went back to the village, embarked on a hunting expedition with some friends and managed to kill a deer. I took the whole animal to the headmistress and secured my admission into her school. I did not know then that it would take me three years to finish the two year course. And oh, what glorious years those were, for I hardly attended the classes and spent my time in my *other* education. And my uncle with whom I stayed was none the wiser.

I learned the ways of the street. I was introduced to Swedish, British and American porn in the video halls by a classmate who had been staying in Kohima for the last year. And my, oh my, did I start to love

Kohima! I loved European porn all the more because they go all the way, and then some more. As soon as my mate and I returned from school (those rare times when we did go to school,) we would change our school uniforms, buy a packet of bidi and head straight for the video halls.

I also explored the steps and drains of Choto Basti and New Market areas where local booze joints abound. We couldn't afford IMFL, Indian made foreign liquor, so we had to make do with mugs of the local brew – zutho or pucca ruhi. Another "in thing" with our generation was to do drugs. Guys either chased brown sugar or injected heroin, but no local hooch. Booze demeans, these druggies claimed. But each to his own kicks. Thank god for that.

And talking of kicks, I had my other kicks as well. I joined a martial arts institute and trained for about three months. I felt martial arts was a way of life since every night I had to protect myself from the riff raff in the booze joints I frequent. Let me get my martial arts straight, I thought to myself, and I shall teach those oversmart buggers a thing or two about fighting. And being the genius that I am, or so I thought, I soon learned more than the instructor and was literally kicked out of my institute. But I wasn't worried. There is only one person in the world who knows about kung fu, and he was dead.

One night I was in my usual hangout, The Dream Corner, when an acquaintance dropped in with several of his friends, all dressed in jeans, sneakers, T-shirts and leather jackets. The peculiar thing was that their jackets were zipped up all the way and their waistline bulged as though they carried bottles of booze or something. By the time they came I had already downed a couple of zutho mugs and was in no position to clearly make out who my new acquaintances actually were. Anyway, we had a good time together talking of nothing in particular but everything under the stars, the moon and the sun. God gives wisdom to the drunk, or so someone once said. We parted ways with promises to get together some other day.

Next morning, my friend came to my room and told me that those with whom we had spent the previous night were a crack unit of the NSCN, conducting an operation codenamed Operation King Cobra. They were no different from me. I could very well be one of them, I thought to myself, and with my ingenuity, I reasoned, I could be their leader! But no thanks, I didn't want to have any dealing with it.

The nineties saw the growth of both the NSCN factions – the NSCN-IM and the NSCN-K. By 1995, both the factions could assassinate just about anyone in Nagaland – anywhere, anytime. And that's when all hell seemed to break loose. It seemed to me that all my friends and acquaintances were in one faction or the other. And there were factions galore. The most popular faction, it seemed to me, was the one with the least control over its cadres. The regoods – recruits, if you please – went to Bangladesh or Boorma – Myanmar – trained for a few months and came back as crack units. Easy as that, someone told me. I must confess I once seriously thought I should join up, get a gun and make a peaceful, easy life with it. These days, with extortion rife and popular, there was an unlimited range of what one could do with a gun.

I had my first taste of a militant's life when this particular friend of mine asked me to hand over a letter to the manager of a bank. No

---

NSCN: The National Socialist Council of Nagaland (NSCN) is the main insurgent group operating in Nagaland. It was formed on 31 January, 1980 by Isak Chisi Swu, Thuingaleng Muivah and S S Khaplang opposing the Shillong Accord signed by the then NNC (Naga National Council) with the Government of India. Later, differences surfaced within the outfit over the issue of commencing a dialogue process with the Government of India and on 30 April, 1988, it split into two factions, namely the NSCN-K led by S S Khaplang, and the NSCN-IM led by Isak Chisi Swu and Thuingaleng Muivah. Clannish divisions among the Nagas are also held as one of the reasons behind the split, NSCN-K being the Konyak faction and NSCN-IM being the Tangkhul faction. Presently, both factions are holding peace talks with the Government of India.

problem, I said and was told that it would be worth the trouble. Suddenly, a thought crossed my mind – it could be an extortion letter. I was reluctant, and my friend saw it. What about the room rent your landlord has been asking you to pay up for the last few months, he asked. Yes, now I saw the logic. After my uncle gently asked me to leave his house, I had rented a small room. I had not cleared the rent even once, and the landlord was after me for a long time now. It wasn't that I need any reminder but his words struck me and stuck to me like glue. Moreover, my parents had been asking me to return to the village.

So I delivered the letter and nearly dirtied my pants in fear. How my friend collected the money or how much it was, I do not know. But I was given five hundred. My joy knew no bounds for it cleared my rent and I was able to pay off some of the debts I had incurred. If it was as easy as that to get money, I thought to myself, I shall be a rich man very soon.

My parents had been telling me to come home. But I did not have any inclination to toil in the fields. No way. I was made to be something different – something better than my rustic brothers who had all left school and were now farmers, through and through.

"Your brothers and both your mother and I work from can see to can't see," Apuo had said the last time I was in the village. "We get no time for rest. We can't work our fields by ourselves and we all are members of a peli group. All the days of the week are scheduled beforehand and we can never shirk from these responsibilities whether we like it or not, whether we are sick or well ... And what do you do? You said you are studying, but where is your service ticket, your certificate? You are living off us like a parasite."

That did it. "Parasite?" I shouted back, "I'm never coming back. And without me who'll respect you? I'm the only literate person in the family. You'd do well to remember that." With that I stomped off and headed for a girlfriend's house at the other end of the village.

The next day, my father sold a cow to the local butcher for one thousand and two hundred rupees. My mother said she would keep two hundred to buy kerosene, sugar and a kilo of meat. I took the remaining amount, went to a joint and had half a bottle of rum. I was quite drunk by the time someone informed me that a truck loaded with firewood was headed my way. When the driver saw my condition he let me sit in front with him. I reached Kohima, paid my rent and bought some kitchen stuff. How I transacted the money in my drunken state baffles me, but I just hope I did right.

The next morning, I counted my money and found that I had only three hundred left. That wasn't going to last long. I had to come up with a money generating scheme, and fast. For weeks, I schemed, tested and failed. No bureaucrat was willing to give the likes of me a second glance, let alone help. But still, I kept on scheming. I was desperate, and I came up with what some people call "a desperate plan."

Very soon, I was looking up friends who I knew possessed guns. We were birds of the same feather – we all needed money. They came up with impressive looking writing pads and seals. We were in business.

We served demand letters to those whom we knew possessed too much for their own good. Our favourite line was that we had come from the 007 Battalion of the Naga Army and that we were carrying out a top secret operation against the "occupationary forces." Our leader, Captain so and so, had directed us to approach you saying that you will surely help the Naga nation ... blah, blah – this line never failed. Anyway, many said OK when approached with an AK. We collected nearly a lakh the first month alone. And oh boy, did we blow it! The parties and orgies in hotel rooms were worth every paisa we spent.

There was a time when it was more or less prestigious to receive an extortion letter. If you did not receive one, you are a social nobody. So, we told ourselves that by demanding money from an individual we were sort of issuing him a certificate of social status – the bigger the amount, the higher the social standing. And we took it upon ourselves to identify the haves in the society. We were social workers. Or so we thought of ourselves.

But people were getting wise to us. They started posting gunmen in their compounds and began cooperating with the police and the army – a totally unheard of thing in this region. Very soon, our Robin Hood days were arrested, so to speak, when one of my gang members pointed me out to army commandos.

That fateful day, I was standing outside a paan shop chewing a paan like a gentleman when a Gypsy of the colour the army fancied, pulled up nearby. I saw someone in the vehicle point to me and my stomach sank. I hoped to heaven it wasn't true. But it was, and I had to get away. I tried to run away, but tripped and fell face down. I tried to get up, but something hard hit the back of my head and I went off straight to la la land. I came to when I felt someone slapping my face over and over again. Looking around, I saw that I was surrounded by none too good looking commandos in plainclothes, their fingers on the trigger of deadly AKs.

I looked around for help, but none was forthcoming. I might as well look for a drop of water in hell. A commando kicked me from behind and told me to get up. I got up, and this football player, I mean the fellow – kicked me again and pointed towards the Gypsy. The pain in my leg was excruciating. One of them grabbed me by the hair and another grabbed me by the legs. They dumped me into the back of the vehicle. Three of them got into the backseat and trampled me with their boots. By the time we reached the army camp a mere five minutes' drive away, I felt I had been stampeded by a herd of cattle. These plainclothes were playing pain gods, and they were playing it too damn well.

I was blindfolded and pushed into a room. They started punching and kicking me. Excreta flowed freely from my body as a result of the beatings, and I was forced to eat it up. Very soon, I collapsed and fainted. I regained consciousness after some time and found I was still blindfolded, my hands tied behind my back.

I died a hundred deaths in the few hours before the soldiers came to take me into what seemed the interrogation room. I was made to sit on a chair and then they gave me hell. They put wires on my private parts and switched on the current. I screamed, cried and whimpered. They asked me a lot of questions about the NSCN, but I couldn't tell them anything since I had never been a part of it. I wished to hell I was one so that I could tell them something ... just to stop all this torture. I told them I was just an extortionist, and told them the names and addresses of the persons from whom we had extorted money. I revealed the names of my friends as well. I had to somehow get out of the situation.

It went on for two days and two nights. And when they released me I was barely the shadow of the man I was before landing up in their parlour. By the time they handed me over to the police I was a sight to behold. The police refused to accept me seeing the precarious condition I was in. I was then taken to the Naga Hospital in Kohima where I was looked after with a certain degree of sympathy and pity by the doctors.

I have been in the hospital for nearly a year now, and I still cannot walk unaided. My kneecap is smashed, and several ribs broken. My head has internal injuries – I get dizzy spells. I can hardly sleep, for whenever I close my eyes, images and experiences I'd rather forget keep coming to my mind.

Azuo is here with me. But I don't know how long she can manage to stay here. I just wish this chapter of my life had never taken place. I can see the pain and sorrow in my mother's eyes. Many things that have happened in the last few years have been beyond the comprehension of my parents. Azuo especially had very high hopes of me. I was the eldest in the family and my parents had expected me to lead and support their younger children.

Their world has come crashing down.

And I yearn for the days when Azuo was all I needed in the world.

I am told I have been booked under the National Security Act and also under National Security Regulation. I am an extortionist, they say, and also a member of the NSCN. My foot! I was never a part of the NSCN, I said, but no one seemed to care.

Ceasefire has been declared, I hear, and talks are going on at the highest level. Ceasefire may become a permanent reality and peace may finally return to these hills.

Perhaps, I may be dealt a fairer card tomorrow.

I wish, I hope, and I pray.

SEBASTIAN ZÜMVÜ writes poems on folk and romantic themes, and short stories based on the contemporary Naga setting of political conflict and the problems of rural-urban transitions. A senior journalist, he also publishes the *North-East Herald*, a leading newspaper in Nagaland. He writes only in English.

SON OF THE SOIL was first published in English as "Son of the Soil" in the Silver Jubilee Souvenir magazine of the Angami Public Organization, 1997.

ABOUT KATHA

Katha, a registered nonprofit organization set up in September 1989, works in the areas of education, publishing and community development and endeavours to spread the joy of reading, knowing and living amongst adults and children. Our main objective is **to enhance the pleasures of reading for children and adults**, for experienced readers as well as for those who are just beginning to read. Our attempt is also to stimulate an interest in lifelong learning that will help the child grow into a confident, self-reliant, responsible and responsive adult, as also to help break down gender, cultural and social stereotypes, encourage and foster excellence, applaud quality literature and translations in and between the various Indian languages and work towards community revitalization and economic resurgence. The two wings of Katha are **Katha Vilasam** and **Kalpavriksham**.

KATHA VILASAM, the Story Research and Resource Centre, was set up to foster and applaud quality Indian literature and take these to a wider audience through quality translations and related activities like **Katha Books, Academic Publishing**, the **Katha Awards** for fiction, translation and editing, **Kathakaar** – the Centre for Children's Literature, **Katha Barani** – the Translation Resource Centre, the **Katha Translation Exchange Programme, Translation Contests. Kanchi** – the Katha National Institute of Translation promotes translation through **Katha Academic Centres** in various Indian universities, **Faculty Enhancement Programmes** through workshops, seminars and discussions, **Sishya** – Katha Clubs in colleges, **Storytellers Unlimited** – the art and craft of storytelling and **KathaRasa** – performances, art fusion and other events at the Katha Centre.

KALPAVRIKSHAM, the Centre for Sustainable Learning, was set up to foster quality education that is relevant and fun for children from nonliterate families, and to promote community revitalization and economic resurgence work. These goals crystallized in the development of the following areas of activities. **Katha Khazana** which includes **Katha Student Support Centre, Katha Public School, Katha School of Entrepreneurship, KITES** – the Katha Information Technology and eCommerce School, **Iccha Ghar** – **The Intel Computer Clubhouse @ Katha, Hamara Gaon** and **The Mandals** – Maa, Bapu, Balika, Balak and Danadini, **Shakti Khazana** was set up for skills upgradation and income generation activities comprising the Khazana Coop. **Kalpana Vilasam** is the cell for regular research and development of teaching/ learning materials, curricula, syllabi, content comprising **Teacher Training, TaQeEd — The Teachers Alliance for Quality eEducation. Tamasha's World!** comprises **Tamasha! the Children's magazine, Dhammakdhum! www.tamasha.org** and **ANU – Animals, Nature and YOU!**

THE NORTH EAST WRITERS' FORUM

Established in 1997, the North East Writers Forum is the probably the first literary body that has a membership base across all the seven northeastern states of India. The members are writers who work in English (though not necessarily exclusively in that language) and have a minimum number of published works in English – English, because the languages spoken throughout the region are so varied and numerous, and because, again, it is a widely used language in the region, and is placed, uniquely, in a position that serves to link together the literatures produced in the different states of the region.

The Forum was established with several objectives in mind, the chief among them being to encourage creative writing in English in the region, to translate the treasure trove of writings of this region into English, and bring them, in their English translations, to the notice of people outside the region. Another important aim was to get members from all the states to interact with each other, and with writers from outside the region to ensure a continuous learning process. All members have been greatly enriched through this interaction, both intra and inter region.

Among the varied activities of the Forum, the one accorded most importance is the annual publishing of its journal, *NEWFrontiers*. This journal, whose editorship rotates from state to state throughout the region bi-annually, focuses on original writings in English as well as English translations of works from the various regions. Over the years, the Forum has also interacted with literary luminaries, both of the region and outside, writing in English and/or other languages. Among the luminaries who have graced important occasions of the Forum have been Padma Shri awardees writer James Dokhuma, playwright and theatre person Ratan Thiyam and writer M K Binodini, besides poet Hiren Bhattacharya, fiction writer Atulananda Goswami and children's writer Arup Kumar Dutta, among others.

The Forum also organizes translation workshops lasting one or two days, for it helds that only able and sensitive translators can do justice to the vast literary wealth of the region, which are yet to be mined. It organizes interactive sessions with renowned writers from outside the region like poets Jayanta Mahapatra and Ron Price and novelist Amit Chaudhuri as well as story and essay competitions for school children and screenings of films on the lives and works of poets and writers.

BE A FRIEND OF KATHA!

If you feel strongly about Indian literature, you belong with us! KathaNet, an invaluable network of our friends, is the mainstay of all our translation related activities. We are happy to invite you to join this ever widening circle of translation activists. Katha, with limited financial resources, is propped up by the unqualified enthusiasm and the indispensable support of nearly 5000 dedicated women and men.

We are constantly on the lookout for people who can spare the time to find stories for us, and to translate them. Katha has been able to access mainly the literature of the major Indian languages. Our efforts to locate resource people who could make the lesser known literatures available to us have not yielded satisfactory results. We are specially eager to find Friends who could introduce us to Bhojpuri, Dogri, Kashmiri, Maithili, Meiteilon, Nepali, Rajasthani and Sindhi fiction. And to oral and tribal literature.

Do write to us with details about yourself, your language skills, the ways in which you can help us, and any material that you already have and feel might be publishable under a Katha programme. All this would be a labour of love, of course! But we do offer a discount of 20% on all our publications to Friends of Katha.

Write to us at –
Katha
A-3 Sarvodaya Enclave
Sri Aurobindo Marg
New Delhi 110 017

Call us at: 2652 4350, 2652 4511
or E-mail us at: info@katha.org